A WISH AT THE CHRISTMAS VILLAGE

A MRS WISHMORE NOVEL

ALIX KELSO

LAKE FALLS PUBLISHING

Cover design by dmeacham design.

ISBN (paperback): 978-1-913098-10-0

Published by Lake Falls Publishing

For my husband, David.

PROLOGUE

The December afternoon was already dark as Mrs Wishmore gazed out of the bus windows at the scenery passing by outside. The twisting road wound through the Cotswolds towns and countryside as the last light of the winter sun disappeared behind the hills and hedgerows. Stars glittered in the twilit sky as a crescent moon rose on the horizon and white frost settled on the fields and rooftops. Mrs Wishmore watched it all from the bus window, admiring the quiet beauty of the land that stretched beyond the road and wondering when it would be time to disembark.

The bus was quiet, with just a few other passengers along for the journey. In the seat across the aisle, a small boy sat beside his mother. Although focused on the action figure clutched in his hand and on the whispered conversation he'd been conducting with it for the last few minutes, the boy threw occasional glances in Mrs Wishmore's direction, his expression curious.

When Mrs Wishmore smiled at the boy, he quickly looked away. But a few seconds later, he was once more slanting his gaze in her direction. His eyes roamed across her bright red coat and cloud of silvery hair. Mrs Wishmore sensed the question behind his eyes and wondered if he might pluck up the courage to ask it.

The boy's mother took his hand and together they rose from their seat and walked towards the bus doors, the mother asking the driver to let them off at the next stop. As the bus slowed, the boy looked back at Mrs Wishmore and then, in a sudden move, ran back up the aisle towards her. Before his mother could even turn and call her son back, the boy was beside Mrs Wishmore's seat.

"Do you know Santa Claus?" the boy asked, his eyes wide.

Mrs Wishmore laughed softly. "My goodness, that's quite a question to ask, young man."

The boy tilted his head, considering her. "You *do* know him, don't you?"

Before Mrs Wishmore could answer, the boy leaned closer and whispered in her ear.

"Tell Santa I was good this year and that I want a new bike for Christmas and although we don't have a chimney at our house, he can just use his Santa magic to get inside."

The boy's words tumbled out in a rush. Laughing, Mrs Wishmore nodded. "I'll be sure to tell him."

"Noah! Come back here this instant!" the boy's mother cried from the front of the bus. "What have I told you about running off like that?"

The boy traipsed back down the aisle. The mother raised her hand towards Mrs Wishmore, an apologetic wave for her son's behaviour. As the bus doors swung open, the boy glanced at Mrs Wishmore one last time.

Mrs Wishmore winked, making the boy's face light up in a grin. As the bus moved off, she waved out of the window to the boy and his mother, hoping the child wasn't in too much trouble for running off the way he had. Children often saw in Mrs Wishmore something that grown-ups either couldn't see or didn't want to see. And at Christmas, children often got a little muddled about just what that something was exactly. Considering the excitement of the season, that was entirely understandable.

The bus trundled on along the darkening Cotswold roads. Soon it reached the outskirts of a little town called Hollyford, where a welcome sign decorated with strings of twinkle lights announced it to be the Famous Cotswold Christmas Village where a very merry time was waiting for everyone who visited.

Mrs Wishmore smiled at the warm and festive welcome. As the bus drove deeper into the little town, she admired the endless Christmas lights that lit up the streets and the warm seasonal cheer of the place.

And she sensed, too, that this was her destination and that it was time to get off the bus.

Mrs Wishmore rose from her seat as the bus pulled into a stop on the high street. Thanking the driver, she stepped off, taking a moment to adjust the big blue handbag on her shoulder and tighten the scarf at her neck before looking around. The high street was lined with shops and cafes and restaurants, most of them still open and busy at this late hour in the afternoon. Along the high street, Christmas-themed light features were attached to the lampposts—in the shape of holly leaves, jingle bells, snowmen—each one casting a warm glow onto the damp pavement below.

Although the high street was bustling, Mrs Wishmore found herself drawn to the market square at its southern end. There, she found crowds of people gathered around a tall fir tree, many of them putting the final touches to the decorations and lights hung on its boughs. The tree lights were not yet lit, and there was a sign draped across the low wooden fence around the tree announcing that today was the grand switch-on of the Christmas tree lights, an event organised by the Hollyford Christmas Village committee.

That explained all the people hurrying around and looking rather busy and official, Mrs Wishmore thought with a grin as she took in the activities.

Beside the unlit tree there was an illuminated Santa Claus in a sleigh pulled by reindeer, which had already attracted much interest from the children running around the market square. There were stalls selling hot chocolate and festive treats, little wooden cabins selling gifts and crafts, and it looked like there might be some carol singing scheduled later, too.

Everything looked wonderfully busy and festive. As Mrs Wishmore glanced around, she wondered what her work here in this sweet little town might involve. She would enjoy spending time here in Hollyford, of that she had no doubt.

The people in the crowds mingled and meandered around the market square. The folks who appeared to be in charge of the Christmas Village committee hurried around, issuing orders to one another, a few of them clutching clip-boards and looking very official. Children raced here and there, excited by the prospect of the tree lights soon being lit up.

Few of those gathered in the market square seemed to notice Mrs Wishmore standing at its far edge, watching the comings and goings. But, inevitably, some of the children began looking her way, their expressions curious and speculative, just as the expression on the face of the little boy on the bus had been.

Two little girls wearing Christmas-themed woolly hats and gloves and matching purple coats conferred with one another in hushed whispers before leaving the Santa Claus display behind and shyly walking towards her. They were sisters, Mrs Wishmore could tell, perhaps even twins, considering how similar they looked. Their father, who was chatting with another parent, didn't notice them wandering off, but that was quite all right. Mrs Wishmore knew they were perfectly safe.

The little girls approached her, nudging one another. When neither said anything, Mrs Wishmore chuckled.

"Hello, girls. Are you enjoying today's festive fun?" Mrs Wishmore asked.

They nodded shyly, still nudging each other. Finally, one of them spoke.

"Are you Mrs Santa Claus?" the little girl asked.

This wasn't the first time Mrs Wishmore had been asked this. She gave a soft laugh as she answered. "No, I'm afraid not."

"But you look just like her!" the other little girl said.

"Do you think so?"

Both girls nodded, warming to their theme. "Are you the Christmas fairy? The one who sprinkles the special Christmas magic dust to slow down time so that Santa Claus can fly around the world and deliver all the presents on Christmas Eve?"

Mrs Wishmore hadn't heard this particular version of the Christmas Eve story before, and she smiled at the charming details. "No, I'm not the Christmas fairy either."

The girls gave each other puzzled looks. "If you're not Mrs Santa Claus or the Christmas fairy, who are you?"

"Well, I'm just a visitor passing through."

The two girls considered this before whispering to each other again. Once they'd finished their consultation, they drew closer and reached out to touch Mrs Wishmore's hand.

"We think you're an angel," one of the girls said in hushed tones.

Her sister nodded. "You are an angel, aren't you? A Christmas angel."

Mrs Wishmore only smiled. "I think your father is looking for you two girls. Why don't you run along now, before you miss out on all the fun?"

In a flash, the two girls sped off back to their father. Mrs Wishmore watched them running around as they struck up a new game of tag with a couple of other children, their encounter with the kindly older lady on the edge of the market square already forgotten.

Mrs Wishmore looked across the gathered crowds, wondering what had led her here and when her work would begin. There was so much excitement and happiness in the market square as people got ready for the Christmas tree light switch-on, but Mrs Wishmore knew that not everyone welcomed the festive season with open arms.

For some, Christmas was a difficult time filled with loneliness, or heartbreak, or grief.

Mrs Wishmore sensed those feelings here, somewhere in the market square, even in the midst of so much joy. Closing her eyes, she let her mind wander to their source.

When she opened her eyes again, her gaze settled on a young woman on the other side of the square. She stood alone, her expression uncertain as she glanced at the crowds waiting for the Christmas tree lights to be switched on.

Mrs Wishmore wondered if this young woman was the reason she'd come here and whether she needed some help. If so, the young woman only had to ask.

She only had to *wish*.

Too often, people didn't know how to ask for help when they needed it. Mrs Wishmore had a feeling, though, that the young woman across the market square was very much on the cusp of making a Christmas wish, even although she feared that wish would never come true.

But beneath the fear, Mrs Wishmore also sensed a bright beat of hope in the young woman's heart.

The young woman was right to hope. After all, Christmas was a time for magic and for miracles.

But until the young woman made a wish, Mrs Wishmore had to wait. Only then could her work begin.

On the edge of the market square, Mrs Wishmore watched the festive fun unfold and waited for a Christmas wish to be sent out into the world.

CHAPTER ONE

The market square in the heart of Hollyford looked like a scene from a Christmas card, and Millie Dawson doubted whether even the North Pole could look any more festive.

The Christmas tree in the middle of the square was decorated with lights that would soon be switched on, the nativity scene beside it was illuminated with a soft white glow, and the merry plastic Santa Claus on board his sleigh and grinning at his galloping plastic reindeer had captured the attention of the little children wandering around the square, their eyes wide with wonder as they gripped their parents' hands.

At the edge of the market square, Millie stood alone. Thrusting her hands into her pockets to ward off the chill, she took in the sights that surrounded her—the roasted chestnut cart scenting the air with its delicious aromas, the festive carols being sung by the church choir on the far side of the square to entertain the visitors, and the little wooden cabins from which traders were selling Christmas decorations, handmade arts and crafts, and other festive goodies.

It was a picture-perfect wintry scene. Yet despite the Christmassy atmosphere and the sight of so many cheerful people wandering around the town square, Millie couldn't shake off the deep loneliness that was her constant companion these days.

In a few moments, the mayor of Hollyford would switch on the tree lights and the town's Christmas celebrations would officially begin. Although she was a newcomer to the village of Hollyford, Millie couldn't have failed to notice just how important the Christmas tree light switch-on was to the town. There were posters pinned up everywhere, announcing the time and date and inviting everyone to come along for an afternoon of festive fun.

The little Cotswold town of Hollyford had made a name for itself as a Christmas destination thanks to the work of the Hollyford Christmas Village committee and its dedicated volunteers, and Millie was amazed at how thoroughly they'd transformed the town into a winter wonderland. Judging by the overflowing car parks, people had come from far and wide to see the market square dressed up in its festive finery, and visit the lovely shops with their alluring window displays, and eat in the quaint cafes and pubs dotted up and down the high street. The posters Millie had noticed also listed some of the special Christmas events that would take place throughout December to attract visitors, and the Christmas tree light switch-on at the start of the month was the first on the slate of activities.

From her spot at the edge of the square, Millie watched the bustling festive fun taking place around her. She saw families enjoying the nativity scene, and little children shrieking with delight at the illuminated penguins and polar bears that stood guard beside the Christmas tree, and couples wandering around hand-in-hand, and groups of friends admiring the treasures for sale from the traders inside the little wooden cabins.

Everyone was here in the company of friends or family or loved ones. Realising she was probably the only person who'd come here by herself made Millie feel awkward and out of place. The work colleague who she'd invited along to the Christmas lights switch-on had cancelled at the last minute because of a family issue. Millie had already been on her way to the market square when the text message pinged on her phone. Not wanting to miss out on the celebrations, she'd taken a deep breath and come along by herself.

Now, she wondered if she ought to have just gone home. She felt silly lurking around the outskirts of the event by herself. Although she wanted to be part of the festive fun, it wasn't easy to just throw herself into the midst of things when she didn't know anyone.

Everyone here looked like they belonged. Millie ached to feel that way.

Everyone here looked like they were excited about Christmas, and Millie ached to feel that way, too. She wanted desperately for this Christmas to be better than last year's.

Although that wouldn't exactly be hard. Last Christmas had been the worst of Millie's entire life.

"Well, doesn't this Christmas tree look splendid?"

Millie turned and saw an older lady standing on her left, her gaze fixed on the Christmas tree across the market square. She was bundled up in a red winter coat and scarf to ward off the frost that was already chilling the air as the afternoon darkened, and a gentle smile creased her lips as she shifted the big blue handbag clutched at her side. With her cloud of silvery hair and bright blue eyes and warm expression, Millie couldn't help thinking that the older woman looked just like Mrs Santa Claus, and the thought made her return the lady's smile.

"It really is a beautiful Christmas tree," Millie agreed. "I'm sure it will look even more amazing when they turn on the lights."

The older lady nodded. "It will be spectacular."

Together, they gazed across the market square at the Christmas tree. Several women were fussing with the large sparkly baubles dangling from the branches and making final adjustments to the positioning of the tree lights. The badges pinned to their coats identified them as members of the Hollyford Christmas Village Committee, and judging by the seriousness with which they approached these last minute tasks, Millie could see how much the work meant to them.

"The ladies on the Christmas Village Committee have done a wonderful job with the tree decorations," the older lady beside Millie said.

"It must take a lot of work to decorate such an enormous tree."

"Oh, absolutely. And I think those tree baubles are very tasteful and also expertly dispersed amongst the branches."

Millie smiled at the older lady before glancing back at the Christmas tree. The tall fir was perfectly proportioned, with lush branches and thick needles, and she felt sure that even if the members of the Christmas Village Committee had simply propped it up in the middle of Hollyford market square and done nothing further to it, the tree would still have held its own. But with the enormous shiny baubles dangling from the branches and catching the streetlamps around the market square, the tree looked just lovely.

Once the Christmas tree lights were switched on, it would look lovelier still.

Millie wondered what her mother would have thought of the Hollyford Christmas tree. Caroline Dawson would no doubt have insisted that there weren't enough decorations and that every empty space ought to have its own bauble.

Millie's mother hadn't approved of understated Christmas decorations or elegant colour-coordinated themes. Every December, their house had always looked like an explosion inside a tinsel factory, and Caroline hadn't rested until every available branch on their Christmas tree was groaning with baubles, every picture frame on the living room wall was festooned with garland, and every available surface boasted some festive trinket or snowy ornament.

Memories of those Christmases spent with her mother swirled in Millie's head as she gazed up at the tree in the market square. Every year, they'd listened to their favourite Christmas music while turning their house into a winter wonderland, singing along to old Bing Crosby songs and cheerful Christmas carols. Once Caroline was satisfied that the house couldn't possibly look any more festive, they'd shared a little ceremony as they turned on the fairy lights, oohing and aahing at the soft coloured lights twinkling on the tree.

With the house decorated to within an inch of its life, and with the excitement of the season bubbling in the air, the next part of their ritual had involved settling on the sofa with mugs of hot chocolate and plates of mince pies, and beginning their December-long marathon through their favourite Christmas films. They'd always started off with *The Santa Clause,* which Millie had loved ever since she was a little girl. She'd curl up beside her mother and the two of them would laugh at Tim Allen's antics as he grappled with the mystery of how he'd become Father Christmas and what he was supposed to do once he put on the Santa suit.

Millie felt a bolt of loss rush through her as those memories swirled. Her throat closed with emotion as she thought about how she'd never spend another lovely afternoon with her mother fussing over the Christmas tree and eating mince pies while Bing Crosby sang from the stereo speakers. All she had now were memories that made her heart ache with bittersweet longing.

"Are you okay, dear?"

Pulled from her thoughts, Millie glanced back at the older lady still standing beside her, and who was now watching her with a curious expression on her face. Millie offered a broad smile.

"Oh, I'm fine." She gestured to the Christmas tree. "I'm just excited to see how it will all look once they turn on the lights."

"It will be wonderful. There's nothing quite like twinkle lights on a dark December afternoon to make everything feel festive and magical." The older lady tilted her head and looked thoughtfully at Millie. "Are you new to Hollyford, dear?"

Millie nodded. "I moved here a few months ago to start a new job."

"And are you settling in all right?"

"Just fine, yes," Millie said, even although this wasn't exactly true. "Hollyford must be one of the prettiest towns in the Cotswolds."

"I couldn't agree more."

Millie had come to Hollyford after accepting a job in a residential care home for the elderly on the outskirts of the little town. The first few weeks spent finding her feet in the new location hadn't been easy, and the tiny bedroom she rented in a flat share was a far cry from the terraced house in Bristol where she'd lived with her mother for her entire life before that. As autumn had turned into winter, she'd started to settle more into the new life in which she'd found herself, but she still couldn't escape the feeling of isolation that enveloped her. Although she enjoyed the company of her work colleagues, and got on just fine with her flatmate on the rare occasions their shift patterns brought them together, she still felt frighteningly alone in the world.

She often had to remind herself that the move to Hollyford was all about making a new start, the way her mother had wanted her to do.

The way her mother had *told* her to do.

This time last year, things had been very different. When Millie thought back to those terrible days last December, it was like remembering a nightmare. Except the nightmare had been real, and Millie hadn't had the luxury of simply waking up and shaking off the bad dream as if it had never happened.

That nightmare had stolen her mother and left Millie all alone in the world.

Caroline Dawson had died on the first day of December last year, six months after receiving a cancer diagnosis that had come too late for treatment to be of any help. The shock and grief of the loss had hit Millie like a wrecking ball straight through her gut. Even as her mother's health had deteriorated, Millie had hoped for a miracle.

But that miracle had never come.

Last Christmas had passed in a blur of tears and stunned disbelief. The months that followed had been long and hard and lonely. In the end, though, Millie had had no choice but to pick herself up and get on with her life again. With no other close family members to help her through the tough time, she only had herself to rely on.

It hadn't taken her long to realise she couldn't afford to stay in the house she'd shared with her mother and would have to find another place to live. While searching for something more affordable, she'd stumbled upon the job ad for an assistant carer in a care home for the elderly, nestled in the chocolate-box Cotswold village of Hollyford.

When the interview led to a job offer, it seemed like the

fresh start Millie needed. Although the pay wasn't great, the care home job was full time and permanent, and offered an escape from the zero-hours contracts she'd worked during her mother's illness. A new job and a new place to live would help kick start her life again and help her get over the devastating loss she'd suffered. Her mother had made her promise she wouldn't wallow once she was gone, and that was a promise Millie wanted to keep.

Her mother had insisted that Millie make another promise, too.

"Millie," Caroline had said one afternoon in late November while propped up in bed at the hospice where she spent her final weeks. "This Christmas won't be like the ones we used to have."

"We'll make the most of it," Millie had answered and gestured to the small plastic Christmas tree by the window, one she'd bought in an attempt to bring early festive cheer to the hospice room. "We've got some decorations to enjoy at least."

Caroline hadn't even spared the little tree a glance, her gaze focused on Millie. "We always made our Christmases special, and we always had so much fun. Promise me that next year you'll celebrate Christmas properly and you won't look back on this one and be sad because I'm gone."

"Mum, don't say things like." The idea of not having her mother around had been too awful to think about, even although she'd known that's exactly what would soon happen.

"I don't have much time left," Caroline had said, her voice suddenly strong. "Christmas was always our favourite time of year. I need you to promise that next Christmas you'll be happy and that you'll celebrate the season the way we always used to."

"Mum, please..."

"Millie, it's the only way I can face this." Caroline's voice had wavered. "I can only face this if I know you'll come through the other side of it and go on to live the life you deserve. You need to chase after your dreams and live a wonderful life."

"Mum, all I care about right now is you."

"I keep thinking about all the times we've had together and all the Christmases we've celebrated. I don't think I can make it to Christmas. I feel myself slipping away."

Hot tears had rushed into Millie's eyes, but her mother wasn't finished.

"I can face what's coming if I know you'll be okay. I can face it if I know you'll be happy next Christmas and celebrate it the way we always did, and that you won't let what's happening right now ruin the season for you. Promise me, Millie. Please?"

Millie had been lost for words. How could she think about having a happy Christmas when this heart-breaking tragedy hadn't even finished unleashing its terrible devastation on them both?

But the pleading look in her mother's eyes left no room for argument. Through muffled tears, Millie had made the promise her mother asked of her. For a long time after Caroline's passing, she couldn't imagine how she could ever keep that promise.

But time was a healer. Wounds turned into scars and Millie realised she might be able to live with those scars, after all.

She'd made a promise to her mother to be happy this Christmas and to celebrate it the way they once had before life played its cruel trick on them both. Now, all she wanted was to keep the promise she'd made and honour her mother's memory the way she deserved.

But honouring that promise wasn't easy.

As Millie looked around Hollyford's market square, she knew her mother would have loved to take part in the festive celebrations. Caroline might not have thought the village Christmas tree was decorated quite as lavishly as it ought to be, but she would have approved of the atmosphere and spirit of the place. There was joy and happiness here, and Millie wanted to let that joy and happiness inside her heart.

If she could do that, it would mean she was honouring her mother and the memory of all those lovely Christmases they'd shared. Now that her mother was gone, it was the only way she could keep those memories alive.

A murmur of excitement rippled through the crowds gathered around the Christmas tree as the mayor made his way across the market square.

"It looks like it's time to switch on the Christmas tree lights," said the silver-haired older lady, still standing companionably at Millie's side.

"I think you're right," Millie smiled.

After welcoming everyone and saying a few words of thanks to the members of the Christmas Village Committee for all their hard work, the mayor made a show of picking up the large switch that controlled the tree lights and then asked the crowd to count down to the big moment.

As the crowd started chanting backwards from five, Millie looked around at the sight of so many excited people gathered in the market square and waiting for the tree lights to turn on. Her mind filled with thoughts of her mother and the promise she'd made last year during the darkest time of her life.

I promise I'll be happy next Christmas, Millie had said in that quiet hospice room, forcing the words out even as it broke her heart to say them.

Her mother had smiled, pure relief flooding her expression. As long as she lived, Millie would never forget the look on her mother's face that day. Now, she had to find some way to fulfil the promise that had helped Caroline through those last terrible days before the end had come.

Around her, the crowds counted down and excitement built.

Five! Four! Three! Two! ONE!

The Christmas lights switched on in a blaze of festive joy, turning the tree into a spectacular beacon in the middle of the market square. Cheers and applause rippled through the crowds as everyone admired the beautiful lights twinkling against the dark December afternoon.

Millie thought of the little tradition her mother had insisted upon every Christmas when they'd turned on the fairy lights on their tree. As the lights lit up and brought the tree to life, they'd both wished each other a happy Christmas and hugged to mark the start of the festive season.

Now, as Millie gazed up at the beautiful Christmas tree spilling warm light around the market square, she found herself making that same wish once more.

I miss you so much, Mum, Millie thought silently. *And I wish for the happy Christmas that you wanted me to have.*

Making that wish come true wouldn't be easy, but she was determined to feel the joy of the season, even although her mother's absence made her heart sore with grief. A promise was a promise, after all.

The Christmas tree glowed. The church choir began singing *We Wish You A Merry Christmas.* The spirit of the season filled the air with excitement and hope.

"Merry Christmas, dear," said the older lady standing beside her.

"Merry Christmas to you, too."

Just saying the words out loud to a stranger made Millie feel a little less lonely. The silver-haired lady's smile was warm as they stood together at the edge of the market square, and Millie was grateful for her presence beside her.

This would be a happy Christmas, Millie decided, just like she'd promised her mother it would be.

And if it seemed sometimes that the ache of loss and loneliness might force tears to fall at any moment, then she'd simply have to put on a brave face and pull herself back together again.

Because that's what her mother would have wanted.

THE CHURCH CHOIR finished singing *We Wish You A Merry Christmas*, and the people who'd gathered to watch the tree lights switch-on wandered off to inspect the Christmas stalls and the other attractions on offer. As the choir began *The Twelve Days Of Christmas*, the music mingled with the chatter from the meandering crowds and the excited shouts of children as they craned their necks to admire the display featuring Santa's sleigh at the North Pole.

"The Christmas lights switch-on appears to be a triumph!" said the older lady who was still standing beside Millie at the edge of the market square.

"Everyone looks like they're having a wonderful time," Millie replied. "And the tree is so beautiful. It looks like something from a Christmas fairy tale."

The silver-haired lady smiled. "Shall we treat ourselves to some hot chocolate?"

Millie couldn't help but glance at the stranger in surprise. They might have shared a few moments of companionable chit-chat while they waited for the tree lights to be turned on, but she hadn't expected that chit-chat to end in the two of them sharing refreshments together. Registering her expression, the woman laughed.

"How silly of me. We haven't even been introduced," she said, shaking her head as she held out her hand. "I'm Mrs Wishmore. Doris Wishmore."

Taking the woman's hand, Millie smiled. "I'm Millie Dawson. It's lovely to meet you, Mrs Wishmore."

"Please, call me Doris."

As Millie shook the woman's hand, she felt a comforting warmth spread through her fingers. Mrs Wishmore's kind smile made her feel warmer still, and the loneliness that had gripped her just a few moments ago no longer felt so dark and overwhelming. Quite suddenly, the older lady didn't seem like the stranger she'd been just a few seconds before.

"So, how about that hot chocolate?" Mrs Wishmore said. "My treat."

"Thank you, that's very kind."

Together, they left the pavement that ran along the edge of the market square and made their way towards a little pastel-painted vintage van parked on the other side, where drinks and snacks were being sold to the crowds. When they reached the van, Mrs Wishmore ordered two hot chocolates with extra marshmallows, before batting away Millie's hand and uttering a *tsk!* when Millie got out her purse and tried to pay.

"I insist on buying these drinks," Mrs Wishmore said. "After all, I was the one to suggest we ought to have them."

Millie accepted the cup of hot chocolate that Mrs Wishmore had passed to her. "Thanks again."

"It's my pleasure, dear." Mrs Wishmore sipped her drink and smacked her lips together. "Delicious. What better way to make the acquaintance of a new friend than by enjoying a steaming cup of hot chocolate on a frosty December afternoon while admiring the Christmas lights?"

Millie smiled at the older lady over the brim of her hot

chocolate cup, wondering at her oddly charming way of talking.

"Agreed," Millie said, not sure if this was the right response or not. She gestured to the wooden cabins, where festive gifts were for sale and which were attracting plenty of interest from the folks milling around in the crowds. "It looks like people are making progress with their Christmas shopping."

"Quite right, too. Have you done your Christmas shopping yet, dear?"

"Almost," Millie said, feeling her cheeks turn pink at the little white lie.

The truth was, she didn't have many people to buy presents for. Her colleagues at the care home where she worked had organised a Secret Santa, and Millie had already bought a bubble bath gift set as her contribution, along with another one to give to her flatmate. Since moving to Hollyford, she'd struggled to make new friends, her natural shyness combining with the lingering grief over her mother's death to make her feel awkward in the company of new people. Although she kept in touch with a few casual friends from Bristol, the distance had already made it feel like they were slipping out of one another's lives. Millie was only twenty-five and knew she ought to have more people in her life than she did. But since her mother's death, she just didn't have the heart for socialising.

Sometimes it felt like she'd retreated into her own tiny world, and getting back out into the actual world wasn't at all easy. Which meant that, as far as Christmas shopping was concerned, there wasn't much to do.

In fact, there wasn't *anything* to do.

"I've done most of my shopping, too," Mrs Wishmore said and gave Millie a wink. "It's good to be organised and ahead of the curve."

"Absolutely."

Millie sipped more hot chocolate and shuffled her feet, wondering what else to say. Perhaps it had been too long since she'd had to strike up a conversation with a stranger outside of a work setting, and she'd forgotten how to do it. How on earth had she imagined she could enjoy this Christmas like her mother had wanted her to, when she could barely even string together a few words to say to the kind stranger she'd met at the Christmas tree lights switch-on?

"So, Mrs Wishmore, do you enjoy living in Hollyford?" Millie asked, determined to make an effort with the friendly older lady.

"Oh, I don't live here in the village," Mrs Wishmore said. "But when I heard about the Christmas Village events starting today with the tree light switch-on, I simply had to come along. I would have been sad to miss such a lovely afternoon."

Millie nodded. "The volunteers who put this together have done such amazing work, and it's nice to come out and show some support."

"Indeed." Mrs Wishmore's gaze travelled across the market square and a wry smile appeared at her lips. "And unless I'm mistaken, here's one of the Christmas Village volunteers headed in our direction right now."

Millie turned to see a middle-aged woman bustling towards them, clutching a handful of leaflets in one hand and a clipboard in the other.

"Hello, ladies," the woman said with a smile. "I hope you're both enjoying yourselves?"

"Very much so," Mrs Wishmore said. "We were just saying that this is quite an event that the people of Hollyford have put on, weren't we, Millie?"

"Yes, it's really wonderful," Millie agreed.

"I'm glad you think so," the woman smiled. "Because I hope you might be able to help us with something." She waved the handful of leaflets in the air. "I'm Evelyn Fox, chair of the Hollyford Christmas Village Committee. We're short of volunteers to help run some of our forthcoming events, and we're canvassing the visitors who've turned up this afternoon to see if anyone might be free and interested in becoming involved."

"Oh, what a pity that you're short-handed," Mrs Wishmore said.

Evelyn waved this off. "It can't be helped. A few volunteers have come down with a nasty head cold that's been doing the rounds, and one or two others have had to step back because of unexpected work or family commitments. It's just the way of things. Anyway, perhaps you'd like to take a leaflet and look at our upcoming activities and have a think about whether you can lend a hand for a few hours some afternoon?"

The woman smiled at Mrs Wishmore and then at Millie before giving them both a leaflet. Millie glanced at the sheet of paper, her eyes widening at the sheer number of events that were planned as part of the Hollyford Christmas Village between now and Christmas Eve. She'd had no idea the programme was so extensive. The schedule included tree bauble painting, gingerbread men icing, a Christmas carol sing-along, a children's festive story time, a Christmas get-together over tea and cake in the village hall, and more besides. Every weekend between now and Christmas Eve was packed with activities, and there were even a few events happening on weekday evenings too, timed to correspond with the special late night opening hours on the high street. As she scanned the schedule, Millie thought it was little wonder that the committee needed more people to volunteer to keep everything running smoothly. She was only surprised they didn't require the deployment of an entire army regiment in order to stay on top of running the Christmas Village.

"Millie, what do you think?" Mrs Wishmore said, turning towards her. "Shall we put our names down to lend a hand with something?"

Millie was momentarily lost for words. She'd only just met the older lady a few minutes ago, and now she was on the brink of being paired up with her to volunteer with the Christmas Village Committee. It wasn't quite what she'd expected to happen when she'd turned up this afternoon to see the tree lights being switched on.

"Um, well..."

"It really would mean a great deal to the village if you could offer us an hour or two of your time," Evelyn Fox added.

"Uh..."

"Wait a minute," Evelyn said, her eyes narrowing as she studied Millie's face more closely. "I think I recognise you. Don't you work at the care home over on Gloucester Road?"

Millie nodded. "That's right."

"My mother-in-law is a resident there. I knew I recognised your face the moment I started walking towards you. I must say, the staff are very kind at the care home. My mother-in-law can't speak highly enough of everyone who looks after her there. Thank you."

Millie blushed at the generous compliment. "What's your mother-in-law's name?"

"Jean Fox."

"Yes, I know her. She's a lovely lady and always has a smile for whoever is looking after her."

"From what I hear, the carers go above and beyond for the residents, and we all appreciate it." Evelyn nodded at the leaflet in Millie's hand. "As you're an employee at the care home, I don't doubt for a minute that you'll be a valuable volunteer on our committee. So, what do you two ladies think? Are you able to lend us a few hours of your time? The Hollyford Christmas Village needs all the help it can get!"

Mrs Wishmore laughed and turned to Millie. "I'm game if you are, dear."

"Lovely!" Evelyn said, and before Millie could respond, the woman was already pulling a pen from her coat pocket and scribbling something on her clipboard. "Now, give me your phone details and I'll ring you later to find out which of our events you're available to volunteer with."

While Mrs Wishmore rattled off her details and Evelyn jotted them down on her clipboard, Millie felt a bit stunned at how all this had come about. She didn't think she'd actually agreed to do any volunteering, and yet here she was sharing her phone number with Evelyn Fox and promising to look at the list of Christmas activities and work out which ones she could help with. Before she knew it, Evelyn was clicking her pen and thanking them both and moving off to find more unsuspecting conscripts for the Christmas Village cause.

"Well, wasn't that an unexpected but lovely surprise?" Mrs Wishmore chuckled. "Won't it be nice to lend a hand and help these volunteers make a success of the Christmas Village events?"

"I suppose it would be a shame if they had to cancel things because they're short of volunteers." Millie glanced at the lovely market square, which the Christmas Village committee had transformed into a magical place for locals and visitors alike to enjoy. She couldn't help grinning at Mrs Wishmore. "Since you've already signed me up to help, I ought to look at this leaflet and find out which activities I can fit in around my shifts at the care home."

"I'm so pleased you'll be able to volunteer. Perhaps it

would be nice if we coordinate our time, so that we can help with the same events? That way, we'll be able to get to know one another a little better."

"That sounds like a nice idea."

"Wonderful! It's always lovely to make new friends, don't you think? And I have a feeling that the two of us are destined to become very good friends indeed."

Millie was surprised once more by Mrs Wishmore's odd way of talking, which was both old-fashioned and endearing at the same time. But with her kind smile and warm expression, she felt strangely drawn to the older woman and decided it might be fun to spend time with her while lending a hand with the Hollyford Christmas Village committee.

The hand of friendship was being offered, albeit from an unsuspecting source. Right then, Millie was glad to grasp it.

Mrs Wishmore pointed across the market square to a little café. "Shall we finish these hot chocolates inside the café and then order a nice pot of tea and some tasty mince pies to enjoy while we look at these Christmas Village activities and decide which ones to volunteer for?"

"That's a good idea." Millie rubbed her hands together and blew out an icy plume of air. "It's getting a little chilly out here."

Mrs Wishmore smiled. "You're quite right. Let's get cosy indoors and see what's what with this Christmas Village business."

It was an unexpected but not unwelcome twist in her afternoon, Millie thought as she accompanied Mrs Wishmore towards the little café where twinkle light glowed in the windows, drawing them closer like a beacon. Becoming friends with an old lady and volunteering for the Christmas Village committee were the last things she'd planned on doing when she'd turned up to see the tree lights being switched on, but it was far more appealing than wandering around the market square by herself.

And maybe getting involved with some volunteering work would be just the thing she needed to help her make some friends in the community. At the very least, if it helped her stave off the sadness and loneliness of this second Christmas without her mother, then it would be more than worth the effort.

Feeling comforted by this thought, Millie followed Mrs Wishmore across the market square, her mind already turning to the tea and treats they'd agreed to enjoy together in the little café.

CHAPTER TWO

Adam Carter turned the sign on the shop door to 'Closed' and blew out a sigh of relief. The Hollyford Christmas tree lights switch-on always brought an influx of visitors to the village, and he was grateful for the extra custom at the gift shop he owned on the high street. But the compulsory festive merriment and good cheer had begun to grate after a while, and he was glad he wouldn't have to wish anyone else a 'Merry Christmas' for the rest of the day.

His face actually hurt from smiling all afternoon at the endless stream of customers who'd come into the shop. Adam rubbed at his jaw, feeling his cheek muscles sag and wondered how he'd make it through the entire month of December with a fake smile pasted on his face while mumbling insincere Christmas wishes at his customers.

This Scrooge-like attitude wasn't usual for him. Running a gift shop in the quaint Cotswold town of Hollyford, which prided itself on its annual Christmas celebrations, meant that it was all but compulsory to get into the spirit of things. In the past, that hadn't been a problem for Adam, and he'd always enjoyed the fun and excitement of Christmas.

But not this year.

This year, he'd happily forget about the whole thing if he could—forget about the Christmas Village events, forget about the Christmas tree light switch-on, forget about the festive activities lined up throughout December to attract visitors to Hollyford.

But forgetting about those things wasn't an option. This was the busiest time of the year for his gift shop. Visitors who came to enjoy the Christmas tree in the market square and the various festive events laid on throughout the month also spent a lot of money in the town while they were doing it. Adam's shop, Hollyford Gift Emporium, was one of the most popular businesses on the high street, with its classic Cotswold stone-fronted façade and old fashioned glass windows and alluring collection of high quality items for sale inside. Stocking only the best artisan and hand-crafted goods, Adam's shop had built a solid reputation over the years since he'd first opened. From glassware to jewellery, ceramics to original art, wooden toys to scented candles, the shop stocked exactly those sorts of things that were catnip to Christmas shoppers searching for unusual gifts for their loved ones.

A big chunk of the gift shop's revenue was generated in the six weeks before Christmas Day, which meant that unless he wanted to go out of business, he had to at least pay lip service to the seasonal events, even although he had absolutely no Christmas spirit inside him at all.

None whatsoever.

It occurred to him that he ought to wear one of those fake Santa Claus beards while working at the shop, and that way the customers might not be able to tell whether he was smiling or not. He was pondering the practicality of this idea as he closed out the till when he heard a sharp knock on the shop door.

Glancing up, he saw his mother peering through the glass window of the shop. A frown creased her forehead as she scanned the shop's interior, her expression displeased. Adam had already switched off the overhead lights at the front of the shop, happy to rely on the lamp beside the till while he finished his tasks for the day, and he wondered whether he could just sink down beneath the counter and pretend he wasn't there.

Even from a distance, Adam could tell from his mother's face that this wasn't just a social call. Lesley Carter had that look that told him she was annoyed about something and Adam suspected wearily that he knew exactly what that something was. The day had been long enough already without adding a telling off from his mother into the mix.

"Adam, I know you're in there!" his mother called out, shading her eyes with her palm as she peered into the depths of the shop. She ducked her head for a better view. "I can see you at the counter, Adam! Open the door this instant!"

With a sigh, Adam set aside his work at the till and headed for the shop door. As soon as he unlocked it, his mother marched inside, her heels clacking on the floor and her smart silk scarf whipping at her neck as she spun around to face him.

"What on earth is the matter with the front of this shop, Adam Carter?" Lesley demanded, her forehead creased in a deep furrow as she stared him down.

"Nice to see you too, Mum," Adam replied, locking the door again. "I thought you and dad didn't get back from your cruise until later tonight."

His parents had been on a Caribbean winter getaway for the past two weeks, and judging by her bronzed face, his mother had enjoyed absorbing the sun. Despite the hours spent flying back from the cruise and then driving home to Hollyford from the airport, Lesley looked fresh and energised and was obviously ready to do battle.

"I told you we'd be back by this evening," Lesley said. "I didn't think you were listening when I said it."

"Of course I was listening. Did you have fun on your holiday?"

"I'm not here to discuss my holiday. I'm here to discuss what's going on at this shop. When we drove past here on our way home, I couldn't believe my eyes. As soon as we'd hauled our suitcases from the car, I had no choice but to drive back over to find out what's going on. So, tell me—what's going on?"

Adam shrugged. "Nothing's going on. I just closed up for the day."

Lesley's gaze narrowed. "Are you being deliberately obtuse? I'm talking about the front of your shop, Adam! Why on earth is it cloaked in darkness?"

"Because we're closed for the day and I've turned off the lights."

"Adam! For God's sake, what's the matter with you? I'm asking why there are no Christmas decorations up in the windows?"

Adam glanced towards the shop windows. "There *are* decorations up, Mother."

He pointed to the three-dimensional paper snowflakes he'd hung at various heights across the main front window. There was silence for a moment as his mother's gaze swung towards the windows and then back to him. Even although he wasn't looking at her, he could still feel her angry stare as if it were burning a hole in the side of his head.

"Are you telling me those are the only decorations you're putting up in this shop?" Lesley said, her tone dangerously even.

"I thought the understated look might make a nice change this year."

He wasn't even convincing himself with this argument. The appalled look on his mother's face made it clear what she thought of his response.

"You can't be serious." Lesley glanced again at the paper snowflakes dangling in the window. "Every shop on the high street is decorated to the nines except yours. Why haven't you put the little silver Christmas tree in the window or strung up the twinkle lights?"

"Like I said, I felt like a change this year."

Lesley propped a hand on her hip, which Adam knew was never a good sign. "This is about Heidi, isn't it?"

With another sigh, Adam walked back to the counter and resumed bagging cash from the till. "I just don't feel like turning the shop into Santa's Grotto this year. What's wrong with that?"

"Adam, this shop has never looked like Santa's Grotto. It's always been the most tastefully decorated shop front on the high street. You always do a brilliant job and everyone thinks so. But this…" Lesley waved a hand at the paper snowflakes in the window. "This isn't good enough, Adam. It looks like you don't care about the season and that you don't care to be part of the Christmas Village. Is that really what you want people passing by outside to think?"

"That's not what they'll think."

"How can you be so sure? There are plenty of other shops on this street where visitors can spend their money and plenty of other shops doing their utmost to lure customers inside."

"Mother, I was non-stop today in the shop with customers. They're clearly not put off because I've chosen to tone things down this year when it comes to the window decorations."

A pained look crossed Lesley's face. "But you could do so much more to make things festive here, Adam."

"Look, why is it that the first thing you do after getting back from holiday is turn up here and start harassing me?"

"Because you're my son and I'm worried about you, that's why."

The sudden softness in his mother's voice caught him off-guard. "You don't have to worry about me. I'm fine."

"If this is about Heidi, then maybe talking about it would help."

"Can we just leave it, Mum?"

Lesley opened her mouth to say something more, but the look on his face must have made her think twice, because she stayed silent. Adam was relieved. The last thing he wanted to talk about was Heidi.

His mother glanced around the shop. "I could help you put up some twinkle lights if you'd like."

Adam couldn't help but sigh again. "If it makes you happy, I'll run a few strings in the window tomorrow, okay?" If he didn't give her something, she'd only keep on at him until he either surrendered or they fell out over the issue completely. Agreeing to a few twinkle lights might be the easy way out, even if he did loathe everything about the idea.

Lesley nodded, apparently satisfied with this concession. "This is an amazing little business you've built up, Adam. I'd hate for it to hit a bad patch because you foolishly underplay your hand during the Christmas season and miss out on customers."

"I don't want that, either."

"And I also don't want you to miss out on Christmas because of *that woman*." Lesley almost spat the words out as her anger resurfaced. "It's not fair."

"Mum, can we just drop it?"

Lesley held up her hands in a placating gesture. "Fine."

"And anyway, shouldn't you be at home helping dad to unpack instead of here interrogating me? You know he'll get the laundry stuff mixed up and put all your things in the wrong place in the wardrobe if you aren't there to supervise him."

"That's true. And I know how much your father loves it when I supervise him." She smiled at last, and Adam was pleased they were back on easier territory. He hated it when they had cross words. Lately, there had been far too many of them.

Lesley turned for the door. "Why don't you come over for dinner tomorrow night. Your father will want to show you the ten million photographs he took of the cruise ship and the buffet tables on the restaurant deck. Honestly, those buffets were all he could talk about. Come over for six and I'll make beef casserole and mash."

"Okay, that sounds good."

"I'll ask Angela to bring something for dessert."

At the mention of his sister's name, Adam's smile disappeared. "If Angela's going to be there, then I'll give it a miss."

His mother gave him a hard stare. "Adam, how long are you going to keep this up? Don't you think this silliness has gone on long enough?"

"First, there's nothing silly about it. Second, I just don't want to see Angela, okay?"

Lesley threw up her hands in despair. "You don't want to put up Christmas decorations. You don't want to talk about Heidi. You don't want to see your sister. This is ridiculous, Adam. This isn't who you are."

She was right. Adam hadn't always been this way, and the truth was he didn't much like this version of himself. But after everything that had happened, he felt humiliated and sad and stuck, and he didn't have the first idea how what to do about it.

None of that was his mother's fault, though, and he was being a jerk by taking it out on her. She was the one who kept turning up and checking on him and trying to jostle him back into life. He just wasn't sure there was much of a life for him to get jostled back into.

"I'll pop round and see you and Dad some other night, instead, okay?"

"And what about Angela?"

"Mum..."

"Fine, I'll drop it," she said, shaking her head and sighing. After pecking him on the cheek, she opened the door. "Make sure you get those twinkle lights up."

"Okay."

Adam stood at the door and watched his mother hurry across the road to where she'd parked the car. After waving her off, he locked up again and returned to the counter to finish dealing with the till.

The quiet stillness of the shop settled around him as he dealt with his paperwork. Adam was grateful for the silence after the strained conversation with his mother and grateful too for the busy work of the shop that kept his mind off things he'd rather not think about.

Like Heidi, for instance, and the terrible thing she'd done to him.

And all the other awful things that had happened because of it.

Adam scowled, realising he was thinking about exactly those things he didn't want to think about and that he'd lost track of his till calculations. Shaking his head, he backtracked through the numbers and started again.

Movement outside the window caught his eye a moment later, and he looked up to see Gayle and Nathan—who owned the greeting card shop across the road—hauling a miniature Christmas tree into place outside their shop door before switching on the pink lights draped around it. The couple, both in their fifties, clapped their hands in obvious pleasure at the sight of the little tree, before fussing with its position beside the shop door.

They already had acres of coloured lights around their shop window and door frame, not to mention a cheerful illuminated Father Christmas welcoming customers beside the step. And yet there they were, adding yet more festive interest to their little card shop.

Adam's gaze travelled to the chocolate shop next door to Gayle and Nathan's, and then to the florist's further along. Each shop owner had put on their usual Christmas displays to charm visitors and entice customers. Soft yellow vintage lights glowed around the window of the chocolate shop, while vibrant green lights laced their way around the displays of mistletoe and roses and holly that decorated the florist's window.

Adam knew his own shop looked dim and dark in comparison to the displays put together by his fellow business owners. He knew he ought to do what he'd promised his mother he'd do and at least add a couple of strings of white twinkle lights to the windows, to show willing.

But he just couldn't face it. Even although he knew it was stupid and foolish, he just couldn't face it.

Turning back to his shop paperwork and chores at the counter, Adam once more pushed thoughts of Christmas from his head and refocused on work.

But his traitorous mind started thinking about Heidi instead, and no matter what he did, those painful thoughts refused to be silenced.

For a long time, Adam thought all his dreams had come true when he met Heidi Ryan. She was smart, beautiful, exciting, and filled with life and fun, and she'd stolen his heart from the first moment he laid eyes on her across a crowded Cheltenham pub one balmy summer's night. For two years, they'd been inseparable.

Until the day Heidi had dropped her bombshell and walked out of his life for good, leaving his heart in tatters and his world in turmoil.

Although three months had passed since that fateful day when he'd learned the awful truth about her unthinkable betrayal, Adam still felt like his entire world was spinning upside down and that he was barely clinging on to the edges of it.

Shock and humiliation still burned inside him like a searing flame. It hurt to think about the relationship they'd once had and what they'd once meant to each other, because thinking about those things made Adam wonder if he'd been taken for a fool all along.

It hadn't been hard to fall in love with Heidi. With her long blonde hair and emerald eyes and laughing voice, Adam had been bewitched from the start. Heidi had been the one who'd walked the length of the bar counter in that busy Cheltenham pub to talk to him while he'd been waiting to buy drinks for the friends he'd met for a Friday night catch up. Before the barman had even finished pulling the pints he'd ordered, Adam had been halfway in love with Heidi.

They soon became a couple and did all the usual things that couples did together—went on dates, got to know one another, shared their stories and their hopes and their dreams, met one another's families. Heidi filled his life with excitement and passion, and her boundless enthusiasm for living each day to the fullest left him breathless.

On a romantic holiday together on the sun-kissed Amalfi

coast in Italy, eighteen months after they met and six months after they moved in together, Adam got down on one knee and asked Heidi to marry him. The joy on her face as she said yes and let him slip the diamond solitaire onto her ring finger made him dizzy with love.

As they planned their wedding, Heidi said her dream was to get married at Christmas. She wanted a beautiful midwinter ceremony filled with all the fun and excitement of the season, in a pretty Cotswold church decorated with Christmas flowers and white twinkle lights, on a day brimming with so much Christmas romance it would make them both swoon. Her wedding dress would be a December fantasy of ivory silk and soft feathers, her bouquet an explosion of Christmas red roses. They'd dance their first dance to *Have Yourself A Merry Little Christmas*, and then party with their wedding guests to every cheesy Christmas song ever recorded. They'd serve mulled wine and roast turkey for their wedding meal, and give gifts of Christmas tree baubles to their guests as wedding favours.

It would be the most gorgeous and Christmassy wedding of all time, she promised him, and once they were married, they'd both love Christmas more than ever because of it.

Adam had agreed to everything she wanted. He would've caught the moon and stars in his hands and given them to her if he could.

During the sweltering heat of June and July, Heidi had talked non-stop about the Christmas wedding they were planning and all the festive details that were involved. If she seemed to turn quieter as summer dipped towards autumn, Adam simply chalked it up to the fact that by then the wedding was mostly planned, the December twenty-first ceremony date booked and ready to go. He assumed Heidi was just wiped out from all the work involved in organising a sizeable wedding in less than six months, the same way he was. He assumed that with the details fixed in place, she just wanted to revel in the anticipation of the big day.

It was an assumption he soon bitterly regretted making.

One rainy evening in September, Adam returned home after closing the gift shop for the day to find Heidi waiting for him in the living room with her coat on and her bags packed.

I've met someone else, she blurted out. *I'm sorry. I didn't mean to hurt you.*

And then she walked out the door and out of his life for good.

She'd said a lot more than just those three short sentences, of course, but Adam had no recollection of what it might have been. He'd been too stunned to absorb the details.

When those details finally clicked into place and he realised exactly what had been going on for the last two months of their relationship, the shock had only deepened.

Add a nasty dose of raw humiliation and searing embarrassment into the mix, and Adam had been well and truly floored. The autumn months had passed in a blur as he'd tried to come to terms with what had happened and face the new reality of his life. Now though, with Christmas just around the corner and Hollyford in full festive mode all around him, all he could think about was the December wedding day that would never happen.

When he saw twinkle lights, he thought of Heidi's excited face as she talked about stringing thousands upon thousands of them around the hotel function room they'd booked for their wedding reception. When he heard Christmas music, he thought of the cheesy Christmas pop playlist Heidi had compiled for their evening dancing after the wedding meal. When he saw Christmas decorations, he thought of the tree bauble wedding favours Heidi had ordered for their guests and which he'd eventually hauled off at the charity shop, unable to look at the things for even a second.

A thousand times a day, his mind turned to the wedding dress Heidi would have worn, the winter bouquet she would have carried, the vows they would have taken.

The life they might have shared.

Now, instead of counting down to a Christmas wedding with his beautiful bride, all Adam could think about was the betrayal and the humiliation and the shattered dreams.

Everything about this Christmas made him ache for what he'd lost.

More than that, every twinkle light, every Christmas song, every festive greeting made him feel like a fool for being too stupid to see what had been going on right under his nose for all those weeks before Heidi pulled the pin and detonated their relationship.

For months, she'd been having an affair with another man, and he'd been completely clueless. Knowing he'd been so utterly in the dark made him feel like the most foolish man on earth, made him cringe with humiliation, made him ache with the pain of rejection.

And made him hate this Christmas with every fibre of his being.

All this would have been more than enough to deal with, but the chaos Heidi had unleashed in his life didn't end there. It turned out that her affair hadn't been a complete secret, and when Adam learned who else knew about it, he'd been stunned all over again.

His sister, Angela, had known exactly what was going on and yet hadn't breathed a word of it to him. Even now, months after the wedding had been called off, he couldn't get his head around the fact that Angela had known about Heidi's affair and hadn't told him about it.

His fiancé cheating on him and calling off their

Christmas wedding was bad enough. His own sister knowing about all the sordid details long before he did just made him feel like he'd been slapped in the face.

Family was supposed to be about love and loyalty, and yet when he'd needed exactly those things from his sister, she'd failed him spectacularly. He could never forgive Angela for heaping yet another betrayal on top of the one he was already reeling from. Knowing that the disastrous humiliation he'd suffered not only meant the end of his relationship with Heidi and the cancellation of their Christmas wedding, but that it had also caused trauma and bad blood inside his own family, left Adam feeling bereft whenever he thought about all that had happened.

Which was exactly why thinking about any of it was a terrible idea.

Adam finished the last of his tasks at the shop counter and grabbed his jacket and satchel from the back office. After turning on the security system and locking the door, he made his way along the high street towards home. As he passed the festive store fronts of his fellow shop owners, with their twinkle lights left on overnight to add extra cheer to the high street, he couldn't resist glancing back at his own shop front that was cloaked in darkness.

He knew his little shop could look better and that it *should* look better. But if he had to stare at twinkle lights and festive baubles draped all around his shop for the entire Christmas season, he thought it might actually kill him.

All he wanted was to get through this Christmas, put the wretched day of his cancelled December wedding behind him, and then think about making a fresh start once the new year arrived.

He only wished he knew how to do it without looking like a miserable old Scrooge for the next four weeks.

I wish this whole, rotten Christmas was already over, Adam found himself thinking as he buttoned his coat against the December chill.

"Bah, humbug!" he muttered for good measure and allowed himself a wry smile as he turned for home.

ADAM HAD REACHED the corner of the high street when he heard a strange tinkling sound coming from his right where the hill twisted and narrowed into Church Lane.

The street was quiet but for the tinkling sound, with no pedestrians at this late hour in the quieter part of the village. As he peered into the gloom of the lane, the tinkling sound grew louder.

Moments later, Adam was baffled by the sight of a small white ball rolling down the darkened lane, tinkling all the way as it skittered and bounced over the uneven cobbles, before coming to a stop at his feet.

There was no one else around, no other noise, no movement whatsoever. There was just the quiet gloom of the cobbled lane and the December chill in the air and the improbable appearance of the little tinkling ball at Adam's feet.

Puzzled by its sudden appearance on the ground next to him, Adam picked it up for a closer look.

The ball was an iridescent white tree bauble, with a red ribbon attached to a small hook on the top. On one side of the ball there was a painted angel with feathery wings and a halo and a serene smile. The little ball tinkled as Adam turned it over in his palm and he felt the little jingle bell inside the bauble move around to create the sweet musical noise.

Adam frowned at the white bauble, and then peered into the gloom of Church Lane where it wound up the hill towards St. Luke's church, which was cloaked in darkness at this late hour, wondering where on earth the little item could have come from.

He wondered, too, how the bauble could have rolled all the way downhill across the uneven cobbles and landed intact at his feet. The cobbles were edgy and rough, while the bauble was delicate and light, and as he turned it over in his hand, he felt sure it was made of thin porcelain or possibly even glass, although the strange feel of the material against his skin made it a little difficult to tell.

Quite how the tiny bauble hadn't been smashed to pieces on its journey across the cobbles was a mystery.

From the depths of Church Lane, a shadow appeared up ahead, stretching out across the cobbles beneath a single, dim streetlamp as footsteps grew louder. A few seconds later, a figure shuffled around the corner.

"Hello?" Adam called out.

"Oh, hello!" said a woman bustling towards him down the lane. Her gaze flicked to the white bauble in Adam's open palm. "You caught the angel charm! Well done, young man!"

Adam glanced at the bauble and then back at the older lady as she stepped out of the gloom of Church Lane. She was bundled up in a red winter coat and clutched a big blue leather handbag over her shoulder. Her hair was a silvery cloud around her head that made Adam think inexplicably of the halo worn by the angel painted on the tree bauble he held in his hand. She laughed as she drew near, sending a puff of white air into the frosty night.

"I thought I might not find that little charm again on this dark lane," the woman said with a chuckle. "Thank goodness you were here to catch it before it rolled any further."

Adam glanced at the bauble and held it out. "Here you go."

"Thank you very much." The woman took the bauble from him. "I keep this little bauble with me at this time of year as a sort of Christmas good luck charm. It slipped from my bag as I was pulling out a handkerchief and rolled away before I knew what was happening. I'm glad you caught it."

"No problem." He smiled at the lady and then nodded back towards the high street. "Well, I'd better get going. Good night."

But before he could start walking, the woman spoke again. "Aren't you the owner of that lovely little shop further down the high street? Hollyford Gift Emporium?"

"That's right, yes."

The woman nodded. "I thought so. It's a beautiful shop with so many lovely things for sale."

"Thank you."

"You must be very busy at this time of year, with people taking care of their Christmas shopping and looking for gifts for loved ones. Perhaps I ought to pop in sometime and see if I can pick up a few bits and pieces."

"Of course, please do. I'm sure we can help you take care of any gifts you need to buy."

"I'd certainly appreciate that." The woman glanced at the tree bauble and looked thoughtful. "Well, thanks again for catching this little good luck charm."

"My pleasure. Good night."

"Good night, Adam."

With a final smile for the older lady, he turned and resumed his walk along the high street. He'd reached the turn onto Sycamore Street when it struck him that the woman had called him by his name, even although he'd never actually introduced himself.

That seemed a little odd, didn't it?

Frowning, he reminded himself that the woman—whoever she was—had recognised him as the owner of the gift shop, which meant she probably knew his name, too. It was part and parcel of running a business in a small town like Hollyford; plenty of folks recognised you, even if you couldn't quite place them.

Still, something about the way the older lady had spoken to him seemed… what? Strange? Oddly familiar?

And what sort of person carried tree baubles around in their handbags as good luck charms?

He reminded himself that it was Christmas, and that people had all kinds of odd traditions at Christmas.

An image filled his head of the little tree bauble rolling down the dark lane across the hard cobbles and landing at his feet intact. He wondered how had that been possible. Why hadn't the delicate bauble been smashed to pieces?

Adam shook his head at the silly question. It had been a long day and he was tired, not to mention hungry. No wonder he was fixating on the odd incident with the runaway tree bauble and the old lady it belonged to—he'd been up since before six this morning and hadn't eaten since lunch time, thanks to a non-stop day of work at the shop.

It was time to switch off. Adam picked up his pace and turned once more for home, grateful that he'd soon be putting another day of this wretched Christmas season behind him. As he hurried past the brightly lit shop windows of his fellow business owners on the high street, and tried his best to ignore the holly-shaped light displays strung up on the lampposts, he thought of his decoration-free house, where there was not a single hint of the season to be found anywhere.

He could hardly wait to get home and close his front door on the Christmas-obsessed world outside it.

CHAPTER THREE

Two days after the Hollyford Christmas tree lights switch-on, Millie arrived at the village hall for her first stint of volunteering duty. Although she'd just finished a busier than usual seven-to-three day shift at the care home, during which she'd been run off her feet for the entire time, she was excited about the couple of hours she'd agreed to spend helping the Christmas Village committee.

As she walked through the doors of the village hall and saw more than a dozen people already gathered inside and hard at work, she knew she'd done the right thing in getting involved. The little hall was brimming with festive energy, helped along by the Christmas music pumping out from a small speaker set up on a trestle table where Evelyn Fox, the committee chair, was busy coordinating her team.

For a split second, Millie's innate shyness stopped her on the threshold of the door, but before she could think about feeling awkward or out of place amongst these new people, she heard her name being called from the other side of the hall.

"Hello, Millie! Come on in!"

Millie turned to see the smiling face of Mrs Wishmore, standing with a group of women who were immersed in the task of disentangling lengths of tinsel from inside a big plastic bag.

"Hello, Mrs Wishmore," Millie said when she reached the group.

"I told you to call me Doris, dear," the older lady smiled. She held out the end of a strand of red tinsel. "Here, take hold of this while I work through the knots that have tied all these tinsel strands together. I can't imagine who packed all this away last year, but I think if Evelyn Fox finds out who it was, she'll give them an earful!"

Millie took the garland end from Mrs Wishmore and helped her tease out the knots. "What's all this tinsel for?"

"According to Evelyn, it will be used to decorate the raffle stall the committee will set up at the Christmas carol sing-alongs that are happening throughout the month," Mrs Wishmore explained. "In fact, I think Evelyn has a few tasks in mind for us to help with today as far as the sing-along events are concerned."

A few days earlier when Millie had settled down inside the cosy café on the market square with Mrs Wishmore after the Christmas tree lights switch-on, they'd marked off several activities on the Christmas Village schedule when they'd be free to help. Later that evening, Evelyn Fox had phoned Millie to chat about her volunteering availability and had suggested that she and Mrs Wishmore come along to the next Christmas Village committee meeting, to meet some of the other volunteers before jumping in at the deep end with the planned activities. Millie had been happy to agree to the suggestion, although she suspected she wouldn't just be at the committee meeting in order to meet people and that she'd be quickly put to work.

As she helped Mrs Wishmore untangle the tinsel, she

smiled at how her suspicions had proved correct. While the tinsel detangling work continued, Mrs Wishmore introduced Millie to the other folk who were also helping with the task, explaining that she'd arrived early and had already met many of the other volunteers. The older lady had obviously already struck up a rapport with the rest of the team, chatting to them as if she'd known them for ages, and Millie couldn't help but be surprised by Doris's relaxed and friendly ways.

It struck her that she ought to take a leaf out of Mrs Wishmore's book when it came to interacting with people and making new friends. Doris made it all look so easy, and Millie wished—not for the first time—that her own shyness and social awkwardness wasn't such an obstacle in her life.

Millie was saying hello to the mix of middle-aged men and women, and to the other people who looked closer to her own age and who were busy with other tasks elsewhere in the village hall, when Evelyn Fox appeared beside her.

"Hello, Millie, how nice to see you here," Evelyn said, her clipboard in one hand and a pen in the other. "I'm so pleased that you and Doris were able to put your shoulder to the wheel and come along today."

"I'm happy to help and it looks like there's plenty to do," Millie laughed.

"Indeed. I see you've made quick work of that messy tinsel. Well done." Evelyn nodded in approval at the lengths of tinsel now laid out on the floor and then gestured to one of the trestle tables on the other side of the village hall. "I have another task in mind for you two ladies, if you'll both come this way."

Evelyn walked quickly across the hall to the little table and Mrs Wishmore wiggled her eyebrows at Millie as they hurried along in the wake of the formidable woman, her expression causing her to giggle.

"Now, let me explain what I need you to do." Evelyn

pointed to the items spread out on the table. There were several wholesale-sized tubs of sweets—foam shrimps, jelly worms, marshmallows, and treats of that sort—alongside a stack of clear plastic cone-shaped bags and three rolls of Christmassy ribbons decorated with snowmen, robins, and Christmas trees.

"Along with our raffle, we're planning to set up a stall during the Christmas sing-alongs to raise money for the Hollyford community garden fund," Evelyn explained. "The goodie stall is one of our most popular money-makers, and we need to make a head-start on our homemade treat bags. The children love them and adults often buy them as last-minute stocking fillers, so we need to have a plentiful supply available to sell. Now, let me explain what you need to do."

Evelyn grabbed one of the clear cone-shaped plastic bags, filled it with a selection of sweets from the big tubs, then snipped off a length of Christmas ribbon and tied it around the top.

"There's nothing to it," Evelyn said, handing Millie the treat bag she'd put together. "Twenty-five sweets per bag, please, and make sure the mix looks nicely arranged from the outside, so that prospective buyers can see which sweets are inside each one. Any questions?"

"This all looks straightforward enough," Mrs Wishmore said. "It will be a nice easy task to get us into the swing of things."

"Good." Evelyn nodded, obviously pleased with this response, and ticked something off on her clipboard. "If you two ladies can fill forty or fifty of these bags while you're here, that will be a big help."

"Consider it done," Mrs Wishmore said. "Now, where can we wash up before getting stuck in?"

Evelyn directed them to the toilets at the back of the village hall, and once they'd washed their hands, Millie and

Mrs Wishmore settled down at the table and got to work on filling the sweet bags. Doris popped a pink marshmallow into her mouth as she worked and passed one to Millie with a wink.

"I'm sure the Christmas Village committee can afford to give us a sweet or two while we work," the older lady said with a chuckle. "Now, tell me a bit about yourself, Millie. When we enjoyed tea together the other afternoon after the tree lights switch-on, we were so busy studying the Christmas Village activities and whatnot that we didn't have a chance to chat about other things and get to know one another a little better. Tell me a bit about your job at the care home. Do you enjoy it?"

Millie nodded and swallowed the marshmallow she'd been chewing. "It's a lovely place to work. The shifts are often tough, with endless running around, and some of the elderly folk who live at the care home need a lot of care and attention, especially the poor souls who have memory trouble and who get easily confused and upset about things. But I love the job, and the residents and the staff are all wonderful."

"Have you always worked in the care sector?"

"Actually, no. It's a bit of a departure for me, although I've done all kinds of jobs in the past. Waitress, hotel maid, cleaner, call centre customer service assistant, office temp."

Mrs Wishmore laughed. "My goodness, what a wonderful job history!"

"I suppose that's one way of looking at it, although some of those jobs didn't feel so wonderful at the time." Millie smiled and rolled her eyes. "Hospitality work can be really high pressured, and I'm not sure I was ever cut out for it. Angry diners who start yelling about their meals not being up to scratch make me all nervous and sweaty."

"I'm sure they make most serving staff feel that way, no

matter how long they've worked in the industry. Angry people do have that effect on others, unfortunately."

Millie shuddered at the memory of some of the horrible customers she'd served in the past while working as a waitress in a big chain restaurant in Bristol. The job hadn't suited her personality at all and she'd felt anxious and out of her depth during most of her shifts, worrying on the one hand that she couldn't keep up with the frantic pace during the busy spells, and terrified on the other hand that some unhappy customer would make a scene that would leave her mortified and in her shift supervisor's bad books. The other serving staff didn't seem to dwell on these inevitable incidents that cropped up from time to time, but angry customers always left Millie feeling like she was stupid and incompetent. She'd only lasted in the waitressing job for a couple of months before her mother told her to quit and find something else, insisting that there was no point in working at a job if it made her miserable, not when there were other options out there.

"My mother always said that angry people are angry at themselves more than they're angry at other people," Millie said, remembering the words her mother had said one time after Millie had come home from an especially brutal Friday night shift.

"She's quite right," Mrs Wishmore nodded. "Your mother sounds like a very wise woman and you be sure to tell her I said so."

Millie frowned at the half-filled sweet bag in her hand, wondering why she'd mentioned her mother in the conversation when she hadn't needed to. Across the table, she was aware of Mrs Wishmore's gaze on her.

"Are you okay, dear?" the older lady asked.

"I'm fine, it's just..." She took a breath before continuing. "My mum died last year."

Mrs Wishmore's expression crumpled. "Oh, Millie. I'm so very sorry to hear that."

The older lady reached across the table and laid a hand on Millie's arm, squeezing gently. The gesture was comforting and welcome.

"She passed away a few weeks before Christmas," Millie said, turning the half-filled sweet bag over and over in her hands. "I really miss her."

"Of course you do."

"Sorry, I didn't mean to bring it up, but you said I should tell her what you said, and it just suddenly struck me that I couldn't do that."

"I understand. And you mustn't apologise for telling me this. I can't imagine how hard it must have been for you to lose your mother when you're still so young. And for her to have passed away close to Christmas must make it even more devastating."

Millie gulped back against the wave of emotion that was threatening to sweep over her. With no close family in her life, and few friends, she hadn't really talked about her mother's death much since it happened. She'd kept the loss and grief locked up inside. Now, seeing the compassion on Mrs Wishmore's face and feeling the comforting weight of her hand on her arm made Millie feel like those tearful floodgates might burst open at any moment.

Determined not to make a fool of herself, she sniffed back against the swirling emotions. She'd only met Mrs Wishmore a few days ago, and the last thing the kind lady would want was some stranger blubbering all over her, especially considering they'd hardly got to know one another yet.

"It was a tough time," Millie said, and pasted on a smile. "But it was a year ago now, and I'm trying hard to move on and get over it."

Mrs Wishmore gave her a considered look, a mixture of

sadness and understanding. When she spoke again, her voice was soft.

"Grief isn't something we just 'get over', Millie. When we lose someone we love, that loss stays with us, even if the pain eventually recedes. It's okay to feel sad, even now, about your loss."

Millie blinked. "Of course I feel sad, but it's just..."

She couldn't think of what she wanted to say next. Mrs Wishmore's words had taken her by surprise. This wasn't the sort of conversation she'd expected to have while helping with these Christmas Village volunteering tasks. In fact, the whole point of volunteering in the first place was so she could get into the Christmas spirit properly, the way her mother had wanted.

"My mother and I always loved Christmas time," Millie said. "We had our lovely little traditions and things we enjoyed doing together to celebrate the season, just like most people do. My mother was ill for a while before she died, and in her final few weeks, as December got closer, it upset her to think about how her illness and... well, the way that illness would end... it upset her to think that those awful weeks would make Christmas very difficult for me once she was gone. She made me promise that wouldn't happen."

Millie smiled, determined to make her new friend understand. Mrs Wishmore gave a soft smile of her own and patted Millie's arm. Once more, Millie was grateful for that comforting gesture.

"Your mother obviously loved you very much," Mrs Wishmore said.

"It was typical of her to be worrying about me instead of thinking about the awful thing that was happening to her. Which is why it's important that I do what she asked me to do and enjoy Christmas the way we used to. Or at least try to." She blew out a breath. "I know that sounds crazy."

"It doesn't sound crazy, not in the slightest. I understand completely." Mrs Wishmore's gaze roamed Millie's face for a moment before she spoke again. "And I certainly commend your desire to fulfil your mother's wishes. I'm sure she'd be very proud of you making a commitment to the cause of the Christmas Village and lending a hand where it's needed. That really is in the spirit of the season."

"I admit I have selfish motivations too. It's not easy to feel festive when you're all by yourself and don't have any family or friends to turn to."

Millie blushed at this admission and the way she'd just blurted it out without even realising it. Quite why she was sharing all this personal information with Mrs Wishmore was a complete mystery. How had they gone from talking about innocuous things that were the bread and butter of friendly chit-chat, to discussions about death and grief and loneliness?

And why was this conversation all about Millie? She blushed at how one-sided their chatter had become, but before she could do anything about it, Mrs Wishmore spoke again.

"I'm sorry you feel alone in the world, Millie," the older lady said. "That must be incredibly difficult. You don't have any other family members in your life?"

Millie shook her head. "My parents separated when I was a baby and my father didn't stay in my life. He sends text messages occasionally, but we aren't in much contact otherwise."

"That's a shame," Mrs Wishmore said mildly. "There are no grandparents or aunts and uncles in your life?"

"My mother's parents died a few years ago, and she was an only child. So, it's just me now."

Millie stuffed a few sweets into the bag she was filling and wished she wasn't talking about any of this. It made her sad to think about how she had no family around her. She longed for those close connections and loving ties. For as long as she could remember, her mother had been her entire family. Their bond had been strong and Caroline always made her feel loved and safe. She hadn't realised just how much those things meant until they were gone. Now that she was alone, she sometimes felt like she was drifting in a world that didn't care what happened to her. When those feelings crept in, she always had to work hard to push them away again.

Perhaps Mrs Wishmore could see the troubled look on her face because she offered a kind smile.

"I think you've done the right thing getting involved in this volunteering work, Millie. Maybe it will help you make new connections in the village."

"Yes, I hope so."

"I'm sure you've already made new friends here in Hollyford, but a person can never have too many friends."

Millie smiled at Mrs Wishmore's sensible words, but inside, she felt mortified. It wasn't easy admitting that you didn't have any friends because you were too shy and socially awkward to actually make any. Quite suddenly, Millie felt like a big fat failure. Life was supposed to be about making connections and filling your world with loved ones—but she hadn't succeeded at doing either of those things.

Across the table, Mrs Wishmore patted Millie's arm again and gave her another gentle squeeze. The kind smile on the older lady's face filled her with warmth.

"I just hope you know you can already count me amongst your friends," Mrs Wishmore said.

"Thank you, Doris. That's very kind."

With another soft pat on her arm, Mrs Wishmore resumed her work bagging sweets. Millie blinked and looked around at the other folks chatting and keeping busy in the village hall. While she'd been talking with Doris about such personal and difficult issues, it seemed as if she'd almost forgotten where she was and as if the little hall had somehow disappeared from her consciousness for a moment, like it had faded from view along with all the people in it.

Which was a very strange thing indeed.

Clearing her throat, Millie turned her attention back to her sweet-bagging work and decided it was time to direct the conversation away from herself for a while. As she tied a piece of snowman ribbon around the bag she'd just filled, a glimmer of light bouncing off the little brooch that Mrs Wishmore wore on her cardigan caught her gaze. Looking more closely, she saw the brooch depicted an angel, cast in white enamel with a gold trim, complete with elegant wings, a sparkly halo, and a cherubic smile.

"That's a pretty brooch you're wearing, Doris."

"Thank you, dear." Mrs Wishmore glanced down at the accessory and smiled. "She's one of the little guardian angel charms I like to carry around at this time of year to bring some Christmas good luck and good cheer."

"A guardian angel charm? What a lovely idea."

Reaching into her handbag, Mrs Wishmore pulled out a selection of items and spread them out on the table. There was another brooch, similar to the one Mrs Wishmore wore, except this angel's wings and dress were styled a little differently. There was also a slender key ring featuring a herald angel with a gold trumpet, and a pearly white tree bauble decorated with a serenely smiling angel and which tinkled sweetly as it rolled across the table surface.

"Gosh, Doris," Millie said in amused surprise. "You're certainly a big fan of angels."

"Well, of course," the older lady said with a soft laugh. "What's not to like about angels? Perhaps you'd like to choose one of these little good luck charms to keep for yourself?"

"Oh, no, I couldn't do that. They obviously mean a lot to you and I wouldn't feel right taking one of your lovely charms away."

"Nonsense. You're not taking it away. I'm offering it to you. So, which one would you like?"

Millie paused in her sweet-bagging work and glanced at the three pretty items Mrs Wishmore had laid out on the table. Although she found it a little odd that the woman carried so many angel trinkets around with her, the truth was that they were incredibly cute and hard to resist. The angels depicted on each trinket looked similar to one another, as if they all came from the same family of gorgeous little angels as the one featured in the brooch pinned to Mrs Wishmore's cardigan.

"Please choose one," Doris smiled. "It would be my pleasure to give one of these to you. After all, everyone needs a guardian angel, don't you think?"

The warm expression on the older woman's face made it hard to say no. Millie was drawn to the sweet brooch nestled on the table between the tree bauble and the key ring, and had a hard time hiding it.

"Enough said," Doris laughed and picked up the brooch. "I can see you've quite fallen in love with this angel brooch. May I?"

When Doris unclasped the pin on the brooch and gestured to the woollen jumper Millie was wearing, she found herself nodding. With another kind smile, Doris pinned the brooch into place.

"There, now we're brooch twins," Mrs Wishmore laughed. "And I'm sure this little guardian angel will watch out for you."

Millie touched the edge of the enamel brooch, running her fingers over the billowing gown the angel wore and her feathered wings and the curve of her halo. She didn't usually bother with accessories such as brooches, but she enjoyed feeling the slight weight of the sweet angel where it rested against her chest. It brought a strange sense of comfort she hadn't expected.

"Thank you, Doris," Millie said. "You're very kind."

"You're quite welcome, dear." Mrs Wishmore smiled and tucked the other two angel charms back inside her handbag. "I'm rather glad you chose the brooch and not the bauble. I have someone else in mind for that, although I suspect I might have a harder time trying to persuade them to accept the gift than I did with you."

Mrs Wishmore chuckled and although Millie joined in with the laughter to be polite, she hadn't the faintest idea what the woman might be talking about. She really was a strange sort of person, Millie thought. Strange, and yet rather nice to be around at the same time.

They resumed their work bagging the sweets. After adding a few more neatly tied bags to the pile they'd accumulated on the table, Millie looked up to see Evelyn Fox walking towards them with a phone clasped to her ear and a serious expression on her face.

"I see," Evelyn said into the phone as she stopped beside their table. "Yes, of course, that makes complete sense... I couldn't agree more... Well, this is all for the good of the Christmas Village and I'm sure he'll understand that, which is why I think you're doing the right thing... Yes, I'm sure we can rustle up some fairy lights and we'll be over shortly... I'll see you soon, Lesley."

Evelyn ended the call and tucked the phone into her jacket pocket. After casting an approving glance over the table and nodding at the pile of sweet bags stacked there, she gave a quick smile.

"Well done, ladies, this is tremendous work," Evelyn said, looking at Doris and then at Millie. "This is a wonderful addition to our stock levels and much appreciated."

"We're glad to make a contribution, aren't we, Millie?" said Mrs Wishmore.

"Absolutely. Do you want us to keep going and make more? There are plenty of sweets left over."

"Actually, I have another job in mind for you," Evelyn said. "It's just come up, although it might not be what either of you had in mind when you came along to volunteer today."

"We are at your disposal," Mrs Wishmore smiled.

"All right, then. Time is of the essence, so let me gather a few things together and we'll be on our way. Grab your coats, ladies. It's cold outside."

As Evelyn hurried off and began rummaging through some cardboard boxes stacked on the other side of the village hall, Millie turned to Mrs Wishmore.

"I wonder where we're going?" Millie said. "And what we're going to be doing next?"

"Hmm, I wonder, too."

There was something in Mrs Wishmore's tone as she said this that had Millie looking over in surprise as she pulled on her jacket. The older lady sounded wryly *knowing*, as if she understood exactly where they were going and what they'd be doing. More than that, she sounded somehow *amused* by this knowledge, too.

Millie once more shook off the silly thoughts she'd had about her elderly new friend. Mrs Wishmore was just as much in the dark about their new volunteering assignment as she was. Wasn't she?

"Come along, ladies, let's get a move on," Evelyn Fox called out from the other side of the village hall. "I've found what I needed." She held up a box of fairy lights in one hand

and jangled her car keys in the other before turning for the village hall doors.

"Maybe we're off to do some Christmas decorating?" Millie said, as she crossed the floor with Mrs Wishmore. "That would be fun, wouldn't it?"

"It certainly would," the older lady said with a grin. "Yes, I think it would be a lot of fun indeed."

CHAPTER FOUR

Adam hurried down Hollyford high street clutching a large cardboard box with both hands and hoping he'd make it back to the gift shop before the rain started. The sky overhead was grey and ominous, and he didn't want the contents of the box to get wet and end up ruined.

He'd spent the last hour visiting a local painter in her garden workshop near Stow-in-the-Wold and had brought back sample stock for sale in the shop. The woman, a bohemian type in her late sixties who'd discovered her talent late in life, created the most beautiful and unusual watercolour paintings of the Cotswolds that Adam had seen in a long time, and he was keen to add her work to his inventory. Customers would love the eye-catching style and eclectic colour palette. Artwork that not only featured the surrounding area but was created by a local artist too always went down a storm with buyers. It had taken him a few attempts to get the talented painter to allow him to sell her work, which she'd been enjoying largely as a hobby. Adam was convinced that the samples he'd brought back to Hollyford would sell like hot cakes and that discerning shoppers searching for unique Christmas presents for art lovers would be enchanted by the pieces he'd selected.

Assuming they didn't get soaked in a downpour before he made it back to the shop. Although they were wrapped inside the box, Adam wasn't willing to take any chances with his precious new stock.

Because he was focused on beating the rain while not jostling his cargo as he hurried down the high street, it took him a moment to notice there was something different about the way his shop looked. In the late afternoon December gloom, the streetlamps were already on overhead and the festive light displays in his neighbour's shops all cast a warm glow across the damp pavement.

As Adam slowed his pace, realisation dawned.

His own shop, Hollyford Gift Emporium, was also casting a warm glow across the damp pavement, a warm glow that wasn't caused only by the shop's regular indoor lighting.

Adam blinked in astonishment at the white twinkle lights now running around the inside of the gift shop window and the glass panes in the door. Those lights hadn't been there when he left and he couldn't understand how they could be there now, either.

As he continued standing outside on the pavement and staring at the twinkle lights in his shop window, Adam saw something even more confusing—a young woman he'd never seen before stepping out through the door of his shop with a small potted Christmas tree in her arms, followed by an elderly woman carrying a handful of shiny red tree baubles.

Adam watched in baffled amazement as the young woman positioned the potted tree beside the door and adjusted it a few times before stepping back.

"What do you think, Doris?" the young woman said. "Is this spot okay?"

"It's perfect, dear," the elderly lady replied. "Now, let's hang these little baubles on the branches and see how it looks."

Adam blinked. Who were these women and what were they doing to his shop?

"Er, excuse me? What's going on here?"

The two women turned and looked at him. While an expression of perplexed embarrassed crossed the young woman's face as she glanced his way, the older lady had a wry smile on her face along with what Adam could only describe a glint of mischief in her eyes. He thought the older lady looked vaguely familiar, now that he was looking at her properly, although he couldn't think of how he knew her.

"Hello, Adam," the older lady said. "We were just putting the finishing touches to your shop decorations. Don't they look lovely?"

Adam blinked at the woman and then at his shop. "What on earth are you doing decorating my shop? I don't even know who you are!"

"Oh, how silly of me!" the older lady said before cradling the remaining red baubles she was holding into the crook of her arm and offering Adam her hand. "I'm Mrs Wishmore. Doris Wishmore. It's a pleasure to meet you."

Utterly mystified and too polite to do anything else, Adam shook her outstretched hand.

"Although I think we may have already met," the older lady said, looking thoughtful. "Ah, yes, now I remember. We bumped into one another the other evening on Church Lane. You helped catch a little trinket of mine that had slipped from my bag."

Adam now remembered the strange woman and how she'd come bustling out of the dark lane in pursuit of the tree bauble she'd lost. He'd found her a bit odd then, and her appearance here at his shop, helping some other stranger place potted Christmas trees outside the door, only made her odder still.

"Uh..." Adam said, but the woman interrupted him before he could pull his pinballing thoughts together.

"And this is my good friend, Millie Dawson," she said, gesturing to her companion.

"Uh, hello." Adam offered the young woman a thin smile. "But why exactly are the two of you decorating my shop?"

A deep blush darkened the young woman's cheeks and her expression now looked positively agonised as she glanced at Adam and then at Mrs Wishmore.

"I'm so sorry," Millie said. "We thought you knew all about this. Your mother said you'd agreed to let us help."

"My *mother?*"

He almost yelled the words, which only made the young woman look alarmed. Before he could ask any more questions, the shop door swung open and his mother appeared.

"Now before you say anything, Adam, just hear us out," Lesley said, stepping out onto the pavement and waving a hand at the gift shop. "Just take a look at this window. Doesn't it look wonderful? And you must admit, it looks a thousand times better than it did before you left?"

Adam scowled at the shop window, where the twinkle lights glowed and danced merrily around the glass frame. He couldn't deny that it looked lovely, nor could he deny that it looked better than it had before, when the only decorations there had been the understated white paper snowflakes he'd hung up.

But seeing those twinkle lights nevertheless made his stomach lurch with stupid embarrassment, which was exactly why he hadn't put any of them up there himself. His logical brain knew this was ridiculous and that Christmas simply could not be avoided, especially for someone who owned a gift shop. But his emotional brain was already having a toddler tantrum about the sudden appearance of the lights in his shop window and screaming that it just wasn't fair.

"Mum, you had no right to do this behind my back," Adam hissed into his mother's ear, not wanting to be overheard by the two strangers now watching them both carefully. "This is my shop and if I decide I don't want to put up any Christmas decorations, then that's that."

"Pfft, what rubbish!"

Adam turned to see yet another figure emerging from the gift shop. When he realised it was Evelyn Fox, his heart sank. Mrs Fox had been the headteacher when he'd attended Hollyford primary school, and he was no less terrified of her now as he had been back then. Since retiring, the woman had become involved in just about every civic organisation and volunteering opportunity in the village, ascending to leadership positions across the board from where she ruled with tireless passion, ruthless efficiency, and steely determination. She wasn't a woman to be messed with, at any cost.

"Mrs Fox, I might have expected that you'd have something to do with this," he said, hoping he sounded braver than he felt.

"That's enough of your smart mouth, Mr Carter," Evelyn replied and wagged her finger at him. "You're not too old for a clip around the ear, and don't you forget it."

"I invited Evelyn to help me put a few decorations up around the place," his mother said. "If you want to blame someone, blame me."

"I do blame you," Adam snapped back.

"Good grief, you're behaving as if we've done something stupid here, when in fact the exact opposite is the case." Evelyn's tone was impatient. "The absence of Christmas cheer in the window of this high street shop has not gone unnoticed by the members of the Christmas Village committee, Adam. Had your mother not phoned earlier this afternoon and asked for my assistance, I would have come here at some point in the next few days to speak to you and try to talk some sense into you."

"Mrs Fox," he said, still unable to call the woman by her first name even although it had been years since she was his headteacher, and he was now a fully grown adult, not to mention a respected businessman in Hollyford. "The Christmas Village committee does an amazing job here in Hollyford. But this is a step too far. You can't just barge into someone's place of business and change things around to suit yourself."

"The Christmas Village is at its most effective when all the shops and businesses pull together and put on a united front. And the Christmas Village committee works hard to make sure that's exactly what happens."

"Well, the Christmas Village committee is starting to sound an awful lot like a totalitarian regime!" Adam barked back.

"Adam Carter, that's a disgraceful and insulting thing to say!" Evelyn said, tilting her chin.

"Now, let's all just take a moment to calm down, shall we?"

Adam turned at the voice and saw Mrs Wishmore shuffling closer with an alarmed frown on her face.

"I think I speak for all of us when I say that no one wanted to step on your toes or tell you how to run your business," the older lady said. "And I know for certain that your mother only wanted to help you do what's best for your business, and Evelyn only wanted to do what's best for the village. As for myself and Millie here, well, we just wanted to lend a hand and make ourselves useful. We're sorry if that has resulted in you becoming upset."

When the older lady smiled kindly at him, Adam was left

feeling like an idiot. These women had given up their free time to help cheer up his gift shop, and instead of swallowing his stupid feelings about the whole thing and thanking them for thinking of him, he was standing here arguing and having a strop.

Was that really what Heidi and their abandoned Christmas wedding had turned him into? A man who had a hissy fit in the middle of the street and caused such a scene that it left people literally cringing with embarrassment?

He glanced at the young woman still standing by the shop door. Millie, that was her name, if he'd heard right amid all the confusion. Her cheeks were burning red because of the altercation, and she looked like she wanted the ground to open up and swallow her whole.

Shame flooded through him in an instant. He'd embarrassed this young woman, when it was obvious she'd only been doing what his mother and Evelyn Fox had asked her to, alongside the other volunteer, Mrs Wishmore, who'd got caught up in all of this. They must both be new volunteers with the Christmas Village committee. After his outburst, they'd be wondering why they bothered giving up their spare time to help with the good cause.

Adam sighed. "I'm sorry for how I reacted. I didn't expect to see anything like this, and…" He gestured to the window and the dancing twinkle lights. "You've done a really great job. Thank you."

"You're quite welcome, dear," Mrs Wishmore said.

"It's just that I didn't want any more decorations this year, you see, and um…"

"And yet, there they are!" Mrs Wishmore chuckled and gave his arm a friendly pat.

He'd been about to say something else, something about how he really didn't want to be surrounded by Christmas decorations every day while he worked at his shop, but something about the kind look on Mrs Wishmore's face stopped him. As the older lady patted his arm again, the gesture seemed almost soothing and the churning sensation he'd felt inside his gut ever since he'd clapped eyes on the twinkle lights began to ebb away.

"I think if you take a moment to look at these twinkle lights and let yourself admire them, you'll feel fine about this whole thing," Mrs Wishmore said.

Adam held Mrs Wishmore's gaze for a long moment, her enigmatic smile making him realise he ought to do what she'd suggested. Turning, he looked at the window of the gift shop, really looked at it.

It was lovely. Bright and merry and festive, and certainly impossible for passing shoppers to ignore.

As he gazed at the transformed window, Adam knew he'd been foolish to resist putting up the decorations he'd always hung up every year. But he'd known all along that he was being foolish, even if he'd been unable to help it.

Now, though, with the twinkle lights actually in the window and with the entire shop looking transformed, he felt like an idiot. His mother had been forced to conscript village volunteers to intervene and make him see sense. That was embarrassing.

And yet, even as Adam acknowledged how lovely and Christmassy his gift shop now looked, he knew too that working there every day would now be even harder. He'd wanted to ignore Christmas, and yet it had refused to be ignored. He'd wanted to get through the season without paying any more heed to it than he had to, and yet the season was now twinkling merrily in the shop window, taunting him with a countdown to the Christmas wedding that would never happen and serving as an unwelcome reminder of all the humiliation it had caused him.

Beside him, Mrs Wishmore smiled kindly. "I think you're

going to be just fine, Adam," she said quietly, her voice almost a whisper. "Just don't be so hard on your poor heart."

Adam glanced at her in astonishment, but before he could ask the strange woman what she was talking about, she'd already shuffled off to adjust the red baubles she'd hung on the little potted tree beside the shop door.

"Now, Adam," Evelyn Fox said. "I don't want any bad blood between us. I hope you understand we just want your shop to look the part."

With a sigh, Adam nodded, knowing he'd been well and truly defeated in this whole infuriating business of the Christmas decorations.

"Thanks for your help. I appreciate it." He nodded to the lights in the window. "How much did you pay for the twinkle lights? I'd like to reimburse you."

"They were going spare in the committee's decoration stock," Evelyn said. "Just make sure you get them back to me once Christmas is over."

"What about that little potted tree by the door?"

"That's a gift from me and your father," Lesley said. "The garden centre had a special deal on and as I was buying one for myself, I thought you might like one, too. When I came round to the shop this afternoon to drop it off and saw you still didn't have any Christmas lights up, despite promising me you'd sort it out when I saw you the other night, I decided to take matters into my own hands."

"Lorraine shouldn't have let you do any of this," Adam frowned, referring to his shop assistant who'd been holding the fort while he visited the painter over by Stow-in-the-Wold.

"Don't you dare give that poor girl a hard time about this, Adam Carter," his mother warned him. "I told her you'd given me the go ahead to put a few lights up around the place and what else could she do except take me at my word? I'm your mother, after all. And if I'd known where you kept your shop decorations, I wouldn't have had to rope Evelyn and these kind Christmas Village committee volunteers into helping me source other twinkle lights at short notice." Lesley grinned at the two women by the door. "I'm very grateful to you both."

"It was our pleasure to help," Mrs Wishmore replied. "Wasn't it, Millie?"

"Um, sure."

But it was clear to Adam that the young woman didn't mean what she'd said. All this bickering out on the street probably wasn't what she'd been expecting to get dragged into as part of her Christmas volunteering duties with Evelyn Fox's army of festive elves. Yet again, he felt a pang of shame for reacting in a way that had left this stranger feeling awkward.

"Why don't you all come inside and I'll pop the kettle on?" Adam said, wanting to smooth things over. "I picked up a batch of cookies from the bakery this morning and you should all have some, as a small thanks for what you've done here."

He smiled at Millie as he said this, hoping to convince her he wasn't some kind of grumpy ogre who spent his free time arguing with well-intentioned pensioners in the middle of the high street. But the young woman was glancing at her watch and clearly getting ready to make a swift getaway. Adam could hardly blame her.

"That sounds like a lovely treat, doesn't it Millie?" Mrs Wishmore said, hooking her arm into Millie's and steering her towards the door.

"Uh, it's getting late and I should probably go home," Millie said, glancing up the high street.

"Don't be silly," Lesley said. "I insist you come inside and have coffee and cookies after all the hard work you've done this afternoon."

"Well..."

Before she could object further, Mrs Wishmore had opened the shop door and was leading them both inside, with Evelyn Fox and Adam's mother close on their heels. As the four women piled back inside, fat raindrops began falling from the dark afternoon sky. Putting a protective hand over the top of the cardboard box containing the framed watercolours, Adam took one last look at the window of his gift shop.

It looked so bright and festive. He knew he ought to feel buoyed by the Christmas spirit, thanks to the impromptu work of his mother and the Christmas Village committee. But even although he accepted the wisdom of adding those twinkle lights to the shop window, the happiness and cheer of the season still eluded him.

With a sigh, he hurried inside his shop before his box of new stock caught anymore rain, and to make sure his mother's festive meddling went no further than it had already.

MILLIE CLUTCHED the mug of coffee Adam had handed her and nibbled on a cookie, trying her best not to feel her usual awkward self and failing spectacularly.

She might have managed just fine in the company of these older women while they enjoyed hot drinks together if things had been different. After all, she already knew Doris Wishmore and Evelyn Fox, and Lesley Carter was clearly a warm and friendly sort of person who'd made her feel welcome from the moment they'd arrived at the gift shop to help put up the Christmas lights.

But the unpleasant quarrel that had taken place out on

the high street when the shop owner, Adam Carter, returned had left Millie wishing she'd never agreed to be part of this.

If she'd had any clue that the shop owner hadn't agreed to allow the Christmas Village committee to lend a hand with the twinkle lights, she wouldn't have come here. Realising that Adam's mother had pulled something of a fast one on her son, and that she herself had been an unwitting co-conspirator, left Millie embarrassed beyond words. Her toes actually curled inside her shoes when she thought of the astonished look on Adam's face when he'd arrived outside his shop and demanded to know what they were doing there, hauling potted Christmas trees into place outside the door without his knowledge or consent.

Now, as she sipped her coffee in the little office at the back of the shop, she could hardly look the man in the eye. Although he'd apologised for his reaction, she sympathised with his irritation about the whole thing. This was his shop, after all, and it stood to reason that he wouldn't want his mother, not to mention a couple of strangers, sticking their noses in where they didn't belong and taking over the decoration work.

Becoming involved in the Christmas Village committee was supposed to help Millie enjoy the festive season and make a few new friends. If this afternoon was anything to go by, she'd be doing neither of those things.

Still, as Adam passed around the plate containing the cookies and insisted that everyone take a second one, she couldn't help but wonder why he hadn't put any lights and decorations up in his gift shop himself. Hollyford Gift Emporium was an elegant addition to the high street and one that Millie had admired on many occasions since moving to the village. Although she'd never gone inside and browsed, not wanting to be tempted by the beautiful items for sale when she knew she couldn't afford anything on her tight budget, she usually eyed the lovely shop window whenever she passed by. As a gift retailer stocking many unique and high quality things for sale that must appeal to Christmas shoppers, Millie wondered why Adam Carter hadn't made sure he attracted those shoppers with maximum festive kerb appeal.

When she'd arrived outside the shop an hour earlier, it had struck her just how bare the windows looked compared to the others on the high street. The mystery of the undecorated shop had only deepened when Adam Carter had returned and looked in dismay at the twinkle lights Millie had spent half an hour wrangling into place around the sweet bevelled windows.

It was almost as if the man didn't like Christmas, and Millie wondered why. After the devastating loss she'd suffered last December, she knew only too well how difficult the festive season could be for some people and how much of a challenge it could be just to get through it. Had something awful happened to Adam Carter to make him dread Christmas?

Or was he just moody and unpleasant all the time?

As Adam swung the plate of cookies in her direction and smiled, Millie felt sure it couldn't be the latter. When he wasn't bickering with his mother out in the street, he seemed like a nice guy and his smile looked genuine enough.

"Go on, have another cookie," Adam said, jiggling the plate in front of her. "You know you want to."

This was true. The cookies were flavoured with white chocolate and some sort of sweet spice mix that Millie couldn't pin down, and they were irresistible. Taking a second cookie, she smiled in thanks.

"These should come with a health warning," Adam said as he bit into his own cookie. "May cause addiction and uncontrollable, dog-like salivation."

The unexpected quip made Millie laugh and then choke on the bite she'd just taken of her cookie.

"These definitely should have a health warning," she said after clearing her throat with a gulp of coffee.

Adam gave a quick grin. He glanced at his mother, Evelyn Fox, and Doris Wishmore, who were engrossed in conversation together about some forthcoming event in the Christmas Village schedule of activities, and then looked back at Millie and spoke in a quieter voice than before.

"I want to apologise again for making a scene outside the shop. I was being stupid."

"It's fine," Millie said.

"It's not fine. I'm sorry I embarrassed you with my outburst."

Now she was embarrassed all over again, remembering the angry look on his face and her own unwitting part in putting it there. Focusing on the mug of coffee, she took a long sip and glanced around the tiny office, trying to think of something else to say to change the topic.

Her eyes met Mrs Wishmore's. The older lady's expression was soft and the smile she offered almost seemed like one of encouragement. When Doris's gaze flicked to the cardboard box Adam had set down on the floor when they'd all stepped into the office, Millie caught her drift and cleared her throat.

"So, were you picking up some new stock for your shop?" she asked and nodded to the box, hoping the diversion might turn the conversation towards more neutral topics.

An enthusiastic smile crossed Adam's face, and he opened the box lid. "I'm hoping to start working with a local painter. She agreed to let me sell some pieces and see how it goes. I was over at her workshop this afternoon."

He pulled a framed watercolour from the box and loosened the bubble wrap around it. Turning the painting around, he showed it to Millie. Her eyes widened in admiration.

"Wow, that's beautiful."

The watercolour depicted a Cotswolds scene of a row of stone cottages winding along a meandering lane towards an ancient church surrounded by oak trees, beyond which rose verdant fields lined with twisting hedgerows, and beyond that, the sky dipping to twilight. But while the scene was traditional Cotswold, the colours used had transformed the painting into something so eye-catching that Millie couldn't stop staring.

"I know nothing about art," Millie said. "But I know I love that painting."

Adam smiled again and glanced at the framed piece. "I know what you mean. The artist has a tremendous eye for colour. She's true to the Cotswold palette, and captures the honey-coloured stones of the buildings and the bright greens of the countryside, but she brings them to life with unexpected highlights, like those pinks on the church roof from the setting sun and those bursts of gold on the boughs of the oak trees."

"You sound like you know a lot about art."

"Not especially, but, just like you, I know when I like something. And I know when my customers will like something, too. I know they're going to love the work this artist creates, although she doesn't believe me."

"Really? Why?"

"She paints as a hobby. She had no plans to sell her work at all until I met her at a summer fair a few months ago where she'd donated one of her paintings for a raffle prize. I've been hounding her ever since to let me sell some of her pieces. She thinks her work has to be at the level of the old masters for it to be any good, but I'm trying to prove to her that there are many people out there who'd love to see these paintings hanging on their walls or be able to give them as a gift to loved ones. If I can sell a few before the end of the year, it will be the proof I need to convince her she has a nice little money-maker here that, if nothing else, will keep her in paints and brushes for a while."

Adam laughed and looked again at the painting.

"It's nice that you support local artists and give them space in your shop," Millie said.

"People expect unusual items and gifts when they visit my place, so I need to make sure that's what they'll find. Scouting for undiscovered craftspeople and creatives in the local area is a big part of my business."

Millie smiled, surprised at how much she was enjoying this easy chit-chat. Adam was passionate about his gift shop and the suppliers he worked with. Now that he was no longer scowling and getting upset about his mother's interference in his shop's Christmas decoration decisions, he seemed like a nice guy.

Turning back to the watercolour again, Millie let out a wistful sigh.

"I feel like I could step into that painting and walk around there, and be very, very happy."

When Adam glanced at her with a surprised look on his face, she felt herself blush.

"That probably sounds stupid," she said, feeling embarrassed.

"It doesn't sound stupid, not at all." His gaze softened. "When I tell the artist what you said, she'll be touched and flattered."

"Oh, well..."

Millie found herself tongue-tied. She glanced back at the box of framed paintings and saw another one tucked there that looked even prettier than the last. Noticing her interest, Adam pulled the painting from the box.

The watercolour depicted a magical woodland wonderland of snowy fir trees, starry skies, and scurrying woodland creatures peeking out between the trees. Looking up at the frosted fir in the centre of the painting stood a young woman, bundled up in a cosy coat and scarf and with wonder etched across her face.

"This watercolour is different from the others," Adam said. "The artist painted it with the idea of using the image on Christmas card prints to send to her friends and family, but she didn't get around to it. She was surprised when I said I'd take it to sell in the shop, because there isn't always a good market for seasonal artworks. But I thought I'd give it a shot and prove to her I can sell her work."

Millie smiled when Adam laughed, but she found her eye drawn back to the painting. The wintry woodland scene caught her imagination.

"I think it's just lovely," Millie said. "It's hopeful and dreamy and very Christmassy. And I'm sure the right owner for the painting is out there somewhere, waiting to find it."

Adam lifted his eyebrows. "That's a nice way of thinking."

He held her gaze, as if he was considering what she'd just said. A long moment spun out while his eyes stayed on hers. Millie was saved from having to think of something else to say by Mrs Wishmore.

"Well, that is a wonderful painting you've got there, Adam," Doris said cheerfully.

Evelyn Fox and Lesley Carter both paused in their conversation to look over in their direction. At the sight of the pretty Cotswold watercolours, both women asked to see more of the stock Adam had brought back from his visit with the painter.

For the next five minutes, he unpacked the other pieces from the cardboard box and showed them off. Millie saw how pleased he was when Evelyn Fox insisted on purchasing a painting of a thatched cottage nestled beside a gurgling stream, declaring it to be the perfect gift for her sister who lived in just such a cottage of her own. While Adam dealt with the impromptu sale, requesting that Evelyn allow him to display the painting as sold in his shop for at least a week to demonstrate the popularity of the artwork, everyone else gathered their coats and prepared to leave. It was almost five o'clock, and Adam's assistant, Lorraine, had already stuck her head around the office door to ask for a hand in getting things ready to close for the day.

"Well, thank you for the coffee and cookies," Mrs Wishmore said to Adam as she buttoned her coat and hoisted her blue handbag onto her shoulder.

"You're welcome, Doris," Adam replied. "And thanks again for the, uh, sudden Christmas decorations."

Mrs Wishmore laughed and turned to Millie. "We were only too happy to help, weren't we Millie?"

"I had fun stringing up all those twinkle lights in the lovely front window," Millie said. "And it was a nice chance to see inside your shop. I haven't visited before."

"Well, I hope you'll drop by again," Adam said as they walked through to the front shop. He waved a hand at the shelves and displays. "Whatever your Christmas shopping needs, we can help."

He laughed as he said it, and it was obviously meant as no more than a throwaway conversational comment, not an oily sales pitch. Something about his relaxed stance as he thrust his hands into his pockets and rocked on his heels made Millie feel at ease in his company. If she actually had any Christmas presents to purchase, not to mention the spare cash to stretch for the lovely items on sale in Adam's gift emporium, she'd be back here like a shot.

"Adam, I'm pleased you've graciously accepted our help

with your shop's Christmas decoration needs," Evelyn grinned as she pulled on a pair of gloves.

"Thanks again for what you've done," Adam said and looked towards the shop window where the lights twinkled against the December darkness outside.

Yet even although he seemed sincere in his thanks, Millie detected uncertainty in his tone and a strange sadness in his eyes as he glanced at the twinkle lights. She wondered again about what had caused that sadness.

"So, what's next on the agenda for the Christmas Village activities?" Adam asked as he walked them all to the shop door.

"We have our first Christmas carol sing-along on Thursday evening, to tie in with the late opening hours on the high street," Evelyn said. She gave him a thoughtful look. "Perhaps you'd like to come along and take part, Adam?"

He spluttered out a stunned laugh. "No, thanks."

"Oh, but it will be fun," Evelyn said.

"I'm sure it will," Adam replied. "But I'll be busy here with the late shopping hours."

Evelyn looked set to press the matter further. Millie braced herself for another falling out between the two strong-minded folk. So when Mrs Wishmore intervened, she was glad.

"I can only imagine things must get very busy around here with the Christmas shopping crowds," Doris said to Adam. "Perhaps you'll be able to take part in something another time?"

Millie watched as Mrs Wishmore offered Adam a kind smile and a wink. A look of relief and gratitude crossed his face.

"Yes, perhaps," he said, and returned the elderly woman's smile.

"Adam, you haven't popped round yet for dinner and a

look at your father's holiday snaps," Lesley said to her son. "Why don't you come over tonight once you've shut up the shop? I've got bolognaise in the slow cooker."

Adam seemed to consider the offer. "Will it just be you and dad there?"

Some sort of silent conversation was exchanged between the mother and son as they eyed one another, and Millie saw Lesley's smile evaporate.

"Angela said she'd come round."

At this information, Adam gave a curt nod. "In that case, I'll give it a miss. And I want to stay late here anyway and get those new watercolours displayed in the shop."

It was clear that Lesley was about to say something in response, but at the last moment she seemed to remember they were in company.

"Suit yourself," she said.

Millie glanced at Adam and saw the unhappy expression on his face. She wondered what all that had been about. One minute he was arguing with his mother on the street about her interference at his shop, the next minute the two of them were having strained conversations about dinner invitations and why Adam refused to accept them. Clearly it had something to do with this Angela person, whoever she was.

Whatever it was all about, it was obvious that there were conflicts of some sort in Adam's family. Although it was none of her business, Millie couldn't help but wonder why.

They all piled out onto the high street and Adam waved them off. While Evelyn Fox headed in the direction of the village hall and Lesley Carter walked off towards her car, Millie pointed down the street and turned to Mrs Wishmore.

"I'd better head home," Millie said. "I'm going this way. What about you, Doris?"

"I'll catch my bus on the other side of the market square,"

she replied. "That was quite an afternoon we had in the end, wasn't it?"

"You can say that again. I feel bad for sticking my nose into Adam's shop affairs just because Evelyn asked us to. He obviously didn't want any help."

"People don't always know what they want," Mrs Wishmore said. "I think Adam is already making his peace with the new twinkle lights in the shop window and will soon be glad there were people around who cared for him enough to step in and do the right thing."

"Hmm, I hope you're right. But I also hope we don't get sent to perform any other Christmassy errands that people haven't agreed to."

Mrs Wishmore laughed, then pulled back her coat collar and tapped a finger to the angel brooch pinned on her cardigan. "Perhaps that brooch I gave you earlier has made you an honorary guardian angel for the day, and pointed you in the right direction in order to lend someone a helping hand. Although I should let you know that the work of a guardian angel is never done, Millie. Who knows what tasks and adventures might lie ahead for us?"

As Mrs Wishmore chuckled, Millie laughed too, but she found herself wondering at these strange comments. Perhaps the old dear was a little more fixated on this angel stuff than she'd realised. When Doris had emptied those angel trinkets out of her handbag back at the village hall, Millie hadn't thought much of it. Now, given what Doris had just said, she wondered if the woman might be a bit batty.

Still, there were worse things in the world than having a soft spot for angel trinkets. Pushing aside the unkind thoughts she'd had about the sweet silver-haired lady, Millie smiled.

"Will I see you on Thursday for the Christmas carol singalong?" Mrs Wishmore asked.

"I'm already looking forward to it."

"Lovely. Well, good night, Millie."

"Good night, Doris."

Millie made her way along the street towards home. She'd only taken a handful of steps when it occurred to her that she hadn't asked Mrs Wishmore if she was planning on arriving early to help set up the tea and cake stalls that would serve visitors in the market square once the sing-along got underway. She turned to retrace her steps on the high street to confirm the other woman's intentions.

But when she looked up the street, Mrs Wishmore was nowhere to be seen. There were a few hurrying pedestrians and a man walking his dog, but no sign of Doris. Millie glanced across the street, wondering if Mrs Wishmore had already crossed over towards the market square beyond, but couldn't see the older lady anywhere.

Millie peered again in confusion, wondering how Mrs Wishmore could have already made it to the end of the high street and disappeared from sight. The older lady's shuffling way of walking didn't seem consistent with such a speedy departure. But although she scanned the high street, the woman was gone.

Mrs Wishmore was more sprightly on her feet than she'd given her credit for. Perhaps the woman's guardian angel brooch gave her the gift of superhuman speed, Millie thought with a quiet laugh, before turning again for home.

CHAPTER FIVE

After two days of grey skies and chilly rain, the weather cleared just in time for Hollyford's first Christmas carol sing-along of the season. Thursday brought wintry blue skies and a sharp bite in the air that promised frost by nightfall. Millie was pleased about the fair weather because it meant her next stint of volunteering duty wouldn't involve standing around in the market square while getting drenched.

"These homemade cakes all look delicious!" Mrs Wishmore declared as she made space for an iced lemon sponge someone had donated to the refreshment stall. "Our sing-along participants will be spoiled for choice."

"I must admit, it's taking a lot of willpower not to devour a slice of something," Millie said as she added a plate of orange and cranberry muffins to the stall. "The home-bakers of Hollyford are a talented bunch."

"They certainly are. And all these treats will raise a lot of money for good causes around the village."

It was almost six o'clock in the evening and the market square was already buzzing with visitors milling around and waiting for the scheduled festivities to kick off. The dazzling Christmas tree in the centre of the square provided a wonderful backdrop for the carol sing-along, and the church choir was gathered around it and waiting for the signal to begin singing. Once the carol sing-along started, the refreshment stall would officially open, serving tea, coffee, and hot chocolate from vast urns carted over from the village hall, along with the cakes, cookies, muffins, and traybakes donated by the generous home-bakers of the village.

Millie and Mrs Wishmore had been assigned to the refreshment stall for the evening, after spending the last half hour helping to carry everything over from the village hall. There was a merry atmosphere in the air and a wonderful zing of Christmas excitement. Everywhere she looked, Millie saw happy, relaxed faces as people clutched the carol lyric sheets that had been handed out and admired the festive decorations around the market square and made friendly chit-chat with neighbours and visitors alike.

"I think we're all set," Mrs Wishmore announced as she squeezed a plate of chocolate cookies on to the refreshment stall. "We couldn't fit any more treats onto this table if we tried."

"I hope people are hungry," Millie laughed, glancing at the groaning table.

"They will be." Mrs Wishmore peered around the canopy covering their refreshment stall and frowned. "Oh, we forgot something."

Shuffling to the edge of the frame that supported the canopy, Mrs Wishmore leaned into the corner and fiddled with something there. Millie wondered what she was up to. A moment later, the stall was filled with a multi-coloured glow from hundreds of fairy lights that were draped around the canopy edges. Millie gasped in stunned surprise.

"I had no idea there were lights around the stall!" she

exclaimed, staring in wonder at the pretty lights. "When did these get put up?"

"Oh, a little while ago when you were busy ferrying cake boxes from the village hall," Mrs Wishmore replied.

Millie didn't think she'd been gone on her cake transportation errands long enough for someone to have hung up all these lights. Her longest trip there and back had only lasted about seven or eight minutes. Remembering the time it had taken her just to hang the twinkle lights in the window of Adam Carter's shop a few days ago, she couldn't help but think that whoever put up these much longer lengths of lights around the refreshment stall must be some sort of miracle worker.

The thought made her glance at Mrs Wishmore. For a tiny instant, she wondered if there was more to these unexpected Christmas lights than met the eye. Mrs Wishmore had an odd smile on her face, a sort of *knowing* smile, as she admired the coloured lights around the stall canopy. It was a curious smile, Millie decided, as if the woman was rather pleased with herself and the little light trick she'd just performed.

As quickly as this odd thought popped into Millie's head, it disappeared again, and she shook her head at the ridiculous notion she'd just entertained. Had she just imagined that Mrs Wishmore had… magicked the lights into existence? It was an insane thought, and Millie wondered what was wrong with her.

Yet, she frowned again at the coloured lights just the same. She was sure they hadn't been there the last time she'd looked. How could that be?

Before she could think anything more about it or ask any further questions about the unexplained appearance of the lights around the canopy, two women arrived at the stall and rubbed their hands together as they admired the cake selection and eyed the hot drink urns. The younger of the two women looked a little older than Millie, maybe in her late twenties, while the other appeared to be in her mid-fifties or thereabouts. Their physical similarities were striking, from their chestnut bobs to their sea-green eyes, and from their high cheekbones to their warm smiles, and Millie knew that they had to be mother and daughter. A moment later, she was proved correct.

"Ooh, these cakes look delicious, don't they Mum?" the younger of the two women asked the other.

"Too good to resist," her mother agreed, and rubbed her hands together. "What shall we get?"

"I'm surprised you even have to ask. That fruitcake has my name written all over it."

"Your words, not mine."

With a laugh, the younger woman batted her mother affectionately on the arm before smiling at Millie. "Can we have two hot chocolates and two slices of that wonderful fruitcake, please?"

"Coming right up."

Millie filled two cups from the hot chocolate urn, listening while the mother and daughter continued discussing the other treats for sale at the refreshment stall and debating whether they ought to take a couple of slices of something home to enjoy the next day. When the mother quipped that the young woman's father would eat whatever they bought before they even had time to put it in the cake tin, they added a third slice of cake to the order that Mrs Wishmore was now handling. The young woman's father was a fan of coffee and walnut cake, apparently, which was what they chose to take home for him as a special surprise.

As Millie added lids to the hot chocolate cups and the women's chatter continued, she found herself longing for the chance to have just one conversation like this with her own mother—just one of those routine, day-to-day conversations about nothing in particular, but which were the stuff of normal life. Those shared understandings and deep knowledge were reminders of what it meant to have a mother, and to have a family, and reminders, too, of what it meant to have someone in your life who knew you inside and out.

Millie imagined the conversation that would have taken place if it was herself and her mother who were standing on the other side of the stall, instead of these two cheerful strangers. Caroline would have wanted a piece of chocolate brownie, her favourite treat, and Millie would have teased her for always choosing the same thing whenever they treated themselves to cake.

I know what I like, Caroline would have insisted. *Why fix something that isn't broken?*

She could almost hear her mother utter those words, her voice clear and filled with humour and warmth, just as it had always been.

"Are you all right, dear?"

Millie blinked and saw Mrs Wishmore beside her, her gaze flicking to the hot chocolate cups Millie had placed lids on and then forgotten all about as she'd become lost in her daydream.

"Sorry, I was miles away."

Millie handed the hot drinks to the women, who thanked her before wandering off into the crowds.

"Penny for your thoughts," Mrs Wishmore smiled.

"I wasn't thinking about anything in particular," she said with a smile. It wasn't true, but the Christmas carol sing-along was about to begin and a queue of people was forming at the refreshment stall, and Millie wasn't about to start recounting wistful memories of her mother when she was supposed to be getting immersed in the festive spirit.

Mrs Wishmore gave her a thoughtful smile and nodded at

the urns. "In that case, I need two cups of tea for the next customers in our line."

"Coming right up."

Across the square, the church choir began singing *I Saw Three Ships,* and the gathered crowds joined in. Amused by the tunelessly charming rendition being performed by the Christmas Village visitors, Millie turned her attention to dealing with the eager customers searching for tea and cake to enjoy as they rustled their song sheets and got into the spirit of things. At her side, Mrs Wishmore proved to be a more than competent co-worker, bagging cakes and muffins, and taking payments, while always ready with a smile and a 'Merry Christmas' for everyone she served.

Millie savoured the feeling of being part of something so lovely, something filled with such obvious good cheer. Across the market square, she saw the mother and daughter she'd served a few minutes earlier tucking into their cake and hot chocolate and laughing together. She saw couples hand-in-hand, families with young children, older folks singing along with the carols and enjoying themselves.

It occurred to Millie that although she was part of this festive scene and helping to make it work by volunteering on the refreshment stall, she wasn't actually a part of it at all. She was on the side lines, watching others have fun. She'd come here by herself and she'd leave by herself, too. A wave of melancholy hit her as she thought about that fact.

"Millie, are you quite sure you're all right?"

Mrs Wishmore was looking at her again, this time with barely concealed concern on her face. With a jolt, Millie realised she was once more standing around doing nothing and just staring into space, while people waited to receive the hot drinks she was supposed to be serving.

"I'm so sorry," Millie said with a forced laugh. "These

Christmas carols are so cheerful, I keep getting caught up in them and forgetting I'm supposed to be working."

This explanation didn't seem to convince Mrs Wishmore, who continued watching her carefully. When Millie applied herself once more to the task at hand, she resolved that this time she wouldn't let her mind wander off into silly daydreams and sad thoughts. She'd joined the Christmas Village committee in order to take part in the festive merriment, and there was no point wasting that opportunity by feeling sorry for herself.

Half an hour later, the hot drinks urns were empty, every crumb of cake on the stall had been bought and enjoyed, and the Christmas carol sing-along was ending with a rousing last chorus of *We Wish You A Merry Christmas.*

"Well, that was an experience to remember," Mrs Wishmore laughed as she stacked empty plates and folded the table cover. "I haven't been kept so busy in ages. And judging by the amount of money now stashed in the cash box, the Christmas Village committee now has a small fortune to spend on their various good causes."

"It's a shame there's no cake left over," Millie said. "I'd planned on taking something home to enjoy later."

"Great minds think alike." With a wink, Mrs Wishmore produced a plastic box from beneath the stall which contained two of the orange and cranberry muffins Millie had set out at the start of the sing-along.

"Perfect choice," Millie grinned. "I had my eye on those."

"I know you did, dear. I popped some coins into the box to cover the donation. Once we've handed over this cash box to Evelyn back at the village hall and helped tidy everything away, let's enjoy a walk together while we eat our muffins."

Millie checked her watch and was surprised to discover it was almost seven o'clock. "Isn't it a bit late for a walk? Not to mention a bit dark?"

"Not in the least. There are Christmas lights everywhere, and what with all this volunteering I've been doing, I've hardly had a chance to enjoy the light displays and take it all in. I think a late evening meander will be just lovely, don't you?"

It did sound nice, Millie had to admit, especially after the time they'd just spent rushed off their feet on the refreshment stall. Volunteering in Hollyford wasn't for the faint hearted, and a stroll beneath the Christmas lights might be a nice reward and provide a welcome wind-down before heading home.

There was nothing to hurry home for anyway. Her flatmate was working a late shift until midnight, and the idea of being alone for the rest of the night after time spent in the midst of so much bustle and activity made Millie feel sad.

"Okay, let's do it," she said.

Mrs Wishmore smiled. "That's the spirit. And perhaps we ought to stop off for some dinner, too. I doubt this muffin will keep us going for long after all this hard work. There's a lovely pub on the high street which serves wonderful food, or so I've heard. It will be my treat."

Millie thought about the kind invitation. She enjoyed spending time with Mrs Wishmore and decided it would be nice to share dinner together in a cosy pub, rather than return to her tiny bedroom where her meal plans involved nothing more exciting than cheese on toast.

"I'd like that, thanks Doris."

"Wonderful!" The older lady clapped her hands together, clearly pleased with this response. "I can't remember the last time I ate out."

"Me neither."

"In that case, we'll make sure it's a memorable occasion."

Mrs Wishmore winked and chuckled. What an odd lady

she was, Millie thought, even although she couldn't resist joining in with her laughter.

The woman's cheerful disposition was positively infectious.

THE ORANGE and cranberry muffins were delicious, the sponge moist and buttery and with a zing of orange zest that made Millie's taste buds explode with every bite. She strolled around the market square beside Mrs Wishmore, the two of them pausing to admire the Christmas tree again and then the nativity scene, before turning towards one of the pretty cobbled lanes that connected the square to the high street.

The narrow lane was lined with quaint shops on either side and decorated with strings of white lights that criss-crossed overhead between the stone buildings. They passed shopkeepers who were closing their doors for the day, the late night Thursday opening hours now over. Shoppers bustled by with bags of Christmas purchases and cheerful grins. Frost hung in the air, making their breaths plume white as they walked.

"You seem a little thoughtful tonight, Millie," Mrs Wishmore said as she finished the last bite of her muffin and tossed the cupcake case into a nearby bin. "Is there something on your mind?"

"Not really," Millie said. "It was a long shift at the care home today, and I'm just a little tired."

Mrs Wishmore considered this for a moment. "It seemed to me that, after seeing that lovely mother and daughter who were our first customers at the cake stall, you became melancholic."

Doris's perceptiveness surprised her. She saw no point in denying the truth of what the older lady had said. "They were so chatty and cheerful together, and it made me think of my mother. That's the sort of relationship we had. She was my mother, yes, but she was my best friend, too."

Emotion surged as Millie spoke, but the gentle look on Mrs Wishmore's face kept her talking. "My mother was always the first person I thought of when I had news to share, or a problem to solve, or a decision to make. But she was also the first person I thought of when I just wanted to be with a friend and have some fun and share a conversation with someone who knew me, and who knew my faults and quirks and didn't require an explanation about any of them."

"She was a big part of your life. I can't imagine how much you must miss her."

"It was only ever the two of us in our own tiny family unit and we mostly kept to ourselves. I've never been great at socialising and making friends. I'm quite introverted, and although I've always had casual acquaintances, I always loved and preferred my mother's company. No one was more fun than she was and I never felt as comfortable with anyone as I did with her. When she died, she left a big hole in my life."

Millie felt bad for once more dominating the conversation with sad stories about her late mother. "I don't mean to dwell on any of this. The whole point of volunteering with the Christmas Village committee is because I want to find lots of lovely ways to fill my time and make sure I have some fun. There's no point doing that if I'm just going to keep reminding myself of painful things."

"Christmas is meant to be a happy time, that's true. But when we miss loved ones, and when we're still grieving a loss, it isn't easy to just switch on the festive spirit. And it might not be healthy to do that, either."

"I know."

"I just hope you aren't expecting too much of yourself this December, Millie."

"My mother wanted me to be happy and not to dwell endlessly on what happened last Christmas and everything she went through before she died. I just want to do what she asked." Millie shrugged sadly. "That's the only Christmas present I can give her now."

"You're a brave young woman, Millie. I know your mother would be proud of you."

Millie said nothing for a moment, choked by Mrs Wishmore's kind words. After almost a year without talking to anyone about her mother and how much her death had affected her, she'd now shared her thoughts on several occasions with Doris. Although she'd known the woman for less than a week, Millie was struck by how easy it was to chat with her, and how comfortable she felt in the older lady's presence, comfortable enough to open up like this about her mother. It hurt to remember Caroline's death, and it hurt to think about her being gone forever. But it was also a relief to share her emotions with someone else. Confiding in Doris felt like confiding in an old friend who'd known her forever, even although Millie knew that made little sense.

They reached the top of the cobbled lane and turned onto the high street to continue their stroll towards the pub where Mrs Wishmore had suggested they have dinner together.

"And, for the record, I know your mother would be doubly proud of you spending time with an old lady like me and extending the hand of friendship in the way you have," Mrs Wishmore said. "Not many young women your age would be interested in tolerating an ancient specimen such as myself."

"You're not that old, for goodness' sake," Millie laughed.

"Well, I'm grateful for your company, just the same."

"Likewise, Doris. I'm rubbish when it comes to meeting new people. In fact, you're my first proper friend here in Hollyford."

"The first of many, I'm sure." Mrs Wishmore looked up the street and a bright smile curved her lips. "Speaking of which, there's another one of your new friends, right over there."

Further ahead, Adam Carter was locking the door of his gift emporium, a satchel slung over his shoulder and a plastic bag wedged between his feet as he dealt with the keys.

"I doubt he thinks of me as a friend, Doris," Millie said. "We only met once and hardly even know each other."

"Well, let's remedy that right this instant." Mrs Wishmore waved to catch his attention. "Hello there, Adam! What a nice surprise to bump into you here."

Adam finished locking up and slid the heavy keyring into his satchel. "Hello, Mrs Wishmore. Hello, Millie. Were you two enjoying some late night shopping?"

"Actually no, we just finished our volunteering duties with the Christmas Village sing-along over on the market square," Mrs Wishmore told him.

"Good for you," Adam said. "Was there a decent turnout?"

"Oh yes, the square was packed. I hope you saw the benefit of extra footfall in your lovely gift shop?"

"We had a busy evening, so no complaints there."

Glancing at the gift shop window, Millie saw that the twinkle lights she'd hung up were still in place and the little potted Christmas tree Adam's mother had given him was now on the other side of the locked door, presumably to stop it being pinched by night-time opportunist ne'er-do-wells. She was glad he'd kept the decorations in place. After his initial reaction the other day, she wouldn't have been surprised to discover that he'd taken everything back down again, leaving only those lonely paper snowflakes in the window.

Adam saw her inspecting the shop window and smiled. "The customers have commented on the much-improved

Christmas decoration situation. I owe you a debt of thanks."

"No debt owed," Millie said. "We were happy to help."

"Millie and I are planning to pop into that nice pub on the other end of the high street for a quick spot of dinner after putting in our volunteering shift," Mrs Wishmore said. "Would you care to join us, Adam?"

"Uh, well…"

Judging by his expression, it was the last thing he wanted to do. When Mrs Wishmore persisted with her invitation, Millie wondered if the woman was tone deaf.

"I, for one, would love to hear more about these wonderful craftspeople and artists you discover in the course of running your lovely gift shop," Doris said. "So, what do you say? Will you join us? Dinner is my treat, especially as it means I don't have to go back to my quiet little house by myself just yet."

Until she'd added those last words, Millie was sure that Adam would decline the invitation. But Doris's little stroke of emotional blackmail in alluding to herself as a lonely old woman clearly had the desired effect, and his expression softened.

"In that case, how can I say no?"

"Splendid!"

Looking pleased with herself, Mrs Wishmore resumed her walk along the high street.

"You don't mind me tagging along, do you?" Adam asked Millie as they fell into step together.

"Of course not. The more the merrier."

Millie almost felt sorry for him, getting roped into having dinner with an old aged pensioner and some young female he'd only just met. He probably had many more interesting things he could do with his time and many far more interesting people he'd rather be doing them with.

When they reached the pub at the bottom of the high street and went inside, they found it busy with drinkers and diners, some of whom had come from the carol sing-along judging by the song sheets set aside on their tables. After finding a free table, they shed coats and sat down to study the menu.

"Well, I must say I'm tempted by the macaroni cheese," Mrs Wishmore said. "That sounds like the perfect meal for a chilly December night. What takes your fancy, Adam?"

"I like the burgers they serve here."

"That sounds good to me, too," Millie said, scanning the burger options. "I'll push the boat out and have a cheese on mine, with a side of chips."

"Let me place our order at the bar," Mrs Wishmore said, and when Adam attempted to get up from his seat to deal with the task, she waved him away. "I said this was my treat, didn't I? Now, what would you both like to drink?"

Once they'd given their soft drink orders, Mrs Wishmore bustled off to the bar. Millie glanced across the table at Adam, feeling suddenly awkward about being alone with him and anxious about whether she'd be able to think of something to say.

But her inept social bungling didn't give her the problems it usually did.

"I keep thinking about those lovely watercolour paintings you showed me in your shop the other day," she found herself saying. "And I keep thinking it must be amazing to be so talented and to create something so special."

Adam smiled. "Me, too. It's one of the best things about running the shop, getting to meet and work with these creative types. I don't have a creative bone in my body, so I'm pretty much in awe of these people."

"It must be a great feeling, knowing you're helping them get their craftwork into the hands of people who'll enjoy it."

"It is. Many of them sell things direct online, of course, but a lot of the folks who enjoy their craft as a hobby aren't interested in the business side of it and can't be bothered organising sales pages on websites and dispatching orders and dealing with payments. For many hobbyists, like that watercolourist, they're happy to let someone else do all the dull grunt work of finding customers, because they aren't in it for the money, anyway. They still get a fair deal from me though, not just because word gets around if you're a shark out to fleece the creators, but because stocking high quality, unique pieces is the entire essence of my business."

Adam frowned and threw her an apologetic look. "Sorry, I went off on a bit of a speech there."

"Don't apologise. It sounds like you love your work and you're passionate about it. How long have you owned your shop?"

"Four years. I used to work in a department store in Cheltenham and thought I'd be there for a long time, working my way up the management ladder. But when they had a big round of redundancies, I got the chop."

"I'm sorry. That must have been horrible."

"It gave me the push to go in a new direction. I'd been a junior manager in the home décor department and I'd seen how the quality of the merchandise had fallen during the years I worked there. The business was under pressure and trying to cut costs, but their customers expected high quality items and they were no longer offering them. It became a vicious spiral of retail failure. When I got my redundancy money, I threw it into a business of my own."

"Wow, that's incredibly gutsy."

Adam grinned. "There have been many moments when I wondered if I made a mistake. Retailing is hard and high streets aren't what they used to be. But Hollyford still has a lot going for it and people come to visit and explore and do some shopping, which means a business like my gift shop has a chance to thrive, along with the other independent shops we have."

"So that's why the Christmas Village committee is so important, I guess?"

"All those activities they organise give visitors another reason to come here and make an afternoon, or even a day, of it. And the committee has been running at full speed since Evelyn Fox took charge." He shook his head, as if amused. "She might get a bit carried away from time to time, and barge into people's shops and insist on putting up decorations without the owner's consent, but her heart's in the right place."

Millie felt her face flush. "Yeah, listen, sorry again about being a part of all that. I had no idea you hadn't agreed for those lights to be put up."

"I wasn't taking a dig at you." Adam's gaze was relaxed as he said this, his smile easy. "I probably needed a kick up the backside anyway, as far as the window decorations were concerned."

"The lights do make the shop look even lovelier than it already is."

"Agreed."

Perhaps it was because she'd been so taken with his lovely shop when she'd helped hang the twinkle lights there, or perhaps it was Adam's natural enthusiasm for his business that made the conversation flow, but Millie couldn't remember the last time she'd managed an exchange like this with a new person close to her own age without already tripping herself up by either saying something silly or failing to say something altogether. After their tension-filled first meeting during the Christmas decoration debacle, their easy conversation now was more than surprising.

"I was amazed you didn't already have lights up in the

window," Millie said. "You obviously know what you're doing when it comes to running a shop, and Christmas lights seem like an easy win at this time of year."

He looked away, his expression clouded. "I'd just wanted to tone things down a little this year, but…"

When he said nothing further, Millie wasn't sure why the conversation had become strained, but it had.

"I don't know anything about how to style and decorate a shop," Millie said, keen to smooth over the odd bump in the flow of their conversation, especially as she'd just been congratulating herself on how well it was going. "But the display you have in your window is so gorgeous that I'm sure whatever decorations you opted for this season, they would have done the trick."

His smile returned. "Thanks for that."

Mrs Wishmore reappeared at the table with a tray bearing drinks. When Millie saw only two glasses of lemonade, she gave Doris a puzzled look.

"You're not having a drink?"

"It turns out I can't stay and have dinner with you both after all," Mrs Wishmore said as she set the glasses down on the table.

"Oh no, why not?" Millie asked, disappointed by this unexpected revelation.

"It seems I got my bus times mixed up and the last bus home leaves in ten minutes, so I'm afraid I'll have to say my goodbyes."

"Well, if you're not staying to eat, then maybe we should all just leave and I'll walk you to the bus stop," Millie said.

"I insist you both stay and enjoy your meals." Mrs Wishmore's tone was firm. "After all, I was the one who invited you here. And I've already ordered your food and paid for it, too. The barman said it should be with you in ten minutes."

"Mrs Wishmore, that's far too generous," Adam said, pulling out his wallet. "Let me pay you back for the food."

"Put that wallet away," Doris scolded him. "I'll take offence if you try to give me money, and when I make new friends with a person, I make a point of not falling out with them over something so silly." She glanced at her watch. "I'd better skedaddle if I'm to catch my bus. I'll see you both later. Good night!"

With a wave, Mrs Wishmore bustled through the pub and disappeared through the doors.

"Gosh, that was unexpected," Millie said.

But was it really? she thought to herself. Since meeting her, Millie had been repeatedly surprised by Mrs Wishmore's unusual behaviour and odd comments and general... strangeness?

Millie blushed. It was mean of her to think of the kindly older lady as strange.

But she *was* strange. The fact that she'd insisted on taking them all to dinner, only to ditch them both after ordering the food, that was strange, wasn't it?

And as for this business about mixing up her bus times... Millie was sure there'd been a sly twinkle in the older lady's eyes as she'd offered this explanation for her sudden departure, and Millie couldn't help but wonder why.

"Listen, we don't have to stay if you don't want to."

Across the table, Adam was watching her uncertainly while she peered across the pub to the doors Mrs Wishmore had vanished through. She realised she probably looked sorry to be left there alone with him, when in fact she was just downright confused by Doris Wishmore's unpredictable antics.

"I'd love to stay," Millie said. "Unless you'd rather go?"

"To be honest, I was quite looking forward to a burger. Let's stay and eat."

Millie smiled. "Fine by me."

Adam picked up his lemonade glass and held it out. "Cheers."

"Cheers," she said, tapping her glass to his.

With Mrs Wishmore gone, Millie thought it might feel weird sitting in the pub with a man she barely knew and that her social awkwardness would finally rear its evil head in order to make her look like an idiot. But as they returned to their conversation, there was no awkwardness at all, and by the time their food arrived, Millie had decided that Adam Carter made for pretty good company.

They might even become friends, she thought, as she tucked into her cheeseburger. It was a prospect she liked the sound of very much.

First, Mrs Wishmore. Now, Adam Carter.

From almost no friends, to two new friends in one week. For an awkward introvert like her, that was a personal record.

After the embarrassment of that first meeting at Adam's shop and being caught decorating the place against his will, the idea of becoming his friend and putting that embarrassment behind her filled her with a lovely, warm feeling.

Perhaps volunteering for the Christmas Village committee was finally helping her turn a corner that would steer her towards the happy Christmas she hoped for.

When their food arrived, Adam couldn't help laughing at Millie's stunned expression as she stared at her plate.

"Good grief, how could anyone ever eat all this?" She lifted the burger bun and gaped at the cheese and toppings piled high on the thick burger inside, before gesturing to the towering stack of chips beside it. "This could feed four people, never mind one."

"Once you get a taste of that burger, you'll want to eat the lot. This place is famous for its burgers."

They ate for a few moments, passing ketchup and vinegar and proclaiming on the tastiness of the meal.

"So, how long have you been involved with the Christmas Village committee?" Adam asked.

"Just a few days. I turned up on Saturday to see the Christmas tree lights being switched on, and the next thing I knew I'd been signed up as a new volunteer."

His lips twitched in amusement. "Sounds about right."

"It was unexpected, but I'm enjoying it and it's a nice way to meet people." She smiled and shrugged. "I'm new to the village and I'm still finding my feet."

"What made you move to the sprawling metropolis of Hollyford?"

Laughing, she popped a chip into her mouth. "I got a job at the care home over on Gloucester Road."

"That must be tough work."

"It is, but I like it. The elderly people who live there are lovely and I enjoy helping to look after them. Some of them don't have any family to look out for them, and so it's our job to make sure they're safe and well and that they have as happy a life as possible. At their age, that's the least they should be able to expect."

Adam was touched by what she'd said. "You have a kind heart to care that way."

She flushed at this, colour blooming at her cheeks. "Caring is what the job is all about."

Maybe, but Adam had heard enough horror stories in the news over the years to know that not all homes for the elderly were filled with kind and caring staff.

"Where did you live before moving here?" he asked, not

wanting to prolong her embarrassment by offering another compliment.

"Bristol."

His eyes widened at this revelation. "Bristol's a terrific city. What made you want to leave?"

"Well..."

At his question, a sudden look of sadness crossed her face, but whatever she'd been about to say in answer was quickly swallowed back, Adam could tell that much. The sadness that had flashed in her eyes was replaced by a brighter look and a wide smile.

"I just thought it was time for a change of scenery," she said. "Plus, the care home was short-staffed and offered a starting bonus and special skills training, so I figured, what have I got to lose?"

"Good for you."

But he wondered what she'd kept out of that answer and what she'd been about to say before she caught herself.

Adam was halfway through his burger when it occurred to him that this was the first time he'd socialised with a woman since Heidi had ended their relationship and walked out of his life. Sipping his lemonade, he let that sink in.

This dinner had been out of the blue and instigated by the other lady from the Christmas Village committee, Doris Wishmore. But it represented something significant, even if it was only inside his own head.

Across the table, Millie was telling him more about her job at the care home. Although he'd only just met her, she seemed like someone who was perfect for work that involved looking after people who were vulnerable and in need of thoughtful attention. There was something tender-hearted about Millie Dawson, that much was obvious just listening to her speak.

And he sensed, too, some sort of wound within her that made her feel like a kindred spirit. The way she'd held back when he'd asked about her move to Hollyford made him think there was more to her decision to relocate than just a good job opportunity. Maybe Heidi's betrayal had made him more sensitive to the undercurrents raging inside other people than he'd been before. When he looked at Millie and when he listened to her talk, he sensed a wound that hurt, and hurt terribly.

Not that he knew her well enough to dig into her personal life and ask what that wound might be. This was only the second time they'd met, and they were only having this meal together because Doris Wishmore had invited him along at the last minute. Once they'd eaten, they'd go their separate ways.

Adam realised he'd be sorry not to see her again. Not because he was attracted to her—he wasn't, not like that. She was pretty, that went without saying, with that dark hair and those eyes that seemed almost violet in the dim light of the pub. He could acknowledge she was attractive without being attracted to her.

After what Heidi had done to him, he suspected he'd never be able to feel romantic attraction to another woman ever again, anyway.

So, it wasn't about attraction. Instead, the simple reason he'd be sorry not to see Millie again was because he enjoyed her company. He liked their easy conversation, which, much to his surprise, had continued after Mrs Wishmore had departed. He liked the way he felt relaxed sitting here with her. That simple peace of mind had been hard to come by since Heidi left. The gnawing humiliation and hurt he felt about the disastrous ending of their relationship, and the cancelled Christmas wedding left behind in its wake, somehow seemed less awful during the half hour he'd spent in this pub booth with Millie, eating hamburgers and talking about nothing much in particular.

Over the last few months, he'd pushed everyone in his life away, too embarrassed to face their sympathetic looks and words of commiseration. In a small town like Hollyford, everyone who lived there knew what had happened to him, thanks to the gossip mill.

But Millie didn't seem to know anything about his status as a dumped fiancé and abandoned Christmas groom. As a newcomer to Hollyford, it was unlikely she'd have heard his humiliating personal story, and Adam was grateful for that. For months, every conversation he'd had with the people in his life was freighted with his failed engagement and its catastrophic end. But now, talking with Millie while they ate their food, that freight was nowhere in sight. Its absence from their conversation left Adam feeling lighter and freer than he had in a long time.

"I'm stuffed," Millie said, pushing back her plate. "I'm going to regret eating all those chips."

"They're good for you. Chips are potatoes, which makes them a vegetable and therefore officially healthy."

She laughed. "If you say so."

Adam was about to suggest coffee, but when Millie drained her lemonade and reached for her coat and bag, he kept his mouth closed. It was late and time to go, and as much as he'd enjoyed her company, he had a pile of shop paperwork to take care of tonight.

"Tell Doris I said thanks for the dinner," he told Millie as he grabbed his satchel and the plastic bag containing the paperwork he needed to look at. "I'm only sorry she wasn't here to enjoy it with us."

"Me, too. She's a sweet lady."

"Do you have far to go? I'd be happy to run home and fetch my car if you need a lift."

"My flat's a ten-minute walk away. I'll be fine, but thanks for the offer."

"Take my number and text me when you get home, just to be safe."

Outside the pub, they stood for a minute, swapping numbers and adjusting their hats and gloves. The night had turned frostier since they'd been indoors, and the pavements were white and glistening beneath the streetlamps.

"It was nice chatting with you," Adam said.

"Yeah, you too."

"Good night, Millie."

"Bye, Adam."

Her smile was warm as she waved and turned along the high street in the other direction. Adam watched her disappear around the corner before heading for home.

He'd had a nice time, the first proper nice time for months. As he walked, he realised he hadn't even been irritated by the Christmas music playing on the house system in the pub. In fact, he'd been enjoying his chat with Millie so much, he'd barely even registered that the Christmas music was playing.

That had to count as progress, he decided. First the twinkle lights in his shop and now the Christmas tunes he'd unwittingly endured while eating dinner.

Maybe this Christmas wouldn't be as grim and as tough to get through as he'd feared.

CHAPTER SIX

"Everyone at their stations! It's almost time to open the doors!"

Millie watched Evelyn Fox march across the village hall towards the doors, her clipboard and pen poised for action. Drawing in a deep breath, Millie wondered what the afternoon might hold. She wasn't entirely sure she was cut out for what was coming next.

"You look terrified, dear," Mrs Wishmore said beside her, and gave her arm a friendly pat. "But I'm sure there's no need to be."

Millie gestured to the items spread out on the trestle table they were seated behind. There were boxes of tree baubles in a mix of shiny and matt colours—red, white, green, blue, purple, pink. There were also containers of glittery Christmas shapes—stars, presents, angels, Santas, candy canes, snowflakes—and countless tubes of glue and glitter pens.

"I can't help thinking this place will be a real mess once this is all over," Millie said. "And that we'll all be covered in glue and glitter and who knows what else?"

"I dare say," Doris chuckled.

"Do you think Evelyn and the rest of the Christmas Village committee have thought this through?"

"We can only hope."

It was Saturday afternoon, and the next Christmas Village activity—tree bauble decorating—was about to begin. The session in the village hall was scheduled to last between two and four o'clock, and visitors were invited to drop in during their Christmas shopping to have fun decorating their very own tree bauble, which they could then take home and hang on their Christmas tree as a fun reminder of their afternoon in Hollyford. Once the bauble decorating was over, the church choir would assemble once more over in the market square to wrap up the afternoon by performing some Christmas carols for everyone to enjoy.

On the face of it, the tree bauble decorating idea sounded like a lovely and festive activity for people to take part in. But the more Millie looked at the tubes of glue on the table, and all those glittery Christmas shapes visitors would be invited to stick onto the bauble of their choice, the more she wondered at the mess that was about to be unleashed in the hall, not to mention on everyone in it.

The job of the volunteers was to staff the tables set out around the hall, encourage and help the visitors with their bauble decoration activity, and generally make sure that everyone had a fun time. It had all sounded perfectly reasonable to Millie until one of the Christmas Village committee members had given them a lengthy first aid briefing, advising on what to do if anyone got glue in their eye or accidentally swallowed any glitter, followed by another briefing from the head of the clean-up crew detailing the process they'd invoke afterwards to sweep the floors and scrub the tables in order to avoid a telling off from the village hall custodian.

"I can't wait to decorate a bauble of my own," Mrs Wishmore declared. "I like the look of those cute silver angel shapes and think they'll work perfectly when glued to one of the blue baubles." She gave Millie a wry smile. "You know I like my angel ware."

"I know you do."

Doris's gaze fell to the angel brooch Millie was wearing again. "I'm glad you like that little brooch I gave you, dear. And I hope that little guardian angel is doing a good job for you, too."

Millie laughed. "We'll find out soon enough once all this glue and glitter is being put to use. If I survive this without finding myself covered in glitter, or glued to the table, then I'll know she's up to the challenge."

"We'll be just fine." Doris nodded towards Evelyn, who was tucking her clipboard beneath her arm and signalling for their attention. "Oh, I think we're about to begin."

"Volunteers, I'm about to open the doors," Evelyn announced. "Repeat, I'm about to open the doors. Here we go!"

With a flourish, Evelyn threw open the heavy doors of the village hall and a line of people hurried inside, a mix of parents and children, couples, and a few groups of giggling teenagers with their phones at the ready to capture their festive creations for social media.

"Welcome!" Evelyn called out as the visitors poured in. "Please make yourselves comfortable at a free table, pick a bauble and some Christmassy bits, and have fun! Our volunteers are there to help, so don't be afraid to ask them to lend a hand."

There were a dozen tables set out around the village hall, each one with space for four or five people to sit down and enjoy the tree bauble decorating, and within a minute of the doors opening, every space was claimed, with a queue already forming. Visitors popped coins and notes in the donation tin to cover costs.

A family of four sat down at Millie's table, and the two small toddlers grabbed for the box of shiny baubles, mesmerised by the bright colours. Catching the box before it tipped over, Millie was treated to an ear-splitting scream from the thwarted youngster before the child reached instead for one of the glitter pens.

"Wait a minute!" the child's mother said. "Don't grab at everything, Harry!"

Harry screeched in response and his sister joined in as she got her hands on a bauble and tried to shove it into her mouth.

"Caitlin, don't put that in your mouth!" her father said. "We're going to decorate them, see?"

The mother threw an exasperated look at Millie and Doris. "Sorry, you must wish we'd sat somewhere else."

"Nonsense," Doris said, smiling at the two youngsters. "They just want to have fun and we're going to make sure that's what happens, aren't we, children?"

The kids screamed in delight and banged their fists on the table. It had only been thirty seconds since the event started and Millie already felt shellshocked.

"Your face is a picture," Doris said with a chuckle and handed Millie a purple bauble. "Here, you help little Caitlin and I'll help little Harry."

"Purple's her favourite colour," the mother said and smiled at Doris. "Good choice."

"I knew it would be," Mrs Wishmore said with a wink. "And how about green for Harry?"

"Perfect," the mother replied, her eyebrows raising. "That's the same colour as his favourite tractor."

"Well, isn't that lucky?"

Enchanted by the shiny baubles in their favourite colours,

the two toddlers were happy. As Millie helped the parents pop the lids from the glitter pens, she stole a glance at Mrs Wishmore.

That strange smile was there on Doris's face again and Millie couldn't help thinking that the older lady had known just which bauble colours to pick to help the little ones calm down.

Millie shook her head at the stupid thought and wondered why she kept having these odd ideas about Mrs Wishmore. The little kids would no doubt have been happy with any of the coloured baubles.

Across the table, Doris smiled at her. "Come on, Millie. Let's help these youngsters decorate these pretty baubles and send them home with happy memories to hang on their Christmas tree."

What a lovely way to put it, Millie decided, and joined in with the festive fun.

"I FORGOT to ask if you and Adam enjoyed your meal the other night," Doris said a little while later. By then, they were helping their third set of visitors of the afternoon, and as this group comprised all adults who didn't need any supervision, Doris and Millie were having fun decorating their own tree baubles.

"The food was terrific and my cheeseburger was a real treat," Millie said. "Thanks again for buying our meals even although you couldn't stay. We were sorry you left."

"It couldn't be helped." Doris added a silver angel to the cluster she'd glued to her tree bauble and turned it this way and that to inspect how it looked. "And anyway, with me out of the picture, I'm sure it gave you a nice opportunity to chat with someone closer to your own age. Adam Carter strikes me as a very nice young man."

"We had a lovely time, and I enjoyed getting to know him better."

It had been the longest conversation she'd had with someone in months and yet the time had flown by. The last person she'd talked to for that long had been her mother. She'd felt comfortable and at ease in Adam's presence and liked hearing him talk about his business. His passion for the gift shop was hard to miss, and it was only later that she realised he hadn't said anything especially personal about himself. Apart from mentioning his redundancy from the department store where he once worked, she hadn't learned much about him beyond his life at the gift shop.

Although she hadn't exactly shared lots of personal information with him, either. She'd talked about her move to Hollyford and her job at the care home, and it stood to reason that when two people who didn't know each other suddenly found themselves alone in a pub eating dinner together, the safe conversational terrain would involve jobs and work.

But she also knew that she'd held back on sharing too much about herself. When Adam had asked why she'd moved to Hollyford, she hadn't told him the whole story. Yes, it was about finding a more secure job with better pay. But the move to Hollyford had been triggered by her mother's death, and yet she had said nothing about that.

That had been a conscious choice. She'd almost told him about Caroline's illness and death, but had stopped herself at the last second because she hadn't wanted to talk about sad things. Their chatter had been relaxed and enjoyable and she liked Adam's company. Telling him about her upsetting bereavement would have put a cloud over their evening and she hadn't wanted that.

"I'm glad you're making new connections in the village," Doris said. "You deserve to have lots of lovely people in your life."

"Thanks, Doris." Millie held up the bauble she'd finished decorating. A scattering of stars and candy canes glittered against the pink bauble she'd picked. "What do you think? Is this gaudy enough?"

Doris laughed. "I'd say so. I'm sure it will look very nice indeed on your Christmas tree." She looked at Millie, her expression thoughtful. "Do you have a Christmas tree where you're staying?"

"My flatmate hauled an ancient gold-tinsel miniature tree out of the cupboard the other night and plonked it on the living room windowsill. She claims that it's so naff, it's cool."

"It sounds charming," Doris chuckled. "I'm sure that pink bauble you've just finished will look quite fetching on it." She held up her own tree bauble again and gave a satisfied nod. "And mine's is finished, too. What do you think?"

"It's lovely and elegant and angelic."

"Just like me," Doris winked.

A new set of visitors arrived at their table, a rowdy family with grumbling children who looked like they'd rather be anywhere than there, accompanied by obviously exhausted parents. Millie guessed the adults were just trying to give their kids a lovely afternoon of festive fun, but struggling to make it happen. Christmas could be a tough time, with too many expectations, as she knew only too well.

"We've got our work cut out with this lot," Doris whispered to Millie. "Let's spread a little Christmas magic, shall we?"

With a grin, Doris turned to the new visitors at their table, and with warmth and humour soon had them enjoying the activity, their earlier unhappiness quickly forgotten. As Millie helped one of the kids use the glitter pen, she wondered how Mrs Wishmore had once again sprinkled oil on troubled waters.

She was like some sort of tree bauble decorating miracle worker, Millie thought with a quiet laugh as she once more turned her attention to the messy craftwork.

At the Hollyford Gift Emporium, Adam was having his busiest Saturday of the year so far. The shop had been packed all day, the till hadn't stopped ringing, and he'd barely been able to keep some of the most popular items stocked on the shelves. His selection of hand-printed scarves, artisan soaps, and carved wooden toys had proved especially popular, and as soon as he finished replenishing the display stock, the customers grabbed it up and happily carted it off.

Throughout the afternoon, he'd reheated the same cup of coffee in the microwave about four times, and still hadn't finishing drinking it. His shop assistant, Lorraine, had stayed on beyond her usual three o'clock finishing time to help serve a crowd of tourists who'd descended on them, but Adam didn't want her to give up any more of her Saturday than she already had. He only hoped he could handle the last hour by himself before closing.

He loved these busy days in the gift shop, but he'd also be glad when this one was over. As the shop would reopen again the next day, with Sunday being a crucial trading opportunity in the run-up to Christmas, he'd need to work late tonight to get the shop back in order and make sure all the stock displays were in tip-top condition.

"Adam, that's me leaving," Lorraine called out. "Unless you need me to stay? I can work for longer if it helps?"

"No, you get home," Adam insisted as he finished ringing up a customer at the till. "I know you've got family coming round to your place tonight, and it's not fair to muck up your plans. You should already have left by now as it is."

After grabbing her jacket from the back, Lorraine pointed to a display rack across the shop. "I've tidied those scarves that someone unfolded and left strewn all over the place. And I've rearranged those boxes of hand-finished chocolates those tourists were picking up and examining and then putting back down all higgledy-piggledy."

She tutted at the actions of the thoughtless customers, making Adam grin.

"You're a star, Lorraine. Thank you. Now, off you go before we get another deluge of shoppers and you end up stuck here."

"Good luck!"

With a quick wave, she left the shop, leaving Adam alone with a few browsers who were inspecting some ceramics by the window, and a couple admiring the prints hung on the wall in the area he liked to think of his as the emporium art gallery. He'd rearranged the frames during the week to accommodate the new watercolours from the Stow-in-the-Wold artist, and had already made a sale, in addition to the one that Evelyn Fox had insisted on buying that day when she and his mother had stuck their noses into his Christmas decoration arrangements. Adam suspected the 'Sold' sign pinned beneath the watercolour of the thatched cottage beside the gentle stream had helped persuade potential buyers that these were original artworks worth having. Judging by the expressions on the faces of the couple who were now gazing up at the rest of the watercolours, he was about to make another sale.

Deciding to give the prospective buyers another moment to admire the artwork before asking if they needed any help, Adam turned to the counter to tidy a pile of paper gift bags that had been upended during the day's busyness. As he finished the task, the shop door swung open and his mother walked in.

"Has the shop been busy?" Lesley asked by way of greeting. "The village has been packed all day, and when I popped to the butcher's this morning to get sausages for your father's tea, I could hardly walk down the pavement without bumping into people."

"We've been non-stop," Adam said. "Lorraine had to stay late to help me keep on top of things. I might need to take on a temporary employee at this rate."

"The Christmas Village activities are drawing people to Hollyford, which is just wonderful. And I'm sure your enhanced window decorations are helping to persuade people to come in here and purchase all these lovely things."

Lesley gazed at the twinkle lights in the shop window, and as she was obviously satisfied that putting them there had been the correct course of action, Adam said nothing, content to let her bask in her rightness.

"Anyway," Lesley said. "I popped in to buy a few boxes of those handmade rose and violet creams that you stock. Your Aunty Gloria and your Aunty Trish both love those chocolates, and will miss them if they don't get a box from us for Christmas. I wanted to pick them up now in case you run out."

Adam helped his mother find the boxes of rose and violet creams. The aunties in question weren't actually his aunts, they were great-aunts of his mother's, but she always made a point of visiting them over the Christmas holidays and taking gifts for the old ladies to enjoy. His mother might be a meddling nuisance from time to time, but she had a good heart and always looked out for everyone in their family, even the extended aunts and uncles and cousins who were so distantly related that Adam could barely understand the connection, even when his mother explained it to him and *tsked!* with impatience at his failure to grasp the complex genealogies.

After ringing up his mother's purchases and defusing an argument with her when she insisted she wanted to pay full price instead of the cost price Adam was charging her, he bagged the chocolates, then glanced over at the couple who were still admiring the watercolours in the emporium art gallery. As they turned and caught his eye, keen to speak to him about the items, another customer arrived at the counter ready to pay for their purchases.

His mother must have noticed his dilemma, because she unbuttoned her coat and nodded at the till.

"I'll staff the counter," she said. "You help those nice people who seem interested in the framed art."

"Are you sure?"

"Of course I'm sure."

Lesley moved behind the till and smiled at the waiting customer. Having worked in retail herself before retiring, his mother was familiar with his till set-up, and this wasn't her first time lending a hand during a busy spell. Grateful for her help, Adam turned his attention to the prospective customers over in the art gallery section. Their eager smiles indicated they were only looking for more information about the watercolour artist and the story behind the original artwork, and that they'd already made up their minds to buy.

Ten minutes later, another of the watercolours by his new Stow-on-the-Wold artist was sold and Adam was waving goodbye to the delighted new owners. After hearing about the artist and being charmed by Adam's tale of the ramshackle workshop where she painted at the bottom of her garden, the couple had told him that the painting they'd chosen would take pride of place in their dining nook back home in Manchester, where it would always remind them of the lovely wintry weekend they'd spent in the Cotswolds. As he'd dealt with their payment, they'd also shown him the tree baubles they'd had fun decorating in the village hall earlier that afternoon, remarking on how much they'd loved the festive atmosphere to be found all around Hollyford and how they'd go home with fond memories of the sweet little Cotswold town that they'd always cherish.

"Well, isn't that nice?" Lesley said after Adam had said goodbye to the couple. "It's lovely to hear that all these Christmas activities around the village are having an impact on our visitors. Hopefully they'll come back for another visit next year and spread the word to everyone they know to consider a visit, too."

"Evelyn Fox will be pleased," Adam said as he selected another watercolour from the new stock to hang up in the space created by the latest sale.

"Indeed, she will." Lesley considered him for a moment before speaking again. "You still haven't popped round to the house to visit us since we got back from our cruise. Your father is frustrated he hasn't yet been able to show you his photos of the ship's restaurant buffets. He put together a slideshow with music playing alongside it and everything."

"Sorry, you know how busy things are here in the shop at this time of year."

"What about tomorrow evening, after you close up?"

"I need to sort out the accounts tomorrow night and deal with a stack of emails I haven't had time to reply to."

"Monday, then. The shop is closed on Mondays."

"I've arranged visits to some suppliers on Monday to collect new stock."

Lesley scowled. "Are you making this up just to avoid visiting us?"

"No, of course not. It's just…"

It's just that I feel like a world-class twat whenever I'm with other people, he thought miserably, *because I know that every-*

one's thinking that if my fiancé hadn't dumped me, I'd be getting ready for my Christmas wedding right now, and I can't stand everyone's pitying looks.

He especially couldn't stand those pitying looks from his mother and father. Those were the worst of all, because they left him feeling like he'd let them down. Instead of preparing to be the proud mother and father of the groom, his parents were no doubt fielding their own share of embarrassed glances and whispered gossip about what had happened to their unlucky, jilted son.

Worse, whenever he thought about dropping by their house for a visit, the way he always used to, he imagined his sister, Angela, calling in at the same time. But he couldn't bear to look at her, couldn't bear to even be in the same room as her, knowing she'd kept that terrible secret from him about what Heidi had been up to behind his back.

He'd been so close to his sister once. With only a year between them, they'd grown up together as friends as much as siblings. That's why he'd been so devastated to discover Angela had known about Heidi's affair and yet hadn't told him.

Why hadn't she said a word about it? Why had she left him in the dark? Adam had no idea what his sister could have been thinking. All he did know was that her decision not to tell him had shattered the close relationship they'd always enjoyed and things would never be the same again.

These thoughts and hurts had been swirling so long that they left him exhausted. That was why he'd enjoyed his time so much with Millie the other night when they'd shared burgers in the pub. During the short time they'd spent together, he hadn't been Adam Carter, the man who'd been humiliated by his cheating fiancé and dumped just a few short months before his Christmas-themed wedding. Instead, he'd been the old Adam Carter, the man he was before everything went wrong in his life, or at least as close to that version of himself as it was possible to get.

He wondered if he'd ever make it back to that version of himself. Seeing his mother's unhappy expression as she stood at the shop counter, clearly hurt that her son refused to visit her anymore, made him wish he could lock up all these humiliating feelings, stuff them inside a box once and for all and fling it into the sea, so he wouldn't have to deal with them anymore.

He reminded himself, yet again, that he wasn't being fair to his parents by shutting them out of his life because of these feelings he couldn't get a handle on. Things were different here at his shop, where he was focused on work and running his business, and when his mother popped in during opening hours, like she had today, he was usually too busy with tasks and chores for there to be much time to get into the nitty gritty of why he was behaving like an idiot.

But now, with the shop quiet as the minutes ticked down to closing time, Lesley had once more broached the subject. It wasn't as if she was even asking anything much of him. She wanted him to drop by and eat dinner with them and look at his father's photographs from their holiday cruise. What kind of son refused to do that for his mother?

Adam sighed, knowing this couldn't go on. "I'm not doing anything on Tuesday evening. I could come over then after I close the shop, if you like?"

Surprise mixed with happiness on Lesley's face. "I'll make that casserole I promised you. And mashed potatoes with extra butter. I'll even use the full-fat milk to whip them."

Adam laughed. "That sounds good."

Lesley looked around the shop. "There are no more customers left. Maybe you should close up for the day? It's almost five o'clock."

When he checked his watch, he realised she was right.

The last hour had disappeared in a flash. "Thanks for hanging around to help me here, Mum."

"If things stay busy like this, maybe you ought to look into finding an extra member of staff sooner rather than later."

"It's not easy finding someone willing to do just a couple of hours at peak times."

"Well, if that's all you think you need to get though the rest of the season, I'd be glad to help."

His mother's offer surprised him. "Really? I thought you were enjoying your retirement too much."

"It's not like I'd be working eight hours a day, five days a week. I'd only be popping in for an hour, here and there. You've already given Lorraine extra hours this month, so you're almost covered as it is. It's just these pinch points where you need some help. If it saves you trying to scare up an extra member of staff, I'd be glad to put my shoulder to the wheel."

He couldn't deny that it would save him the trouble of trying to find another part-time worker. Things were busy enough already. Perhaps his mother lending a hand would be enough to see him through the rest of the Christmas shopping season?

And maybe spending a few hours a week working alongside her and focused on shop tasks would help him get past this humiliation and awkwardness he'd felt around his parents ever since the wedding was called off. If he and his mother were busy talking about shop stuff and dealing with customers, maybe it would help him move beyond the crushing embarrassment he felt every time his mother looked at him.

If nothing else, it would see him through the busy Christmas period. Adam was grateful for anything that lessened the load this December and got him through to the

New Year with his mind still intact and all his emotional marbles under control.

"Thanks, Mum. That would be a big help."

Lesley's face softened at his acceptance. "Really?"

"I only need someone for a few spare hours in the afternoons when I'm here by myself. With all these extra Christmas visitors in Hollyford, I need a helping hand."

"Well, a helping hand is what I can offer."

They smiled at one another. Seeing his mother's expression made Adam glad he'd agreed to let her help.

"I'll add you to the payroll tonight."

But Lesley frowned at this. "Don't you dare try to pay me, Adam Carter. I don't need the money. But if it makes you feel better, you can donate to charity whatever you would have paid me."

"It's a deal."

Lesley grinned. "And anyway, being able to say I'm helping you here in the shop will mean I have a good excuse if Evelyn Fox asks me to volunteer for too many of the Christmas Village activities. I'm already doing my share, but the woman is incorrigible."

Lesley's phone rang just then. She glanced at the screen. "Speak of the devil," she said, then answered the call with a cheery, "Hello, Evelyn. How's it going over at the village hall? Adam had customers in here this afternoon who said they had a wonderful time at the tree bauble decoration event."

Adam watched as his mother listened to whatever Evelyn was saying on the other end of the line. Lesley frowned and nodded, then threw a look at Adam.

"That sounds like quite a debacle, Evelyn," Lesley said into the phone. "I'm here at Adam's gift shop right now, so I'll ask him and find out if he can help. Yes… yes… okay, Evelyn, I'll see you in a minute."

Lesley hung up. Adam braced himself, wondering what his mother might have got him involved with.

"Well, the tree bauble decorating over at the village hall seems to have been a triumph," Lesley reported. "However, there have been a few incidents involving glue and glitter, and the hall custodian is having an apoplectic fit about the state of the place."

"Uh-huh," Adam said, wondering where this was going.

"Well, you know that old grouch, Tony Withers," Lesley continued. "He's always moaning about something and grumping about people abusing the village hall. If the old codger had his way, no one would ever be allowed inside the place and that way it would always be kept spick and span. He doesn't seem to realise that being the custodian means it's his job to help tidy up after community events are held there."

Adam wasn't sure he agreed with the logic of this argument—a custodian was a different thing from a cleaner—but wasn't about to interrupt his mother to say so.

"Anyway, Evelyn needs all hands on deck to get the place squared away before they hand the place back over at five-thirty as agreed, or else Tony is threatening to fine the Christmas Village committee a damage penalty. That man really is a despot."

When Lesley only stared at him, Adam raised an eyebrow. "And you're telling me all this because…?"

"Because Evelyn asked if I could scare up a few warm bodies to go over there and help with the clean-up. I thought you might be willing to spare some time for a good cause."

"As soon as I lock up, I need to crack on with my stock work," Adam said, gesturing to the depleted shelves and displays. "We open again at eleven tomorrow."

"But surely you can help for just fifteen or twenty minutes, Adam? And after all, the reason you were so busy today was because of all the folk taking part in the Christmas Village events. The least you can do is give some help when it's needed."

He didn't know why he was bothering arguing about it. If he didn't lend a hand, he'd feel like a selfish jerk. His mother had made a good point, as usual, and if she was going over to the village hall to help clean up, he ought to go with her. She had just agreed to help cover his staffing problems at the shop, after all.

That didn't mean he was happy about it—or, more accurately, comfortable about it. Showing his face in the village hall meant mingling with local folk, enduring their whispered comments about his cancelled wedding and their bad-luck glances. He hated that.

But the alternative was looking like a selfish twat by refusing to help his mother lend a hand for a good cause. And he reminded himself that he'd eaten out in one of the local pubs just the other night without thinking much about whether anyone was talking about his cancelled Christmas wedding, although the more he thought about it, that was probably because he'd enjoyed Millie's company too much for the thought to have occurred to him.

His mother's steely glare was still on him. Adam sighed in defeat.

"Fine, I'll come with you and see what I can do to help."

"Good boy," Lesley nodded. "If you have any cleaning products in the back office, we should take them with us. Evelyn says they're running low and that the glitter glue on the floor is taking some effort to shift."

Adam grabbed his coat along with a couple of bottles of cleaning spray from the back. He wondered what on earth the Christmas Village committee had been thinking, using glue and glitter in the village hall. The more he thought about it, a tree bauble decorating event was only ever going to leave a mess behind, and it was little wonder the hall custodian was upset about it.

He'd do his civic duty and lend a hand and then make good his escape to return to the shop. Hopefully, if everyone there was busy scrubbing and cleaning, no one would even notice him. Turning out the lights and locking the shop doors, he followed his mother up the high street towards the village hall.

The Christmas Village committee did great work for Hollyford, there was no argument about that. But they were also a downright nuisance, when all was said and done.

Not that he was brave enough to share that sentiment with anyone else, he thought with a chuckle as he followed his mother into the village hall and prepared to be put to work.

Millie scraped at a patch of dried-in glue on the floor of the village hall and sighed with relief when it finally detached from the surface. Brushing it into a dustpan, she glanced around to see how much more work remained to be done.

From where she was hunched on the floor she could still see at least half a dozen glistening pools of dried-in glue. Her fingers would have seized up by the time she'd finished all this work to the satisfaction of the scowling custodian who was keeping a beady eye on the proceedings.

"This isn't the festive fun I expected to have when you signed me up for the Christmas Village committee, Doris," Millie said with a resigned laugh.

"I sympathise, dear," Mrs Wishmore replied, sweeping a scattering of Christmas glitter shapes into a pile on the trestle table. "But sometimes it's those unexpected things we find ourselves doing in life that turn out to be the best things for us."

"Are you saying that scraping dried-in glue off the floor of the village hall is good for my well-being?"

"Who's to say it isn't?"

Millie laughed. "I like your positive mental attitude, Doris."

"What other sort of mental attitude is worth the trouble?"

The older lady had plenty of wise words to share, which was just as well considering how they were spending the last few minutes of their afternoon. "I suppose we did have fun together decorating our own lovely tree baubles to take home."

"Exactly. There are always silver linings to be found, even if they are a little hard to see on account of all this sticky glue and spilled glitter."

Mrs Wishmore's expression—a mixture of determination and exasperation—made Millie laugh again. She stretched her fingers against the cramp that was threatening after fifteen long minutes spent working on the glue puddles. Just as she was about to resume her work again, she saw a familiar face come through the doors of the village hall.

It was Adam Carter, accompanied by his mother, Lesley. She wondered what he was doing here. Lesley made a bee-line for Evelyn Fox, brandishing two spray bottles of cleaning liquid while glancing around at the upended village hall. Adam's eyebrow arched as he, too, took in the sight.

There were still glitter and sticky shapes waiting to be swept up, tables to be wiped, and chairs to be stacked. Millie already knew from Evelyn Fox's increasingly pale complexion as the afternoon wore on that the Christmas Village committee had made a serious misjudgement when it came up with the idea for the tree bauble decorating session. What might have seemed simple and fun in theory had turned out to be messy and laborious in practice. After an hour of sweeping and scraping and scrubbing, they were still some way from leaving the village hall in the condition expected by the grumpy custodian.

Millie was surprised to see Adam Carter roll up his sleeves and get to work with one of the bottles of spray cleaner he'd brought along. She was grateful for the extra bodies turning up to lend a hand, but hadn't expected Adam to be one of them. Although she'd seen a different side to him during their pleasant meal together a few nights earlier, she couldn't forget his unhappy reaction when he'd caught sight of the twinkle lights she'd help string up in his shop window. It seemed to her that he tolerated Christmas, rather than embraced it, so quite why he was here helping with this clean-up following one of the Christmas Village events was a mystery.

Still, every pair of helping hands was welcome. Without them, there was no telling how long they'd be stuck here.

"Well, it looks like people are turning up to help us out of this tight spot," Mrs Wishmore said, nodding to the doors where a few more folk were traipsing inside carrying rubber gloves and cleaning supplies. "Evelyn must have put out a call for emergency assistance."

"Thank goodness. If I have to scrape at this glue much longer, I won't have any fingernails left."

"I have a feeling this little Christmas crisis will go down in infamy here in Hollyford."

"They'll have to set up a therapy fund to help us all recover from the trauma."

Mrs Wishmore laughed and shuffled off with her dustpan and brush towards the big black bin bags being filled with detritus on the other side of the hall. As she continued scraping at the floor, Millie saw Adam hard at work with his spray cleaner and cloth, being directed around by Evelyn Fox while she scribbled on her clipboard and barked out orders.

Fifteen minutes later, victory was declared.

"Can I have everyone's attention?" Evelyn called out to the assembled volunteers who'd finished work at last and who were now stretching out their backs and rubbing their sore hands. "Our work here is done. I can confirm that Tony the custodian has finally seen fit to sign-off on the clean-up and hand-over of the village hall. Tony, we are all so pleased that our work and effort has met with your approval and we thank you for your gracious support today."

Evelyn's voice couldn't have dripped with any more sarcasm if she'd tried. Millie exchanged a look with Doris, struggling to hide her giggles that were as much a result of the fatigue caused by all the cleaning as they were of the hilarious antics and rivalries that lay at the heart of Hollyford community organisation.

"You lot should never have been allowed to bring all this glue and glitter in here in the first place!" Tony the custodian snapped. "There are rules, you know!"

A murmur rippled through the crowd and Millie heard an assortment of whispered comments, some siding with the custodian, some declaring him too strict. Evelyn Fox waved her arms in the air.

"All right, that's enough," she called out. "What matters is that the hall is tidy again and everyone's happy. Now, just before we all go, I'd like to remind you that our next event in the Christmas Village calendar is on Thursday afternoon, when there will be a special Christmas story time for the little ones hosted by the Hollyford library."

This news prompted affectionate rumblings from the crowd. Even Tony the custodian's expression softened.

"And then next Saturday we're back here once again in

the village hall, this time for a wholesome afternoon of gingerbread men decorating," Evelyn finished.

"*What?*" Tony the custodian barked. "I didn't agree to that! That sounds just as messy as this fiasco with the tree baubles!"

Before further strife could erupt, Evelyn dismissed the clean-up crew with a flick of her wrist and hurried over to Tony the custodian, taking him by the arm and steering him off to the back where an animated discussion commenced.

"Gosh, it looks like Evelyn hasn't quite won everyone round with the Christmas Village plans," Millie said.

"I think there are lessons to be learned here for everyone," Mrs Wishmore laughed. "But I certainly had fun this afternoon. I hope you did too, dear."

"Yes, lots of fun."

Despite her shredded fingers on account of all the glue-scraping, Millie had enjoyed herself. Every time she turned up to volunteer with one of these Christmas Village activities, she felt part of something bigger than herself and more connected to this sweet little community. She treasured those feelings and the warm glow they gave her at this special time of year that she'd worried would be too hard for her to enjoy.

With their work done, Millie and Mrs Wishmore moved towards the doors, sidestepping small groups of people who were still chatting and pulling on coats before departing. As they neared the door, they crossed paths with Adam Carter.

"Hello, Adam," Mrs Wishmore said, stopping for a moment.

"Hi there, Doris," he replied, and then smiled at Millie. "Hi, Millie."

"I see you got hauled in for cleaning duty," Millie said, nodding at the bottles of cleaning fluid he was holding.

"My mother roped me in to lend a hand." He scanned the

hall, apparently searching for Lesley. When he spied her deep in conversation with someone, he shook his head. "She'll be here yapping for ages, but I need to get back to my shop."

"Oh, I just realised I left my scarf somewhere," Mrs Wishmore said, glancing back across the hall. "Give me a minute, dear, while I find it."

When the older lady shuffled off in search of her scarf, Millie turned back to Adam. "Thanks again for a nice time at the pub the other night."

"I enjoyed it, too."

He gave a quick smile, but Millie noticed the way he glanced around the hall as he spoke, a guarded look in his eye as people moved past them. When he dropped his gaze, it settled on the tree bauble she was holding.

"Did you make that?" he asked, a smile ghosting at his lips.

"With my very own hands." She held up the tree bauble to show it off. "Honestly, I don't think I could have made it look any more tasteless if I'd tried."

Adam seemed to be about to say something about the bauble, but when a peal of laughter rolled through the hall from a crowd of women gathered nearby, his gazed clouded over as his eyes swung in the direction of the noise.

"Uh, I should get back to my shop," he said with a frown.

Puzzled by his obvious discomfort, Millie wondered what the matter was. "Adam, are you okay?"

Another roar of laughter rippled through the hall and the frown on Adam's forehead deepened as he looked over at the gathering of women, his eyes hooded.

"I'm fine, but I ought to go."

"You look like something's wrong. Are you sure you're feeling all right?"

The noise in the hall rose as people moved towards the doors, still chattering to one another and laughing. A couple of women bumped into them as they passed and laughed before apologising and moving off.

"I need to go," Adam said, turning for the door.

Millie didn't like the expression she saw on Adam's face as he spun away from her. It almost looked like… embarrassment? At the very least he looked uncomfortable amongst all these people, and because she knew just how that felt, she couldn't help but want to reach out to him.

"Hey, do you want to grab a coffee or something?" she asked.

"No, sorry," he barked over his shoulder.

She watched in astonishment as he strode through the doors of the village hall and disappeared into the departing crowds.

What had just happened? One moment they'd been saying hello to each other, the next Adam had mutated into a frowning ball of agitation and fled before they'd even finished their conversation.

Mrs Wishmore returned, wrapping her scarf around her neck. "I found my scarf, thank goodness. It looks cold out there." Her smile faded when she saw Millie. "What's the matter?"

"It's that man, Adam Carter," she sighed. "I don't understand him. One minute he's grumpy and rude, the next minute he's friendly and chatty, and then before you know it, he's back to being grumpy and rude again."

"What happened?"

"I wish I knew. We were just chatting while you went to find your scarf, and suddenly he started frowning and scowling before running out of the place without even saying goodbye."

Mrs Wishmore looked thoughtful. "Perhaps he was in a rush."

"Perhaps he was. That doesn't mean he had to be so rude.

I'd just asked him if he wanted to grab a coffee and he literally spun around and ran out the door." A horrible thought occurred to her. "Oh no! Maybe he thought I was asking him out. As in, out on a date."

"Were you?"

Millie gaped. "No! I don't like him that way at all. I mean, I hardly know him." She shrugged and waved a hand at nothing in particular. "It's just that he had this look on his face all of a sudden, as if something was wrong. He said he was fine, but he didn't look fine. So, I asked if he might like to get some coffee. I thought maybe he'd like to get out of the village hall, find somewhere quiet and have a chat. But he just turned and ran. He was so rude!"

Mrs Wishmore adjusted her scarf and smiled. "Perhaps something *was* the matter, but he reacted the wrong way about it."

"Do you think so? Like what?"

"How should I know?" Doris gave a soft laugh. "Maybe you ought to ask him and find out."

"That's what I thought I was doing."

Millie peered out of the hall doors, as if expecting to see Adam Carter still running off into the darkness, but he was already long gone. Mrs Wishmore patted her arm.

"You have a kind heart, Millie, to worry about Adam like this."

"I had a nice time the other night in the pub with him. I thought we might become friends."

"Perhaps you still will become friends. Don't give up on him yet."

Millie arched an eyebrow. "He's hard work, Doris. And he's a bit of a mystery. The way he behaves and carries on, he's like Ebenezer Scrooge."

Mrs Wishmore let out a rumble of laughter. "And what a treasure Scrooge turned out to be in the end." She linked her arm into Millie's. "Come on, let's go and have some hot chocolate as a reward for surviving an afternoon of chaotic Christmas Village fun."

"Sounds perfect."

"And perhaps we should indulge in a mince pie or two?"

"You're a bad influence, Doris."

The older lady grinned and tapped at the angel brooch pinned to her coat. "Only when it comes to cakes and treats. In all other matters, I'm a perfect angel."

CHAPTER SEVEN

The delicious aromas of beef casserole and roasted vegetables greeted Adam the moment he stepped through his parents' front door. It was Tuesday evening, and he'd come round to dinner just as he'd promised his mother he would. The scents of her home cooking made him glad he was here, not just because he loved his mother's casserole, but because this visit was long overdue.

"Mum? Dad?" he called out as he hung his jacket on the hallway rack and shook off the damp evening air.

"We're in the kitchen," came his mother's response.

At the back of the house, he found his mother stirring a pot on the hob while his father sat at the table, peering over his glasses at his laptop screen. When his father looked up, a wide grin spread across his face.

"Adam, you made it!" Roger rose from his seat and pulled Adam into a bear hug, almost choking the life from him. "It's been ages since I saw you, son. How've you been?"

Seeing the sympathetic look in his father's eyes made Adam drop his gaze and shuffle uncomfortably.

"I've been fine, Dad, thanks."

"Arc you sure?"

"I'm sure." Adam gave his father a last hug and searched for a way to deflect his questions and attention. "Looks like you caught the sun on your cruise."

"What a terrific time we had, son. And what a ship we were on. You had to see it to believe it. It was huge, like a city skyscraper floating in the sea. I've been looking forward to showing you my photo slideshow."

Roger tilted the laptop screen so Adam could see it and tapped at the keyboard.

"Give the boy a chance to get through the door and sit down before you start boring him with those photographs of yours," Lesley said from the counter.

"I'm only going to show him the highlight reel for now."

"Well, your highlight reel lasted ten minutes the last time you made me watch it, and dinner will be ready soon."

"It'll be fine," Roger said, waving off his wife's comment. "The lad wants to see some of our holiday snaps. That's why he came round, isn't it?"

"He came for my home-cooked meal."

"Which we'll be ready to eat when it's done. Mind your potato pot. It's boiling over."

"Oh, heck." Lesley scampered to the hob and turned down the heat. "You and your photo slideshow, distracting me yet again."

Adam laughed softly at his parents' bickering. He'd missed this. When he counted back in his head, he realised it had been almost six weeks since he'd last seen his father, and shame flushed his cheeks. His parents' two-week cruise had provided a useful excuse to avoid them as they got packed and ready to leave, and this was his first visit to the house since they'd returned. He loved his parents, and since his break-up from Heidi, they'd been nothing but supportive.

But that didn't stop Adam feeling bone-deep humiliation every time either of them gave him that, *How are you doing, son?* look.

Asking his mother to help at the gift shop during busy spells was a big step forward in returning to some kind of normality when he was around his parents. He couldn't shut himself off from them forever and he was looking forward to having his mother lending a hand in the business. As they'd both be busy and working, there'd be little time for the sort of heart-to-heart conversations Lesley seemed to think he needed to have about Heidi.

But things with his father were a different matter.

Despite feeling glad he'd finally made the effort and put in an appearance, Adam couldn't quite look his father in the eye as Roger clicked through the cruise highlight reel on the laptop. Keeping his gaze on the screen, Adam pretended to be fascinated by the endless photographs of cruise ship buffet restaurants and bars and leisure facilities, and then equally fascinated by another set of photos showing the many new friends his parents had made on their holiday. As his father filled him in on who the various people were and where they lived and what they did for a living, Adam was grateful for the pointless summaries about strangers he'd never met.

His father's chatter and absorption in the slideshow he'd put together meant Adam could avoid eye contact. It was ridiculous that he couldn't look his father in the eye, but that's just how it was, and how it had been ever since Heidi had brought his world crashing down around his head.

These days, anytime his father's eyes met his, Adam felt embarrassed. Embarrassed at being too stupid not to have seen what was going on behind his back. Embarrassed to be the sort of man who'd fall for a woman who was destined to cheat on him. Embarrassed at the reality of finding himself a jilted groom. Embarrassed at the gossip his parents must have been at the centre of on account of their clueless son and his cancelled Christmas wedding.

He felt like he'd let his parents down. Worse, he felt like Heidi's betrayal might make him look like less of a man in his father's eyes. Roger was no alpha male type by any stretch of the imagination, but it had to embarrass him to know his son's fiancé had carried on behind his back and that Adam hadn't known anything about it until it was all too late.

It was the same anxious feeling he'd had the other day at the village hall when he'd helped with the cleaning up after the tree bauble decorating event and then fled the scene before he'd even finished his conversation with Millie Dawson. One minute he'd been fine and minding his own business, and then he'd heard a group of women laughing and giggling, and couldn't help but think they were all laughing and giggling at *him*, gossiping about his cancelled wedding and his cheating fiancé.

He'd run out of the village hall while Millie had been in the middle of saying something to him. He felt bad about that. It wasn't the first time he'd been abrupt or rude in her company, and she probably thought he was a flake.

Adam never used to be this sort of person—brittle, anxious, unfriendly, isolated. He missed the man he'd been before Heidi tore his world apart. If he could rewind the clock and become that man again, he would, in a heartbeat.

"Dinner's ready," Lesley announced, as she carried a serving dish to the table. Welcoming the interruption to his gloomy and never-ending internal conversation, Adam helped his mother bring everything over and poured some wine.

"This looks smashing, love," Roger said and spooned an enormous helping of beef casserole onto his plate.

"I know how much you two love my beef casserole,"

Lesley said, looking pleased. "Although considering how much food your father ate while we were on our cruise, I think we might have to put him on a diet."

"Rubbish," Roger frowned. "There's nothing wrong with indulging in an extra treat or two on holiday. That's what it's all about, isn't it? And anyway, there were so many delicious dishes to choose from, it would've been a crime not to try a bit of everything."

"Those buffet photos you showed me are really something," Adam said. "What were the desserts like? I know how much you like your desserts, Dad."

Roger gave a rumble of laughter. "The desserts were unbelievable! Trifles, cheesecakes, gateaux, sundaes, tortes, and more flavours than I even realised existed."

"If I hadn't been there to keep an eye on him, your father would've had to be airlifted off the ship because he'd eaten too many cakes and had a bad turn."

"Rubbish," Roger said again, waving off her comment with a chuckle.

Adam was happy to let his parents continue regaling him with tales of their holiday while they ate their meal. It was safe conversational terrain, and he enjoyed hearing about their adventures and the good times they'd had. Once they'd cleared their plates, Roger patted his stomach.

"Thanks for a lovely meal, love," he told Lesley. "Since you did all the cooking, I'll do the dishes and brew the tea. Adam will help me, won't you, son?"

"Of course."

"Good," Lesley said, picking up her wine glass and heading for the kitchen door. "In that case, I'll finish this last splash of red wine through in the living room and catch a minute or two of the soaps on television."

Once Lesley was gone, Roger filled the sink while Adam stacked the dirty dishes on the counter. His parents had never owned a dishwasher, preferring the routine of washing and drying under their own steam. Adam grabbed a tea towel and got to work while his father scrubbed at the oven dishes.

"So, you're doing okay, son?" Roger asked. "Everything all right at the gift shop?"

"It's all good. I don't remember ever being this busy before in December. There's never a quiet moment in the shop these days."

"That's brilliant news. I'm glad you've made such a success of your shop. Your mother and I are proud of you."

"Thanks, Dad. Although, if I'm being honest, things probably wouldn't be so busy if it wasn't for the Hollyford Christmas Village events. Those bring in a lot of extra customers who might not visit otherwise."

"It's a grand thing Evelyn Fox and her team have got going there, that's for sure. A great bonus to the town and to all the little businesses we've got around the place." Roger rinsed a pot and glanced at Adam. "Your mother's thrilled you asked her to help in the shop in the run-up to Christmas."

"I'm glad she can pitch in. I'd have to recruit a new shop assistant otherwise. Because Mum knows the shop already, it saves me wasting time training someone new. If I'd had any idea we'd be this busy, I would've got a new staff member in place weeks ago."

"Well, I know your mother's glad for the chance to help out. And I think she's glad for the chance to spend a bit of time with you, too, son. We've missed seeing as much of you as we once did."

Adam shrugged and kept his attention on the dishes he was drying. "Like you said, it's a busy time of year at the shop."

"But that's not the only reason you've not dropped by lately."

"Well, you were on your cruise for a few weeks, too."

"Adam." Roger said his name softly. Setting aside the washing up, he turned from the sink. "Adam, son, look at me."

His father's gentle tone caught Adam in the gut. When he reluctantly did as Roger had asked and met his father's gaze, he saw pain there.

"Son, I'm not going to insult you by pretending I know what you're going through," Roger said. "Heidi did a terrible thing and I can't imagine how much it hurt you."

"Dad…"

"Just listen for a second, son. I need to say this." Roger blew out a long breath. "Don't shut us out of your life. We're your parents and we want to be there for you. We can't do that if we hardly ever see you and if you won't talk to us about what happened."

"I'm here now, aren't I?"

"Yes, you are. But you've scarcely looked me in the eye since you arrived."

The kitchen fell silent as Adam tried to find a response. "I'm embarrassed, Dad," he said at last, his voice a whisper. "What Heidi did ripped me in two and I'm so embarrassed about it all, and so humiliated, and…"

When his words trailed off, Roger smiled sadly. "I hate that she did this to you. But what I hate more is that you think there's anything to be embarrassed about when it comes to your mother and I."

"You both must think I'm an idiot for not realising what was happening."

"Of course we don't think that. If we think anything at all, it's that we're glad you found out what Heidi was really like before you married her, instead of afterwards. She wasn't right for you, and better you know it now instead of months or years after a big, fancy wedding."

"But that's just it, Dad. I thought she *was* right for me. I thought she was perfect."

Roger sighed and nodded. "I know, son. I'm sorry you were wrong. But sometimes we get things wrong in life. That's just the way it is. None of us get through our days without ever putting a foot wrong."

"Maybe. But Heidi was a pretty big misstep."

"You need to stop beating yourself up about it. No good comes from that. And you need to start thinking about moving on from the whole mess."

"I'm trying, Dad."

Roger gave a sad smile and turned back to the washing up. "That's all I can ask for. But there's something else you need to do, too."

"What's that?"

"You need to talk to your sister."

"One thing at a time, Dad."

"It isn't fair to give Angela the cold shoulder like this, Adam."

"And it wasn't fair of Angela to keep a secret from me, not one like that. You know I'm right."

"She said she's sorry."

"Oh, well, that makes it all okay, then."

"Adam, don't be like that."

"Look, I don't mean to sound stroppy or sulky, but Angela should've told me what she knew, when she knew it. Why didn't she?"

"She's explained all that, son, time and time again. She thought she might have made a mistake when she saw Heidi and that bloke together in that bar, maybe got her wires crossed and put two and two together and got twenty. So, to avoid creating a problem where there might not be one, she confronted Heidi before saying anything to you, to see what the explanation was."

"I know all this, Dad."

Adam didn't want to hear any of this story again. He'd already heard it from Angela at the time. It was as gut-wrenching to hear about now as it was then.

The story his sister had told him went like this. One Thursday night last September, after enjoying a quick drink with a few colleagues from the office where she worked in Cheltenham, Angela had been leaving the bar when she'd caught sight of Heidi huddled in a corner booth with a man she didn't recognise. The two of them looked friendly, cosy even, and the way Heidi's hand rested on the man's arm made it seem like they were more than just friends.

According to Angela's account, she'd almost gone over to the booth to find out what was going on there and then. But for all she knew, the man was just an old friend or maybe even some family member, someone Heidi was close to and felt comfortable with. A woman with her hand on a man's arm while they shared a drink could mean many things, not just a romantically intimate relationship. Men and women could be friends, after all, and Angela herself had a close relationship with a guy she'd known since childhood and who she often met for drinks, just the two of them, but that didn't mean there was anything romantic happening between them.

But when Angela sought Heidi out the next day and mentioned seeing her in the bar, Heidi's embarrassed reaction had told her all she needed to know, at least according to the account she'd given to Adam when it all came out in the wash. Heidi had tried to come up with an excuse, but her face had revealed the truth of the matter, and she'd soon admitted to Angela that she was having an affair.

Adam could've understood that his sister just wanted to get her facts straight first and that she'd want to ask Heidi about what she'd seen before jumping to any conclusions. But the story hadn't ended there.

After admitting to Angela that she'd been seeing this bloke for months, Heidi had begged Angela not to tell Adam the truth about what was going on. Heidi said she wanted to do that herself, but needed to find the right moment to break the news. She was about to end an engagement and cancel a wedding and ditch the partner she'd spent the last two years with—and she needed to do it in as kind and gentle a way as she could.

Heidi had begged Angela to give her time to find the right moment. Angela had agreed.

But another full week passed before Heidi dropped her bombshell on him. When Adam later discovered that Angela had known what was going on for days before Heidi broke up with him, he'd been shattered all over again. He'd been wandering around in complete ignorance about his fiancé's betrayal, while his own sister had known the truth the entire time. They'd seen each other twice during that period, once at their parents' house and once on Hollyford high street, and although Angela had seemed in a rush to get away on both occasions, Adam had simply chalked it up to her being busy.

Once he realised the real reason she'd fled his company on those two occasions, he'd been stunned. When they'd bumped into one another at their parents' house, Adam had been discussing some of the wedding arrangements with his mother, and yet Angela hadn't said a thing about what she knew.

He'd felt shocked and stupid and horribly, horribly betrayed. Angela had apologised, and it was obvious that she'd been upset about the whole thing. Needing time to calm down after yet another terrible revelation on top of the one already delivered by Heidi, Adam had walked away from his sister, too angry to look at her for a moment longer.

Weeks later, he still didn't want to see her. There was a

wedge between them now and Adam wasn't sure how to remove it or how to get past what had happened. Right now, all he wanted was to survive Christmas and get beyond the date of his doomed wedding day. He didn't have any head space for dealing with his sister, too, or for thinking about the spectacularly bad judgement call she'd made when she'd chosen not to tell him about Heidi's affair as soon as she found out about it.

Adam finished drying a glass and set it down on the counter, loathing the constant presence of Heidi and her betrayal in his life, even although she was long gone. Beside him, his father gave a frustrated shrug and slid the plate he'd just cleaned into the drying rack on the sink.

"I know Heidi's affair came as a big shock," Roger said. "And I understand why Angela knowing about it and not telling you right away was a big shock, too. But she's your sister and you can't just shut her out of your life. We're a family and families stick together."

Adam saw the unhappiness in his father's expression and felt even more awful about everything than he did already. The ripple effects of his ill-fated engagement and abandoned wedding seemed to have no end.

"Just give me time, okay?" Adam said, his voice soft. "I'm here tonight having dinner with you because I know I'm being stupid by shutting you out. I know I need to try harder. I know I need to get my act together and move on. But one step at a time. The honest truth is that if I see Angela, I'm worried I'll end up saying something I regret and that I can't take back. I don't want that."

"But it's been weeks since it all came out into the open, Adam."

"I know. I wish I could shrug it all off and move on. No one wants that more than me. But I just can't do it. I need time to get over Heidi. I need time to stop feeling mortified every time I think about what happened. And I need time to stop being so angry at Angela before I see her again."

Roger sighed again and nodded. "Okay, son. We're all here for you in the meantime."

"Thanks, Dad."

"We're going to get through this. *You're* going to get through this. And then things can get back to how they used to be between you and your sister."

Adam turned to the dishes waiting to be dried. What if things never went back to how they'd been between him and Angela? Maybe this was something they'd never move beyond. Angela was his sister and she should've had his back, but she'd let him wander around cluelessly for days, yapping on about wedding plans and dealing with ceremony arrangements, and all the while she'd known there would never be a wedding.

How could she have done that? And how could Adam ever forget she'd done that? He feared that the old days when they'd been friends as well as siblings might be gone forever.

Roger must have caught Adam's expression, because he reached out and squeezed his shoulder.

"Everything will be fine, son," Roger said. "I know it will."

"Thanks, Dad. I hope you're right."

They shared a sad smile and then Roger gave a firm nod, as if that settled matters.

"Let's put the kettle on before your mother starts wondering what happened to the cup of tea I promised her."

LATER THAT EVENING, as Adam walked home from his parents' house, the chilly December night air helped clear his head following the strained conversation with his father.

On the one hand, it had been good to put aside his anxieties and talk properly with his dad, be honest about how he felt about things, and start spending time again with his parents the way he used to.

On the other hand, he just *hated* having to talk about Heidi and what she'd done to him. Talking about it only reminded him of how blind and stupid he'd been. And the inevitable discussion about when he would stop shutting Angela out of his life hadn't helped, even although he knew his father meant well. Roger Carter was a good man who'd worked hard to raise his children, and the last thing he'd want was for there to be a schism in the family.

Adam didn't want there to be a schism, either. But he couldn't face Angela, not yet. Like he'd said to his father, he'd take things one step at a time until he could shake off the humiliation he felt and hold his head high again. Maybe then he'd be able to look his sister in the eye once more.

Turning at the end of his parents' street, he walked towards the high street and the market square. Adam lived in a small apartment building on the other side of the centre of Hollyford, a fifteen-minute walk away. He was glad he'd left the car at home. He hoped the fresh air and exercise might stop the endless internal yapping that had been going on inside his head since his conversation with his father after dinner.

Adam was halfway across the market square when he saw Doris Wishmore standing beside the Hollyford Christmas tree, admiring the lights. She turned as he approached and gave him a smile.

"Well, hello there, Adam," Mrs Wishmore said. "What brings you out on such a chilly night?"

"I'm on my way home after having dinner with my parents," he replied. "How about you?"

"I was helping with a few bits and pieces of Christmas Village organisation tonight over at the village hall. I'm just waiting for a friend to come and pick me up to drive me home. The last bus left some time ago."

Adam glanced around the market square, which was quiet tonight on account of there being no Christmas Village activities happening. A few dog walkers skirted around the edge of the square, but otherwise there was no one around. Although Hollyford was a safe place, Adam didn't like the idea of the older lady standing around in the square by herself while she waited for her friend to arrive.

"I'll hang around until your friend gets here," he said. "Keep you company while you wait."

Doris smiled. "That's very kind of you. I'd like that very much."

"So, how are you, Doris?"

"I'm just fine, thanks." She gave him a thoughtful look for a moment before continuing. "Although perhaps I'm the one who should ask you that? Millie mentioned that you hurried out of the village hall on Saturday rather suddenly and that it seemed as if something might be wrong?"

"Ah, no, nothing was wrong. I just..." *I'm just an idiot who's lost all confidence in myself because it seems like everyone is laughing at me behind my back because of my stupid, cancelled Christmas wedding.* "Something just came up and I had to hurry off."

"I see." Mrs Wishmore nodded, as if considering what he'd said. "I'm sure Millie will be pleased to know all is well. She was a bit baffled when you ran off while she was talking to you. And I suspect she was perhaps a little hurt, too."

Adam's cheeks burned with heat. "I didn't mean to upset her."

"Of course you didn't. I'm sure that if you let her know you had a good reason for rushing off, she'll understand."

If only he did have a good reason for rushing off. But he wasn't about to tell Millie—who was little more than a stranger—the sordid tale about his cheating fiancé, his abandoned wedding, and the crumbling self-esteem and churning humiliation he now struggled with on a daily basis. He could hardly talk about those things with his own parents, never mind someone he'd only just met.

"I'll do that," he said, to put an end to the discussion. "Thanks for the heads-up."

If he bumped into Millie again, he'd make something up about a forgotten appointment he'd realised he was late for. He didn't like the idea that he'd left her feeling confused or upset when he'd run off on Saturday, not when he could clear matters up with a word or two of an explanation.

"I got the impression that you two might have struck up the beginnings of a nice friendship when you had dinner together last week in the pub," Doris said.

"We had a nice chat and a fun time, that's true."

Doris smiled, her eyes twinkling beneath the lights of the Christmas tree. "It's lovely when we make new friends, don't you think? And I'm always amazed at how often people come into our lives at just the perfect moment to help us through a tricky patch." She gave a soft chuckle. "Life can be so magical sometimes."

Adam had no idea what to say in response to this rather odd comment. Doris Wishmore had a curiously innocent quality about her and an odd way of talking sometimes. She certainly saw a brighter side to the world than Adam did, at least right now.

"The world *is* a wonderful place, Adam," Doris said, as if she'd read his thoughts. "And most people in it are wonderful, too. I hope you won't let one bad experience spoil your enjoyment of life."

Adam's eyes widened in surprise. "What do you mean?"

But the older lady only laughed. "You know exactly what I mean." She gestured to the Christmas tree, its twinkling lights bringing warmth to the damp December night. "Christmas comes but once a year. It would be a shame to miss this one when you could just as easily open your arms and embrace it and let all the wonder sweep you away."

If Adam had been lost for words before, he was completely speechless now. He'd never met anyone before who talked this way. The older lady's twinkling eyes held him spellbound.

"Anyway," Doris said with a sweep of her hand. "I hope you'll catch up with Millie again soon. I'm sure she'd love to see you again, what with her being a newcomer in Hollyford and keen to make new connections in the village."

"Uh, well…" Adam cleared his throat, wondering what was wrong with him and why the strange older lady had this weird effect on him. "I'm sure we'll bump into one another again."

"Good. I happen to know she'll be helping at the Christmas Village story time at the library on Thursday afternoon. Perhaps you ought to drop by and say hello and clear up this little misunderstanding between the two of you?"

"Hmm, that's a good idea. I'll do that." Adam hadn't meant to say this, but the words popped out before he realised they were coming.

"There's no need to look so terrified at the idea!" Doris laughed. "It will only be some sweet little children listening to the librarian read a Christmas story aloud while a few of us old fogies on the Christmas Village committee hand out juice and biscuits."

"Right, no problem."

Doris tilted her head and smiled. "And I'm sure Millie is an excellent listener, if you decide you want to share a little more about yourself than you have already. After all, that's how strangers become friends."

As Adam watched the expression on the older lady's face, he couldn't escape the feeling that she knew a great deal more about him than she ought to. Had she somehow found out about his cancelled wedding? Did the gossip mill stretch even as far as people who didn't actually live in Hollyford?

Before he could think any more about these disturbing ideas, a car horn tooted on the other side of the market square. Mrs Wishmore turned and waved, then looked back towards Adam.

"Well, my friend has arrived to drive me home. I'd better skedaddle. Good night, Adam."

"Good night, Doris."

"And thanks for keeping me company while I waited. You're a very thoughtful young man."

"My pleasure."

Adam watched Doris shuffle off across the market square to where her friend was waiting in the car. The older lady turned up the collar of her red jacket as she walked and pulled her scarf close against her neck. Adam waited until she'd got into the car before resuming his journey home.

As he turned around, something on the ground caught his attention at the spot where Mrs Wishmore had been standing beside him. Peering down, he saw a pearly shimmery ball reflecting the glow of the white lights on the Christmas tree.

It only took him a second to recognise what he was looking at—it was the miniature tree bauble featuring the delicately painted angel, the same bauble that had rolled across the cobbles of Church Lane and landed at his feet the first time he'd met Mrs Wishmore. The little tree trinket must have once more escaped from Doris's bag, although he couldn't remember hearing it drop while they'd been standing here. The tiny tinkling jingle bell inside the bauble would surely have made a noise when it fell. Yet he'd heard nothing, and neither, apparently, had Doris.

Adam picked up the little bauble and checked it over. The little jingle bell tinkled merrily when he shook it and the serene angel gazed up at him from the pearly surface of the ball. Mrs Wishmore would be sorry to have lost the bauble yet again, and he was glad he'd noticed it on the ground before leaving the market square. The next time he saw her, he'd return the trinket.

Sliding the bauble into his coat pocket, Adam started walking again towards home. Despite its small size and light material, the bauble felt solid inside his pocket, its weight there somehow reassuring.

For reasons he couldn't understand, Adam slipped his hand into his coat pocket as he walked, running his fingers over the smooth edges of the angel bauble and feeling a warm comfort from its presence that was as surprising as it was soothing.

CHAPTER EIGHT

There were many things Millie missed about her mother, too many things to count. But one thing she missed most was all the time they'd spent together curled up on the sofa, each of them with their noses buried in a book. Those snapshots of time formed enduring memories that Millie knew she'd cherish forever.

Caroline Dawson had been a voracious reader, and she'd passed that passion on to her daughter. After a long day at her hospital cleaning job, when Caroline was bone tired and weary from scrubbing toilets and mopping floors, there was nothing she'd loved more than getting lost in a novel, and being carried off into other lives and other adventures filled with romance and mystery and drama. She'd favoured fat paperbacks that promised captivating family sagas, epic love stories, thrilling suspense, and mindboggling mysteries, and the more impossibly ridiculous the twists and turns, the better.

Lacking the spare cash needed to sustain her book addiction in the high street bookshops, Caroline had turned instead to the local library. Millie remembered so many

Saturday mornings spent scouring the library shelves for new books to check out, first as a little girl in the children's section and then as a teenager thrilled by the mesmerising world of the adult section, and then browsing side-by-side with her mother as a grown woman, the two of them suggesting books to one another whenever something caught their eye. Millie had always felt a thrill of disbelief whenever she walked into a library and thought about how, with the aid of a simple library card, she could take home and read anything she wanted to. It always seemed like a little miracle, or an act of magic, when the librarian stamped the books she'd chosen and Millie left with them tucked under her arm.

If it hadn't been for their local library in Bristol, Millie wasn't sure what she and her mother would have done to keep themselves entertained. When Millie was growing up and money was in short supply, the library was their escape. As a single parent keeping body and soul together in a low-paid job, Caroline hadn't had any cash to splurge on trips to cinemas or restaurants. For them, pushing the boat out had involved a visit to the charity shop to see what second-hand books they might find there for a few pounds.

But Millie had never felt like she'd missed out. If anything, her mother's love of books had given her endless places to escape to, and endless stories to carry her far away from a world that could sometimes be too hard on a girl with Millie's sensitive soul and introverted nature.

Which was why she'd missed books so badly during her mother's illness and the months following her death. Where books had once been her escape, they instead became a painful reminder of all that she was losing and then, eventually, all that she had lost. As the cancer had spread, Caroline had lost all interest in reading, telling Millie that her mind could no longer focus on the stories she'd once loved.

Watching her mother push away a stack of unread paperbacks beside her bed—books she would have devoured not long before—while telling her to return them to the library because she didn't want to read them, had been just one more awful reminder of the unthinkable toll the disease was taking.

With Caroline's appetite for reading gone, Millie had lost hers, too. After her mother died, it had been a long time before Millie had been able to pick up a book again and read for pleasure. The first time she'd curled up on the sofa with a book she'd bought as a treat at the charity shop, she'd cried to think of how many times she and her mother had read together, content to be with one another while getting lost in their novels.

But the book she'd picked up that day had grabbed her and pulled her deep into a complicated murder mystery that was so preposterous that Millie had been compelled to get to the bottom of it, while keeping company with the brooding detective whose desire for justice drove him on through every obstacle thrown up by the villains of the piece. Only when she turned the last page of the final chapter did she realise that, during the dark spring afternoon she'd spent immersed in the story, she hadn't thought of her mother's passing once.

The bolt of sadness caused by that realisation was quickly replaced by relief. Her grieving heart had been given a rest from the painful sorrow, and she was smart enough to know that had to be a good thing. A healthy thing. An essential thing if she was ever going to move on from losing her mother.

As spring turned to summer, Millie's love of reading had gradually returned. During the move from Bristol to Hollyford, books had provided a much-needed escape from the upheaval and from her worries about whether she was doing the right thing. While setting off on a new journey in her own life, she'd devoured books filled with people doing exactly the same thing—starting new lives, finding new loves, resolving old hurts—and their stories had helped her find the courage to take the next steps.

Because their reading pastime had revolved around books borrowed from the library, and charity shop purchases that they donated again once they'd read them, there hadn't been many books for Millie to pack up once she'd decided to move to Hollyford. But there was one book that the Dawson family did own and which was very special to Millie.

That book was *The Night Before Christmas.*

A slim, oversized hardback, filled with beautiful illustrations depicting the fantasy of the Christmas Eve tale, Millie adored the book and the festive memories it evoked. Purchased during a visit to a discount bookshop when Millie was seven years old, the book had pride of place amongst the Christmas items that were brought out every December as part of their festive celebrations. Once Caroline and Millie had decorated the Christmas tree, and strung tinsel over every surface, and set out the little ornaments and knick-knacks they'd hunted down in bargain bins over the years, the last thing they did before settling down for their ritual viewing of *The Santa Clause* film was to place that hardback copy of *The Night Before Christmas* on the coffee table. From there, it would be read time and time again throughout the season, because Millie had never tired of hearing the story. Even when she was grown up and much too old for it, she'd still loved listening to her mother recite the gorgeous poem as part of their family Christmas traditions.

The only December during which *The Night Before Christmas* hadn't been read aloud was last year, when Caroline died. It wasn't until many months after her mother's passing, when Millie had been packing up the house and pulling their boxes of Christmas decorations from the back of the cupboard, that she'd realised she hadn't even thought of the book once during that terrible December. Many other Christmas traditions had flickered in her mind that month, but not that one, although Millie couldn't say why.

Although there wasn't much storage space in her rented bedroom in the flat share, Millie had brought the boxes of Christmas decorations with her to Hollyford, including the illustrated hardback copy of *The Night Before Christmas*. But she'd decided against displaying or hanging any of the decorations once December arrived. Her flatmate's main concession to the season was the ragged gold tinsel miniature tree she'd propped up on the windowsill, and although Christmas was supposed to be a time for sharing, Millie didn't want to risk any of her mother's decorations being broken or lost if she brought them into their shared living room. Not only was her flatmate clumsy, but she seemed to have a lot of clumsy friends, too, who were always upending coffee cups or dropping plates on the floor or accidentally knocking things over after drinking one glass of wine too many on a Saturday night.

Caroline's horde of accumulated Christmas decorations might not have been worth much in terms of money—in fact, they weren't worth anything at all—but they were no less precious to Millie because of it. And so the few decorations she'd taken from the boxes had remained in her small bedroom for her own enjoyment only.

As for the hardback copy of *A Night Before Christmas,* Millie had set it out on her bedside table and had already looked at it many times since the December countdown began. She'd flicked through the pages, admired the illustrations, and read the words inside her head.

She'd remembered Christmases gone by, curled up beside

her mother on the sofa while Caroline read the story aloud as the fairy lights twinkled on the tree and the magic of the season filled their tiny living room.

Millie thought of her mother's lilting voice as she'd recited the story, and how she'd always known when to speed up and when to slow down, when to fill the story with excitement and when to fill it with wonder. She thought of the way her mother's eyes had danced with delight whenever Millie, when she was small, had laughed and clapped her hands together as the story unfolded.

Such simple pleasures, now gone forever.

A mixture of fond remembrance and aching sorrow now filled Millie's heart as she stood in the Hollyford library listening to a recital of *The Night Before Christmas*, scheduled as part of the Christmas Village activities. A mix of toddlers and small children sat on the floor of the children's section, their rapt attention focused on the librarian, who was reading aloud. Parents and grandparents lingered at the back, smiling at the storytelling and the expressions on the faces of the children.

After the chaos of the tree bauble decorating event last weekend, Millie was pleased to be volunteering with an activity that hadn't descended into a sticky mess, at least not yet. And although she'd looked forward to the Christmas storytelling session in the library all week, hearing *The Night Before Christmas* still made her feel wistful and more than a little sad.

"Is everything okay, dear?" Mrs Wishmore whispered in her ear.

Millie turned to the older lady and gave a smile and a nod, silently mouthing, "I'm fine," so as not to disturb the storytelling.

Doris searched her face for a long moment, as if she

didn't quite believe her, before laying a hand on her arm and giving her a gentle squeeze and a smile.

A warm feeling of comfort rolled along Millie's arm and into her body and, somehow, into her heart. The ache that had been there just a moment before immediately felt less painful, and the memories that swirled in her head of Caroline as a young mother, reading *The Night Before Christmas* while Millie listened, wide-eyed with wonder, no longer felt laden with bittersweet sorrow.

In that moment, she remembered only the golden glow of those long ago Christmas story-times with her mother, and forgot the pain of Caroline's passing.

She thought of her mother's smile, and the warmth of her voice, and the bright joy in her eyes, and the cosy excitement of their shared tradition of reading the story aloud.

She thought of how her mother had always made Christmas feel magical.

She thought of how her mother had always made her feel loved.

Millie blinked as a round of applause broke out amongst the children and adults assembled in the library, and realised with a start that the reading had ended. The last thing she remembered hearing was the part of the story where St. Nicholas dashed to the window and tore open the shutters and threw up the sash. Now, though, the tale was over.

But she barely remembered hearing any of it. How could that be?

Had she been so caught up in her reminiscences that she'd somehow zoned out for more than half of the reading?

As the round of applause quietened down, Millie wondered what was wrong with her.

She remembered the gentle way Mrs Wishmore had squeezed her arm, and how that simple act had left her feeling soothed and comforted and no longer dwelling on the sadness that too often threatened to claim her.

Perhaps nothing was wrong with her. Perhaps she was simply lucky to have made a kind new friend who knew just when she needed a friendly pat on the arm.

Millie's hand moved to the angel brooch Doris had given her, and which she'd pinned to the snowman jumper she'd worn today for Christmas story time. As soon as her fingers touched the creamy enamel of the angel's billowing dress and graceful wings, Millie once more felt deeply comforted.

She closed her eyes and let the warm sensation flow through her, bringing comfort and strength.

"It's okay to miss your mother, dear."

Millie opened her eyes and saw Mrs Wishmore's kind smile. As Millie glanced around the library, she realised that all the children were now selecting Christmas story books from the shelves to take home and read with their parents. Millie hadn't even heard the librarian tell them to get up and wander around, and hadn't heard the noisy chatter start up and which now filled the space.

Once more, Millie wondered how she could have zoned out like that, neither hearing nor seeing anything that was going on around her. She peered at Mrs Wishmore.

"What did you say?" she asked.

The older lady once more favoured her with a kind smile. "I said, it's okay to miss your mother, dear. I'm sure that hearing this lovely story read aloud must bring back many memories of your own mother reading it to you when you were small."

Millie blinked, wondering how the woman could have known what she'd been thinking. "How do you know my mother used to read it to me?"

"You told me, dear," Mrs Wishmore said with a soft laugh.

Millie frowned. She didn't think she'd said anything to

Doris about how her mother had read *The Night Before Christmas* to her. In fact, when she'd arrived at the library for her volunteering duties, she'd reminded herself to keep such memories to herself, because she'd wanted to enjoy the fun afternoon of Christmas storytelling and not become maudlin because of reminiscences.

After all, everyone had bittersweet memories of Christmases gone by, memories of festive traditions that were once treasured, memories of loved ones who were no longer around.

And what she wanted most of all this Christmas was to feel the happiness and joy of the season, the way she'd promised her mother she would. She couldn't do that if she was constantly looking to the past and missing what had been lost—although she knew only too well that was easier said than done.

"I don't think I said anything about my mother reading that story to me, Doris." She said it with certainty because she knew it was true.

But Mrs Wishmore only waved a hand, as if this minor detail didn't much matter. "Of course you did. How else could I know?"

It was a good point. Still, Millie *knew* she hadn't said anything about it to Doris.

Or had she?

A bright twinkle lit up Mrs Wishmore's eyes, and Millie couldn't escape the feeling that there was something deeply mysterious about the older lady, something she couldn't quite put her finger on.

"Anyway," Doris said as they grabbed their bags and coats now that their volunteering duties were finished. "I wondered if you'd heard from young Adam?"

Surprised by the sudden change in conversation topic, Millie shook her head. "No, we've not been in touch."

"That's a pity. It seemed you two were becoming friends."

"I've been busy at work this week and doing overtime. And anyway, Adam's the one who ran off at the weekend when I asked if he wanted to grab a coffee. I got the message, loud and clear."

"I'm not so sure you did."

At Doris's strange comment, Millie looked up from buttoning her coat and saw a curious look on the woman's face.

"What do you mean?"

"Only that I suspect there's more going on with that young man than you realise, and that he might just need someone to talk to about it all."

Millie wondered how on earth Mrs Wishmore could know this. "It sounds like you know him far better than I do."

"Hardly." Mrs Wishmore smiled. "Just remember what I said at the weekend and give the young man time."

"Time for what?"

The older woman wasn't making much sense today at all, or at least that's how it seemed to Millie. Between zoning out during the storytelling session and being baffled by Mrs Wishmore's cryptic comments, she wondered if she was coming down with a winter cold. She hoped not.

"Oh look!" Mrs Wishmore said, her gaze shifting to the library doors behind Millie. "Now, isn't that a lovely coincidence?"

Turning to see what Doris was talking about now, Millie saw Adam Carter coming through the library doors. His cheeks were red from the chill outdoors as he pulled off his gloves and scanned the space.

When his eyes connected with Millie's, he gave a smile and an awkward wave across the room.

"I'll leave you two to catch up," Doris said to Millie, and hiked her big blue handbag onto her shoulder. "I'm meeting an old friend for an early dinner and don't want to keep her waiting. Bye, dear!"

As quick as a flash, Mrs Wishmore bustled off towards the doors. After saying a brief hello to Adam, she disappeared outside. Adam glanced around the library at the kids who were now lining up at the counter to check out the Christmas books they'd chosen and then made his way over to where Millie was standing.

"Hi," Adam said when he reached her. "I hoped I might find you here, what with the storytelling thing happening this afternoon."

"Yep, here I am." She couldn't help but sound frosty. Images were flashing in her head of the last time she saw Adam, when he'd turned his back on her in the village hall and run off with barely a word of goodbye.

Standing in front of her, Adam shifted from foot to foot. "I owe you an apology for the way I rushed away on Saturday. I was rude and bang out of order. Can I buy you a coffee to make up for it?"

Millie's instinct was to say no. She found it hard enough connecting with new people, her shyness a constant obstacle, but it was harder still when people blew hot and cold and left her wondering whether they really were interested in getting to know her at all.

But Adam looked sorry and hopeful that she'd say yes. Remembering Mrs Wishmore's baffling advice to give the man a chance, Millie softened. "Okay. Coffee sounds nice."

The smile that spread across his face at her answer made her glad she'd said yes.

ALL WEEK, Adam had been thinking about how rude he'd been on Saturday when he'd bumped into Millie at the village hall and she'd asked if he wanted to grab a coffee, and he'd responded by fleeing the scene without even saying goodbye. Every time he thought about the stunned look he'd caught on her face as he'd hurried off, he felt shame burning.

All week, he'd also known he ought to apologise. But apologising would also mean explaining, and he hadn't wanted to do that.

He hadn't run off because she'd asked him to join her for coffee. But if he told her the actual reason why he'd left so quickly, it would just sound stupid.

The dilemma had grated, day after day. He also kept thinking about what Doris Wishmore had said when he'd met her in the market square on Tuesday evening. The older lady had advised him to talk to Millie and explain why he'd run off so quickly that day. She also said Millie had been a little hurt by his sudden and rude departure. Of course she had, and he shouldn't have needed Doris Wishmore to point that out to him.

Adam had picked up his phone time and time again, intending to send Millie a message to say sorry for running off. But as soon as he'd typed out the words, he'd deleted them. Apologies were given in person, or at least that's what his parents had taught him, and a text message just wouldn't cut it.

Last Saturday afternoon in the village hall, Millie had sensed something was troubling him and had asked if he was okay. She'd been kind and thoughtful. Instead of being grateful for that, he'd behaved like an idiot—yet again.

Worse, Millie was a newcomer to Hollyford, and a generous person who was already lending a hand with the endless Christmas Village activities. He should be the one extending the hand of friendship to her, not the other way around. How must she have felt when he'd about-turned and not even given her the courtesy of a proper goodbye? It had to be hard enough settling in a new town without the locals behaving like bad-mannered trolls.

So, all this had been churning since Saturday night, but with every day that passed, it had only got harder to put things right. He liked Millie and had liked talking with her last week when they'd had dinner. He could use a new friend in his life right now, and he wouldn't get the chance to count her as one if he didn't sort this out.

With his mother holding the fort at the gift shop, he'd decided it was time to fix this thing before any more time passed.

"There's something I want to tell you," Adam said to Millie as they left the library and stepped out into the darkening afternoon.

"Okay," she said, giving him an uncertain look.

Now they were just standing in the cold street outside the library, feeling the late afternoon dampness seeping into their bones. His courage fled as he contemplated telling Millie what was going on and the reasons for his behaviour. He could already feel his toes curling in embarrassment at the prospect of relaying the sorry story.

Perhaps it would be better just to forget this whole thing and forget about telling Millie anything at all?

Frustrated, Adam thrust his hands into his coat pocket. His fingers grazed against something round and smooth nestled inside the lining. It was the little angel tree bauble he'd found on the ground at the market square after saying goodbye to Doris the other night. He'd forgotten the bauble was still in his pocket so he could return it to the older lady the next time he saw her.

Adam ran his fingers over the surface of the bauble, thinking of its soft pearly colour and the ethereal way it reflected the light. He thought of the serene expression on the face of the beautiful angel painted on the bauble and the sweet tinkling sound the decoration made when the jingle bell moved.

For reasons he couldn't explain, just running his fingers over the surface of the angel bauble renewed his courage and filled his heart with hope. He looked at Millie, who was obviously confused about why they were still waiting on the pavement and shivering against the cold while Adam stood there and said nothing. With a smile, he gestured to the café on the corner.

"Let's get that coffee first, before we freeze out here."

The café was warm and cosy, and once Adam had ordered their drinks, they snagged a table by the window. After stirring sugar into his coffee, he threw Millie another apologetic smile.

"Sorry again for running off last weekend," he said. "I know that's not the first time you've seen me behaving… strangely. But I want you to know I don't always go around acting like a twat, all evidence to the contrary."

That got a smile from her, which gave him the determination to go on.

"When we had dinner the other night in the pub," he said, "it was the first time in a long time where I felt relaxed and like I could just talk about easy stuff. We didn't know each other, and you're a newcomer to the village and so you didn't know about… What I mean is, I'm guessing you hadn't heard any of the gossip, and so when we were talking together, none of that was an issue, and I could just forget about it all for a minute, and…"

Adam could tell by the baffled look on Millie's face that he wasn't making any sense. Blowing out a breath, he tried again.

"I liked the time we spent together in the pub, Millie. I hoped we could become friends and that you'd never have to know about what happened. But I realise now that's impossible and stupid. I can't keep it a secret."

Millie sipped her coffee, the bafflement in her expression now looking more like alarm as she eyed the door, no doubt wondering if she could make a hasty escape. He was making a proper mess of this.

Why didn't he just spit it out? Why was he turning it into this big deal?

Because it already *was* a big deal, at least it was to Adam.

"Okay," he said on a long exhale. "A couple of months ago, my fiancé ditched me for someone else and cancelled our Christmas wedding. It was the most painful and humiliating thing that's ever happened to me."

The words spilled out in a rush. Across the table, Millie paused with her coffee cup halfway to her lips, her eyes wide.

"Adam, that's awful." She set the cup down, her gaze fixed on him. "I'm so sorry. I can't imagine how terrible that must have been."

"It was… it *is* hard to deal with. Actually, I'm not dealing with it at all. Heidi—my fiancé, well, my ex-fiancé—was everything I wanted. I thought we'd have the big Christmas wedding she planned and then spend the rest of our lives together. I had no idea there was a problem and obviously had no idea she was seeing someone else. When she told me it was over, it was a complete bolt from the blue."

He raked a hand through his hair and gulped down some coffee. His heart was pounding as he spoke, the strain of the explanation making his pulse race.

"I can see how much it upsets you to talk about this," Millie said. "You don't have to tell me any more if you don't want to."

"I want to explain it. You're the first person I feel like I want to talk to about it." The sudden truth of this took him by surprise. "I've kept my head down ever since it happened, and shut myself away from family and friends, because I was too embarrassed and humiliated to face anyone. But for some reason, I want to talk to you."

He hadn't expected that. He'd wanted to apologise for behaving like an idiot and that had required an explanation. But he hadn't expected to *want* to tell Millie what had happened to him.

For the first time since Heidi broke off the engagement, he felt at ease in the company of another person. Maybe it was because Millie was someone he'd only recently met. Maybe it was because he needed a new friend in his life, someone who hadn't known him back when Heidi was a part of his world.

Or maybe it was just because he felt an unexpected connection with the woman sitting across the table from him, the same way he had that night they'd shared dinner in the pub. He sensed something about her that made him want to confide and made him feel that she understood something about the hurt that had carved his heart wide open.

"Ever since Heidi broke off the engagement, I've felt on edge and insecure." Adam frowned, searching for the words he wanted. "Guys aren't supposed to admit to being insecure and feeling embarrassed about things and having their feelings hurt."

"Says who?" It was Millie's turn to frown. "Of course you'd feel those things after what happened, and it's okay to admit it."

"But it's not easy to talk about being a jilted groom abandoned by the bride just weeks before the wedding. It's like there's this bone-deep humiliation inside me that's always there. That's why I flipped out and legged it last weekend from the village hall."

"What do you mean?"

"I've avoided people ever since Heidi broke off the

engagement. In a small town like Hollyford, it stands to reason that a cancelled wedding will make for some juicy gossip. It's just human nature." He shrugged, then got to the heart of what he needed to explain. "When I turned up at the village hall on Saturday to help with the clean-up, it was the first time I've been around so many local people in months. There were a few groups of women laughing and looking over at me, and I couldn't help but think they were talking about me and how I'd been dumped by my fiancé."

When Millie frowned again and opened her mouth to speak, he held up his hands.

"I know what you're going to say—that they probably weren't talking about me at all. And the chances are, they weren't. But at that moment, that wasn't what my brain was telling me. It was telling me that everyone was laughing at the fool who didn't know his fiancé was cheating on him behind his back. It was telling me that everyone was gossiping about the big fancy Christmas wedding that had to be cancelled because the groom was too stupid to realise it was all too good to be true."

He blew out a long breath and looked across the table at Millie. Her expression was soft as she studied him.

"That's why I hurried away without saying goodbye," he finished. "It wasn't anything to do with you."

"I'm sorry for what you've gone through, Adam," Millie said. "For what it's worth, I don't think those women were laughing at you in the village hall on Saturday. In fact, I happen to know they were laughing about how Evelyn Fox was barking orders at everyone left, right and centre, even after she'd just told everyone they were done for the day and could go home."

When he tried to explain further, she held up a hand. "But I understand what you're telling me and I understand why you feel the way you do. That must be very hard."

"I know I should just forget all about Heidi and get on with my life. That's what my mother keeps telling me to do. But it just isn't that easy."

"Of course it's not easy. She was your fiancé, and you loved her."

Emotions tugged in Adam's gut. Millie's simple words and the kind look in her eyes made him feel understood for the first time in a long time.

"Right now, it's like I'm stuck in limbo," he said. "Heidi wanted this big, romantic Christmas wedding. She wanted white roses and holly garlands at the church, and twinkle lights and Christmas music at the reception. We set the date for December twenty-first. Ever since she called off the engagement, I've just been waiting for that wedding day date to pass, so it's gone and behind me. And I've been dreading Christmas."

A look of sudden understanding crossed Millie's face. "That's why you were so annoyed when we decorated your gift shop."

Adam nodded. "I'm not a Grinch, not usually. I like Christmas. In the retail business, you *have* to like Christmas." With a laugh, he waved a hand to emphasis this obvious fact. "But everything about this Christmas just makes me feel sad. I thought I could get away with doing an understated theme in the gift shop this year, because I couldn't face looking at Christmas lights and decorations for weeks on end. But my mother put a stop to that with her meddling, as you know."

"If I'd known any of this, I would never have agreed to help put up those twinkle lights in your shop window. I just thought we were lending a hand to a local shop owner."

Adam shook his head. "You don't have anything to apologise for. And the truth is, I know the shop needed the proper Christmas treatment. Hollyford is the famous Cotswold Christmas Village, after all. It's not as if hanging a few twinkle lights in the window is going to wreck my mental health. It's just that…"

When he trailed off, Millie gave him a soft smile. "It's just that it's hard."

"Yeah."

For a long moment, they looked at one another across the table. Although the café was busy and filled with noisy chatter, Adam forgot about the other people around them. As he looked at Millie, a sense of a connection bloomed, deep and true. Her straightforward and sympathetic responses to his tale of woe touched him and he felt friendship kindle.

"But maybe it's not *quite* as hard as you thought it would be," Millie said. "After all, you like the twinkle lights in your shop window, now that they're up there. And you came along to the village hall to help with the clean-up on Saturday, even although you didn't have to."

"Actually, I did have to. My mother made me do it."

"Ah, I stand corrected," she laughed.

"You know what mothers are like. They always know best, or at least they think they do."

It was a silly throwaway joke, but the moment he said it, Millie's expression clouded and she dropped her gaze and became intensely interested in her coffee cup. Adam couldn't help but wonder at the change.

"Did I say something wrong?" he asked.

She shook her head, then seemed to think better of it. Looking up, she gave a sad smile.

"My mother passed away last year."

Adam wished he could take back the stupid comment he'd made. "I'm so sorry. I shouldn't have said that."

"Don't be silly. You didn't say anything wrong, you were just making a joke." The clouded expression on her face disappeared and was replaced by a smile. "Sometimes it just hits me suddenly that she's gone. I'll be busy doing something or talking to someone, like we are right now, and for a few moments I'll forget that she died. And then it all comes rushing back and takes my breath away again, and I wonder, 'Did that really happen? Did she really *die?*' And of course, she did, and I feel sad all over again." She waved a hand. "Sorry, I didn't mean to say all that. You've got enough problems of your own without hearing about mine."

"Don't say that. You listened to me, and so I want to listen to you." He searched her expression, wary of shifting the conversation into upsetting terrain. When he spoke again, his tone was soft. "What happened to your mum? Was she ill?"

Millie nodded. "She had cancer. They caught it too late to save her. She spent her last few weeks in a hospice before she died in early December."

Adam felt his face drain of all colour at this revelation. "Millie, I'm so sorry. I can't even begin to imagine..." He trailed off, sensing that the words were meaningless. "I feel like an idiot, bleating on about my cancelled Christmas wedding to someone who lost their mother so close to Christmas time."

"It's okay, Adam," she smiled. "It was a year ago, it's not like it just happened. What you're going through is still very raw. And although I miss my mother every single day, I promised her I'd get on with my life, and..."

When she trailed off, Adam frowned. "What were you about to say?"

"Nothing, it doesn't matter."

"Of course it matters."

She gave a shy smile and sipped some coffee before speaking again. "My mother made me promise to life a good and happy life, to take chances and chase after my dreams. When she was ill, I couldn't think about doing any of that. It was too painful. But time passed and the pain of losing her got a little easier to handle each day. And I had to work and earn money and pay bills, so I didn't have much choice but to get on with it."

Adam nodded, wondering what that must have felt like. His gift shop business had kept him going through the worst days following Heidi's bombshell and he'd been grateful for the distraction. But he couldn't imagine what it must be like to lose a parent so young and to have to keep going. He reckoned Millie was only a few years younger than he was. If something happened to either of his parents, he'd be beyond devastated.

Realising that Millie had come through a terrible tragedy, and yet had pulled herself together and faced life with her shoulders squared and her head up, made Adam see her in a new light.

And it made him want to do the same thing as she'd done.

"You've been through something horrible, Adam," Millie said softly. "And although what happened to you is very different to what happened to me, I suppose I just want to tell you that things get better." Shaking her head, she seemed lost in her thoughts. "After my mother died, I didn't think things would ever be okay again. I felt very alone and lost. Last Christmas was terrible, just the absolute worst time of my life. I couldn't imagine ever having a happy Christmas again. My mother's death was just too awful and too close to Christmas and it was all just too hard. I took extra shifts at work throughout the holidays to try and stop myself thinking about it, and to fill up the time. But the truth is, I cried every day, and Christmas Day was... well, let's just say it wasn't merry and bright."

Millie glanced away, as if remembering those days last year and every ounce of pain they'd brought. But a moment later, she looked back up, a half-smile on her lips. "But because I had to get up every day and live every day, eventually, things *did* get better. Things that scared me eventually led me somewhere better. Realising I couldn't afford to stay in the house my mother and I rented together was scary at first. Where would I live? What could I afford? What if I ended up homeless?"

"Homeless?" Adam said, unable to hide his shock. "That wouldn't have happened, surely?"

But Millie only shrugged. "I didn't have much money, and neither did my mother. I had no other family around. The jobs I was working in Bristol were temporary and low-paid. It wouldn't have taken much to push me into a tough situation."

Adam could only stare, unable to imagine what it must have been like for Millie to lose her mother to cancer at such a young age and then struggle alone with financial worries that sounded downright terrifying.

Despite all his bad luck when it came to romance and the humiliation of his cancelled Christmas wedding, Adam realised just how fortunate he was.

"But I found a way through it all," Millie said. "It wasn't easy, and there are no guarantees things are all okay now in my life. I'm still a long way away from chasing after all those dreams my mother made me promise to go after." She gave a wistful smile. "But all I can do is get through one day at a time. I'll always miss my mother. I'll always wish she was here with me. But if I can try to do the things she asked me to do and live my life the best way I can, then that's what counts."

For a moment, Adam was speechless. He wasn't sure what he'd expected when he'd asked Millie to forgive him and join him for coffee, but it hadn't been this. She'd told him things about herself and her life he would never have guessed in a million years.

"You're an amazing person, Millie." The words tumbled

out before he realised they were coming. "And you've completely blown me away."

Laughing softly as a flush coloured her cheeks, Millie dropped her gaze to her coffee cup. "I don't usually talk as much as this with someone I hardly know."

"It seems to me that we know each other pretty well by now."

This only made the pretty blush deepen. The naked vulnerability in her eyes made something shift unexpectedly in Adam's chest, catching him by surprise.

"Anyway," Millie said after drawing in a breath and giving him a shy smile. "The whole point of telling you all of that was because this time last year I was in a terrible place in my life and filled with so much pain I didn't think I'd survive it. Now, everything is different and life feels much better than I ever thought it could. Christmas was always special for my mother and I, and she made me promise I'd be happy this Christmas and celebrate it the way we always used to. Last year, that was unthinkable. This year, maybe I'm halfway there to doing what she asked me to do."

"That takes courage, Millie."

"I don't know about courage. But I know it took time and a lot of good luck. Just a couple of weeks ago, I wasn't sure I could celebrate Christmas much at all. How do you celebrate when you don't have anyone to celebrate with?" She waved a hand, almost like she was apologising. "I'm a bit rubbish at social stuff and making friends. Before my mother died, I didn't need to worry about any of that because we were together and always there for each other. Now, though, things are different."

Adam wondered how someone as lovely as Millie could find it hard to make friends. After only meeting her a few times, he already felt fortunate to know her.

"Your mother left a big hole in your life when she died,"

he said, then wished he'd found a better way to word it. Heidi had left a big hole in his life when she'd ditched him, but that was nothing compared to the gaping chasm that must have opened up in Millie's life when her mother—and, by the sound of it, her best friend—passed away.

But Millie only nodded. "When I came to see the Hollyford Christmas tree lights being turned on the other week, I just wanted to feel part of something, even although I knew I was on the outside looking in. But then I met Doris Wishmore there, and we both ended up volunteering for the Christmas Village activities. I probably wouldn't have volunteered if I hadn't met Mrs Wishmore, and I wouldn't have met Mrs Wishmore if I hadn't taken a chance and turned up to see the Christmas lights being turned on, even although I didn't know anyone and felt like a bit of a johnny-no-mates the entire time."

She laughed, but Adam sensed the lonely ache beneath her words, an ache he'd felt too many times himself lately, albeit for different reasons.

"I'm having a lot of fun being involved in the Christmas Village activities," Millie continued. "It's not what I expected, and it's not what I ever dreamt I'd be doing. This Christmas will be very different from the ones I spent with my mother, but now I feel okay about that. All these mad activities I've volunteered with are helping me remember that there are lots of ways to celebrate Christmas and lots of ways to make it meaningful."

"Wow, that's a lovely way to think."

"I'm getting much more out of these Christmas Village activities than I'm putting in. At the story time session in the library this afternoon, I listened to the librarian read *The Night Before Christmas* to the little children, and it took me back to all the times my own mother read that story to me when I was small. A year ago, those memories would have crushed me. Now, although they still twist my heart, they make me smile, too."

"That's a good thing."

"That's a very good thing." She blew out a breath. "I haven't talked this much in a long time. I'm sorry if I'm boring you with all this stuff."

With a quick shake of his head, Adam frowned. "You're not boring me. We're becoming friends, aren't we?"

Millie's uncertain expression dissolved into a smile. "Yes, I hope so."

"Well, friends share their stories with each other. That's what we're doing."

"I'm sharing more of my story than you are, which isn't fair considering you're the one who bought the coffee."

Her wry smile made him laugh. "I can tell you more about my tragically abandoned Christmas wedding, if you'd like? Maybe I could talk more about the Christmas dinner wedding menu and all the roast turkey I'll still be paying for when I'm a pensioner thanks to the big fat reception dinner deposit on my credit card?"

Millie's laughter matched his own, and he was grateful for the moment of levity. It was the first time he'd been able to find something funny to say about his ditched wedding since Heidi left.

"That does sound pretty traumatic," Millie smiled. "And if you're laughing about it, then you must be on the road to recovery."

"I hope so. I can't keep up my bah-humbug routine forever."

With another laugh, she ran a finger around the rim of her coffee cup, looking as if she was weighing up whether to say something more. "I understand why you'd want to just slog your way through this Christmas and forget it's even happening. But maybe it'd be fun if you got involved with some of the Christmas Village activities."

Adam opened his mouth to reject the idea, but the expression on Millie's face stopped him, that shyly vulnerable look in her eyes once more catching him by surprise.

"What sort of activities?" he asked.

"We've got a gingerbread icing session happening on Saturday afternoon in the village hall. Why don't you come along and help?"

"That sounds messy."

"Horribly messy. And I'm sure we'll all be in trouble again with the village hall custodian and made to work our fingers to the bone to clean up after ourselves, which means we need all hands on deck."

Part of him wanted to say no. The gift shop was too busy on Saturday afternoons for him to waltz off on a whim.

But another part of him wanted to say yes. His mother was now helping in the shop and would no doubt put in an extra hour on Saturday if it meant he was getting out and about again in the world. Maybe Lorraine, his shop assistant, could also switch her Saturday start time and stay on a little later while he was gone for a bit.

And maybe it would be healthy to get out from the shop and show his face around Hollyford for a change. He couldn't hide away forever, and the idea of ignoring Christmas just didn't seem as appealing as it once had. It might even be fun to help with the gingerbread icing.

But Adam knew it wasn't the idea of icing gingerbread men that appealed to him so much as the person he'd be icing them with. Millie felt like a welcome tonic in his life, her shy smile lifting his heavy heart, and he needed that right now.

Letting out an exaggerated sigh, Adam waved a hand in mock resignation. "Go on then, you've twisted my arm."

When Millie's eyes lit up in obvious surprise and delight, he was glad he'd said yes.

"You'll have fun, I'm sure of it," she said.

"Considering the mess I got roped into clearing up last week after the tree bauble decorating fiasco, I'll be sure to bring my hazmat suit."

Millie let out a bright bubble of laughter, the violet flecks in her eyes dancing beneath the café lights.

Adam remembered the conversation he'd had with Doris Wishmore on Tuesday evening when they'd chatted in the market square. The older lady had said something about how he should open himself up to Christmas and let the wonder of it sweep him away.

As he saw those violet flecks dancing in Millie's eyes as she laughed, Adam thought Mrs Wishmore might just have been on to something.

Millie's phone buzzed, and she glanced at the screen in surprise.

"Is that the time already?" she said, turning off the alarm notification. "I need to go. I'm working extra hours this evening at the care home to cover someone who's going to a family Christmas party."

"No problem, let's get out of here."

Rising from the table, they pulled on their coats and headed for the café door.

"So, what time should I turn up for this mad gingerbread thing on Saturday?" Adam asked when they were outside.

"It runs from one until three. Come along anytime you can, for as long as you can." Millie buttoned her jacket and gave him a sly smile. "Evelyn Fox will be so happy to hear she has a new volunteer with the Christmas Village committee."

"God help me."

With a rumble of laughter, Millie turned and hurried up the street, throwing him a wave over her shoulder and a cheery goodbye as she left. Adam watched her until she turned the corner and disappeared from sight.

He'd walked the length of the high street and was pushing through the door of his gift shop when he realised he was still smiling at the sound of her laughter.

CHAPTER NINE

Saturday afternoon brought crisp blue December skies, the Hollyford church choir singing carols in the market square, and a village hall filled with the warm aromas of spicy gingerbread and sweet sugar icing and the delighted chatter of the folk who'd turned up to take part in the festive decorating fun.

Millie wasn't sure how the bakers on the Christmas Village committee had managed to produce the hundreds and hundreds of gingerbread men—and gingerbread women, children, dogs, stars, and Christmas trees—that were laid out on the tables around the village hall, but they had done it. Now, the task was to keep a ready supply of icing sugar and icing decorations to hand for the visitors who'd flocked to the village hall to take part in the latest Christmas Village activity.

At Millie's table, a young mother was helping her children pipe icing onto their gingerbread men, while Mrs Wishmore assisted them by adding yellow sugar disc buttons to the gingerbread men's coats. The children's faces were scrunched up in concentration as they handled the miniature piping bags and applied the sugar buttons, their chubby little fingers sticky from the work. Whenever they completed a portion of the decoration task, the little ones beamed with delight, earning warm praise from the laughing Mrs Wishmore.

It wasn't just children who were enjoying themselves. As Millie glanced around the village hall, she saw plenty of adults indulging in the fun together. At a nearby table there was an older woman who looked as if she was in her sixties, accompanied by two young women who appeared to be closer to Millie's age, their giggling chatter revealing them to be a mother with her adult daughters, the three of them enjoying the decorating activity while taking a break from their Christmas shopping. When an older gentleman appeared in the hall and approached the women, making a show of checking his watch and reminding them they'd be late for their restaurant booking if they didn't hurry up, there was much gentle mocking of the man, who turned out to be the husband and father of the little group. As the family left together with their decorated gingerbread men in paper bags, Millie watched them go with their arms looped around one another, and feeling that familiar longing fill her heart.

"You've got that faraway look in your eye again, Millie."

Turning, she saw Mrs Wishmore watching her with a soft smile on her face as she cleared the table, following the departure of the young woman and her children who'd now completed their gingerbread decorations.

"I was just thinking about how everyone is having a wonderful time," Millie said, wiping some spilled sugar icing and gingerbread crumbs from the table. "These Christmas Village activities might be messy, but people seem to love them."

"It's the perfect way to bring people together." Mrs Wishmore smiled again and patted Millie's arm. "And the perfect way for strangers to become friends. I'm certainly enjoying our time together and helping to run these activities."

"Me too, Doris." Seeing the warm look in the older lady's eyes, Millie thought about asking a question that she'd been thinking about all day, but before she could decide to do it, Mrs Wishmore spoke again.

"We need more sugar decorations," Doris said, pointing to the almost empty containers on the table. "Come and help me find them over there on the supply table, so I don't have to dig out my spectacles to see what I'm doing. These little sugar thingies all look the same shape and size to me."

Laughing at Mrs Wishmore's expression of amused exasperation, Millie signalled to Evelyn Fox, who was coordinating the afternoon with her signature clipboard and pen in full deployment mode, and told her they needed to top up their decorating supplies before anyone else sat down at their table. After grabbing the piping bags to refill them with icing at the supply table while they were restocking anyway, she followed Doris across the hall.

"Right, what have we got here?" Doris picked up a plastic container and peered at the label before handing it to Millie. "I can't tell whether those are sugar stars or sugar holly leaves. You can keep me right, Millie."

Millie hid a grin as she inspected the label and then poured sugar decorations into the little tubs they'd brought from the table. As the older lady laughed as she peered at another container and tried to read the writing on the side, Millie decided to ask the question she'd been wondering about.

"Can I ask your advice about something, Doris?"

Mrs Wishmore looked up from the plastic container, her expression curious. "Of course."

"I've been thinking about something for a while, but I'm not sure if I ought to do it or not."

When Doris's mild gaze stayed on her, her expression expectant, she took a deep breath and continued.

"I've been thinking about asking my father if he'd like to meet up before Christmas."

For a moment, Doris only stared, her eyes wide. "I had no idea you were in contact with your father regularly. You've never said much about him before."

"We're not in contact, not really. We exchange messages from time to time, but he's never been part of my life." With an uneasy shrug, she finished filling a piping bag with icing sugar and set it aside, wiping her hands with a paper towel as she tried to explain. "He and my mother separated when I was just a baby. I got birthday or Christmas presents from him occasionally when I was younger, and there were a few meet-ups now and again, although…"

Although he wasn't interested enough in me to have any regular contact. That was the truth of the matter, but Millie didn't want to say that, because admitting it hurt.

"He moved around a lot, and it wasn't always easy to arrange time together," she said instead.

Doris listened and looked thoughtful. "And now you'd like to reopen the lines of communication?"

"I think I'd like to try." Frowning, she tried to organise her thoughts. "He is my father, after all. He's… family."

The only family I have left. Another thought that hurt, but which she kept to herself.

Doris studied her face for a moment, her kind eyes intense as she seemed to think about what Millie had said. "I can certainly understand why you'd want to make contact with people you consider to be family."

"I didn't think much about my father while my mother was alive. We led separate lives. These last few months, though, I've been wondering if it's time to reconnect." She gave an awkward shrug. "Relationships don't just happen by magic. You have to work at them."

"And you'd like to work at this one." She said it as a statement, not a question, and then gave Millie another thoughtful look. "Tell me about him, your father. What's his name? What's he like? What does he do?"

"He's called Derek. Derek Hill. My parents were never married and my mother gave me her surname when I was born. I'm not entirely sure what his job is right now. He's done lots of things over the years, mostly casual work he picks up here and there, or at least that's the impression I got from my mother. The last I heard, he was working in a warehouse somewhere near Birmingham."

Millie paused, realising this was about as much as she knew about the man who was her father. As if reading her thoughts, Doris prodded gently.

"Did he have any other children after he separated from your mother? Do you have any half-siblings?"

"No, he didn't have other children. He had other relationships after my mother, but none that lasted. He's a bit… chaotic? Maybe that's not fair, or maybe it's not the right word. He hasn't ever *stuck* at things in his life. And I think he might have had some money troubles over the years, although I'm not sure. Again, most of what I know came from my mother."

Doris's expression softened. "Does that trouble you? That you don't know much about your father?"

"I didn't think much about it until I got older. Like I said, my parents were never in touch much with each other after they separated, and I grew up not knowing the man. He was just someone who sent gifts from time to time, someone who occasionally phoned up to say hello. When I was a child, I doubt I saw him more than once or twice a year, and once I was a teenager, I hardly remember seeing him at all." She shrugged and blew out a breath. "Now that I hear myself saying all this, I'm wondering if I should get in touch at all. What do you think, Doris?"

Doris frowned, a troubled look crossing her face. "It would be quite wrong for me to tell you what to do, one way or the other. This is your decision to make. What does your heart tell you to do?"

"I honestly don't know. Part of me wants to jump in and make contact and see what happens. He's my father and that has to count for something. But another part of me thinks that, after all these long years without being in regular touch, he's just a stranger and it might be too late now."

Doris nodded, saying nothing while Millie's conflicting thoughts swirled in her head.

"Does your father know that your mother passed away?" Doris asked.

"Yes, he knows. I called him after she died. He came to the funeral."

Doris's expression lifted at this. "That must have meant a lot to you."

"I suppose it did, although I was too upset at the time to say much to him, or to anyone else, for that matter. But it's true that I hadn't expected him to turn up."

Remembering that bleak December day of gunmetal skies and a freezing damp that had drilled deep into Millie's bones, and the sight of her mother's coffin disappearing behind the curtain at the crematorium, still filled her with sorrow a year later. At the time, Millie hadn't trusted herself to utter more than a few words of thanks to the people who'd turned up to pay their respects to Caroline Dawson. She remembered shaking hands with some women Caroline had worked with before falling ill, and with a kind neighbour who'd told her to keep her chin up.

But all she remembered of her father's unexpected

appearance at the funeral was that it had taken her a long moment to even recognise the man because it had been years since she'd last seen him, and that he'd muttered something as he'd left the crematorium about how sorry he was about Caroline's death and how he'd keep in touch to find out how Millie was doing.

Her father had sent a text message a month later, saying he hoped she was all right. Millie had replied, assuring him she was fine. Both texts had been short and formal, each one a testament to a lifetime of separation. There had been a few brief messages between them since then, but nothing that went much beyond, *Hi, hope you're well* and *I'm fine, how are you?*

"Do you think you'd like to have your father in your life again, Millie?" Doris asked.

Millie searched her heart for the answer to that question, but all she found there was doubt and uncertainty.

When the answer remained elusive, Doris reached out and laid her hand on Millie's arm. At the older lady's touch, calming peace descended across her jumbled thoughts. As she looked into Doris's kind blue eyes, Millie felt the doubts and uncertainties ebb away, to be replaced by the truth for which she was searching.

"I want to feel part of something," Millie said. "I want to feel like I belong somewhere. I don't want to feel so alone."

Doris nodded and gave a soft smile. "You don't feel you belong here in this sweet little village? You don't feel you've already made friends here who help chase away the loneliness?"

"I love Hollyford. Everyone is so lovely and welcoming." Millie let out a soft sigh. "But they're not family."

Mrs Wishmore gave another slight nod and a smile. "Well, it sounds to me like you already know what you want to do."

Exhaling another long breath, Millie realised she was right. She *did* know what she wanted to do, but that didn't mean there weren't still doubts.

"I don't know much about Derek except that he chose not to be part of my life, and that he's had troubles of his own. He's moved around a lot, had problems holding down jobs, and I don't even know if he has other people in his life now or even if he wants to hear from me."

"But?"

"But I want to know for sure." With the decision made, her heart clip-clopped with nervous excitement. "I'll contact my father. I'll find out if he'd like to meet up. Maybe we could have coffee and get to know one another better."

Mrs Wishmore smiled as she patted Millie's arm. "It's a big step. A simple get-together over coffee sounds like the right way to get the ball rolling."

Millie almost pulled her phone from her pocket to send a text to her father right away. Now that she'd made the decision, she didn't want to wait. But before she could do it, Evelyn Fox marched across the village hall in their direction and waved her clipboard at them.

"Come along, ladies, no loitering back here with the icing supplies," she barked. "We've got a queue of people waiting to get to work on their gingerbread men, and the more visitors we welcome into the village hall, the more donation money we raise. Back to your icing station, this instant!"

With a mock swat in their direction with her clipboard, Evelyn shooed them back to their table where a new group was waiting to get stuck into the icing fun.

"Perhaps I'll wait until we're finished here before texting my father," Millie said as Evelyn hurried away to give some other unlucky volunteers a telling off.

Mrs Wishmore returned Millie's wry grin. "I think that's

a good idea, dear. We don't want to get into any more trouble with the boss."

Millie turned her attention to the young mother and her two small girls waiting at their table, the children's eyes wide as they gripped their gingerbread men and stared at the assorted sugar decorations Mrs Wishmore was setting out before them. With another half hour still to go before this latest Christmas Village activity session drew to a close, Millie resolved to focus her attention on helping with the icing fun and putting everything else out of her head.

Maybe it wouldn't hurt to wait a little longer before contacting her father, just to be sure she'd made the right decision.

Although in her heart, she knew she had. The man was her closest living relative. He was her *father*. They may not have been a part of each other's lives in the past, but maybe it was time to change that and reopen the lines of communication, even if that idea scared her as much as it excited her.

At Millie's side, Mrs Wishmore nudged her and nodded towards the doors of the village hall. "Well, look who's here!"

Glancing across the hall, Millie's smile widened when she saw Adam stroll inside, his gaze casting around the space.

"He came!" Millie said. "I thought he wouldn't, but he did!"

"You invited Adam along to today's activities?"

"We had a chat over coffee the other day after the Christmas story time at the library and he told me a few things about himself that explained a lot."

Mrs Wishmore smiled. "Didn't I say there was more to that young man than met the eye?"

"You did, and you were right."

"Well, naturally," Mrs Wishmore said and wiggled her eyebrows.

Laughing, Millie glanced back at Adam, who was now

caught in Evelyn Fox's tractor beam and listening as she issued orders and instructions to him. The astonished look on his face made Millie laugh all the harder.

"It's lovely to hear you laugh like that," Mrs Wishmore said.

"I think Adam might regret agreeing to come here and lend a hand with the gingerbread icing duties," Millie grinned as she watched Evelyn shoo him over to their table.

"I doubt that," Mrs Wishmore said with a wink. "I doubt that very much."

Millie caught the mysterious twinkle lighting up Mrs Wishmore's eyes and the coy expression on her face. But before she could ask the older lady about her cryptic wink or knowing grin, Adam appeared at their icing station.

"Evelyn sent me over to help," he said, taking in the young family seated at the table and who were absorbed in their gingerbread icing, before glancing up at Millie with a smile. "She said if I don't do whatever you tell me to do, she'll swat me with her clipboard."

"I'm glad you came," Millie laughed, feeling an unexpected heat flush her cheeks as she returned Adam's grin.

"Me too," he said.

A long moment passed as they smiled at each other. When Millie looked away, she caught Mrs Wishmore watching her. The older lady gave another of those mysterious winks.

"Let's put you to work, Adam," Doris said. "I think I have just the job for you, too."

CHAPTER TEN

Adam pulled his gaze away from Millie, wondering what task Mrs Wishmore had in mind for him. When she handed him a gingerbread man and an icing bag, Adam took the items from her and she nodded with approval.

"Here's how you can help, Adam," Doris said, and gestured to the small children hunched in their seats at the table and concentrating on decorating the gingerbread shapes they'd chosen while their mother watched over them. "These young geniuses here are doing a fine job with their icing work, but I think they'd love to see how our Christmas Village volunteers like to decorate their gingerbread men. Isn't that right, children?"

The two small girls seated at the table nodded and looked up from their icing task.

"We bet our gingerbread men will look better than yours," one girl said.

"Much better!" said her sister.

"That sounds like a challenge," Adam said and rolled up

his sleeves, unable to resist the girls' beaming grins. "Right, let's see what we can do."

"It's two against one, so we'll win," one of the girls announced.

"All right, don't be cheeky," said the mother, now frowning behind her daughters before offering an apologetic smile to Adam. "Sorry, they've had too much sugar today."

"It's fine," he laughed. "And they probably will win, anyway. I've never iced a gingerbread man before."

"Well, in that case, two against one definitely doesn't sound fair," Mrs Wishmore said. "I think we ought to make sure this contest is run properly." Reaching for another gingerbread man and mini icing bag, she handed them to Millie. "Now it looks we've got two against two."

"We'll still win!" giggled one of the little girls.

"We're the best at gingerbread men icing in the whole world!" said her sister.

"Let's see about that," Millie said. Taking a seat at the table, she gestured to Adam to join her. "I think we ought to show these youngsters a thing or two about icing a gingerbread man."

"And if I actually knew a thing or two about it, that's just what I'd do."

Millie laughed. "It's easy, you'll see."

Adam took his seat, wondering what he'd let himself in for. When he'd agreed to lend a hand at the event, he thought he'd be welcoming visitors, helping keep the place clean and tidy, topping up the icing supplies, and that sort of thing. He hadn't thought he'd actually be doing any gingerbread icing himself.

He almost hadn't made it over to the village hall for the gingerbread icing session. The gift shop had been packed with customers all afternoon, and even with both his assistant Lorraine and his mother working alongside him, they'd barely kept up with the work. With sales booming and with an eager stream of customers to keep happy, he had no business abandoning the shop in order to drop by the village hall.

If he'd only been coming over to help with the gingerbread icing event, he would've ditched the commitment, knowing there would be plenty of other volunteers lending a hand. Evelyn Fox would've made sure she wasn't short staffed.

But that wasn't the only reason he'd come here.

He'd been looking forward to seeing Millie again. The simple truth was that he liked spending time with her. Being in her company made him feel like himself again. The honest conversation they'd had over coffee a few days earlier, when he'd told her the grim story about Heidi and their cancelled Christmas wedding, had been cathartic. After he'd explained it all to her, it felt like a load had lifted off his shoulders.

When she'd then shared her own tragic story about her mother's death a year ago, he'd been stunned, and he'd thought a lot since then about what she'd told him. He'd thought, too, about how she was dealing with the terrible hand that life had dealt her. Despite going through a heartbreaking bereavement less than a year ago, just weeks before Christmas, Millie was now embracing this year's festivities with enthusiasm and a determination to make the most of the season. Her attitude and bravery amazed him.

More than amazed him, actually. She'd bowled him over, plain and simple.

If Millie could get through what she'd gone through and not just survive it, but come out the other side smiling and determined to be happy, then he could, too. Millie had endured something far worse than he had. Her story had made him realise it was time to pull himself out of the dark place where he'd been hiding for all these months and get on with the job of living again.

That didn't mean he was about to start celebrating Christmas the way he once had. He was still dreading the imminent date of his cancelled Christmas wedding, and December twenty-first hung on the horizon like a black cloud. But maybe he didn't have to hate the entire festive season quite so much as he did.

He could put up with it. Putting up with it would be good enough for now. Putting up with it meant he could come along to this mad gingerbread icing event run by the Christmas Village folk and lend a hand for the good of the community.

And since that meant spending more time with Millie, that suited him just fine. He only hoped he didn't make an idiot of himself decorating these ginger biscuits. It all looked a bit fiddly, now that he found himself in the midst of things.

After staring at the plain gingerbread man Mrs Wishmore had given him, he stole a glance at Millie's biscuit to see what she was doing with hers, and then at the two little girls across the table who, judging by the icing work they'd already completed, were a couple of Mary Berrys in the making.

Adam dipped his piping bag towards the gingerbread man and squeezed.

Nothing happened.

"Huh," he muttered, wondering why the icing hadn't come out of the nozzle.

He watched Millie deftly tracing a line of white icing around the edge of her gingerbread man, then glanced at the two little girls who were now applying decorative flourishes to their biscuits, adding curly hair and smiling mouths.

They all seemed to have mastered the art of piping the

icing with no trouble. Adam peered at his icing bag, then at Mrs Wishmore.

The older lady winked and gave him a nod of encouragement. With a shrug, he bent down again to his work, this time giving the icing bag an extra hard squeeze.

There was a sudden *plop!* as the icing bag exploded and a spray of sticky icing splattered across Adam's face. For a second he sat stunned and blinking, wondering what had happened. He hadn't squeezed the icing bag that hard, surely?

Across the table, the two little girls dissolved into shrieks of giggles.

"You're covered in icing! It's up your nose!"

"It's even in your hair!"

They were right. Adam sneezed on account of the icing globules that had shot up his nose, and when he lifted his hand to his hair, he felt great drops of icing all over his head. There was even icing in his eyes.

"Gosh, Adam! Are you okay?" Millie gasped beside him, dropping her gingerbread biscuit and icing bag and reaching for a roll of paper towel.

"Uh, I think so."

Once Adam wiped the wet, sticky icing from his eyes, he saw the two little girls still laughing their heads off across the table, saw the stunned look on the face of their mother as she hid a grin, saw the way Millie was trying—and failing—to keep her own laughter at bay.

Then he saw Mrs Wishmore, her shoulders shaking as she laughed. But beyond the older lady's obvious amusement, there was something else in her expression, too, something Adam couldn't quite put his finger on.

"Let me help you," Millie said, tearing a sheet from the roll of paper towel and handing it to him.

"Thanks."

Feeling foolish, Adam scrubbed the paper towel across his face and hair. When the little girls only laughed harder, he frowned.

"You've spread the icing all over your hair!" one of the girls announced with glee.

"Now it's even messier than before."

Adam realised his mistake too late. Touching his hair, it felt even stickier than it had a few moments ago. The paper towel might have been up to the challenge of scraping the icing from his face, but when he'd run it over his hair, he'd only succeeded in rubbing the stuff even more thoroughly into himself.

"I'll have to go home and take a shower at this rate," Adam muttered with a laugh, tossing the paper towel aside.

He caught Millie's gaze, amusement bubbling in her eyes.

"You've, um, missed a bit," she said, pointing to his cheek.

Adam rubbed once more at his face. "Did I get it?"

Millie's lips quirked, her eyes dancing with laughter. When her hand came up to cradle his chin as she cleared a blob of icing from his jawline, Adam felt a hum of electricity sizzle across his skin at her touch.

Where had that come from?

Adam's eyes met Millie's. For a beat, they just stared at each other.

When laughter finally claimed them both, Adam didn't know whether to be relieved or disappointed.

"The icing's gone from your face," Millie smiled. "But as for your hair… I think that might be a lost cause."

Adam shook his head and prodded at his sticky hair. "You can't take me anywhere."

"The look on your face when that icing bag exploded," Millie said with a soft laugh. "I only wish I'd snapped a photo on my phone."

"Thank God you didn't. I'd never live it down."

They laughed again, and Millie patted his arm. "Poor you."

Out of the corner of his eye, Adam saw Mrs Wishmore wink and give him that wry smile of hers, and a strange thought occurred to him.

Had the older lady planned this little accident? Had she somehow *caused* the icing bag to explode like that?

Of course she hadn't. Why would she knowingly create such a terrible mess? For what purpose? And how on earth could she have made the icing bag explode?

Adam thought of the buzz of electricity he'd felt when Millie's hand touched his face as she wiped the icing from his cheek. He thought of the way her soft laughter had lifted his heart. He thought of the sweetly innocent moment they'd shared…

Across the table, Mrs Wishmore gave him that wry smile again, and in that instant, Adam knew there was something strange going on here, even if he couldn't for the life of him say exactly what it was.

"What on earth happened here?"

Adam blinked at the sight of Evelyn Fox peering over her clipboard at him as she scurried across the village hall towards their table. "Adam, why are you covered in icing sugar?"

"There was a slight incident with the piping bag," Adam said, wiping the last of the icing from his hands.

"Good grief, if I'd known you'd end up in this state, I would've put you on door duty instead." Evelyn shook her head. "Well, you can't stay here in that condition. Your hair looks like you've stuck your fingers in a socket."

The two little girls sitting at the table giggled at this.

"You're messier than we are!" one of them cried.

"Indeed he is," Evelyn said. "Adam, you're excused from

further gingerbread duties. I suggest you go home and wash your hair before the icing dries any further."

Adam pushed back his chair, feeling the weight of Evelyn Fox's bemused stare as he picked up his coat. The woman had lost none of her terrifying head mistress aura in the years since he'd last been her pupil at Hollyford primary school, and he felt thoroughly reprimanded, even although the exploding icing bag hadn't been his fault.

"You'll notice that no one else here has managed to get themselves covered from head to toe in icing, Mr Carter," Evelyn told him sternly.

"Yes, I did happen to notice that." Adam threw Mrs Wishmore a glance as he said this, and couldn't help but notice her obvious amusement.

Yet, even as he frowned, he saw the older lady's expression was nothing other than kind beneath her laughter as she stepped closer to him.

"These things happen," Doris said quietly, and patted his arm. "And sometimes they even happen for the best."

What did that mean? The woman really was a bit of an oddball. He was beginning to wish he hadn't come here to the Christmas Village event after all.

But then Adam thought again of the way Millie had cupped his face as she'd helped clean the smears of icing sugar from his face. The feeling of her hand on his skin had been…

He pushed away the final words that would have finished the thought. That was a road he was not about to walk down. He liked Millie and enjoyed spending time with her—as a friend. No more and no less. End of story.

He was still getting over the humiliation of being dumped by his fiancé, for God's sake! The last thing he should be thinking about was the way Millie's touch had sent a shiver across his skin and…

Stop it!

"Right, I'm off to, erm, wash my hair," Adam said.

When the two little girls sitting at the table with their iced gingerbread men dissolved once more into fits of giggles, he couldn't do anything other than join them in laughing. It *was* funny. Stupidly embarrassing, but funny.

After walking around the table and taking a bow, which prompted more laughter and a round of applause—even from Evelyn Fox—Adam headed for the doors of the village hall.

"Hey, Adam, wait!"

He turned to see Millie hurrying to catch up with him.

"Sorry this ended in a bit of disaster," she said.

"It's my own stupid fault. I shouldn't have squeezed the icing bag so hard. I obviously don't know my own strength."

Millie laughed, then tucked a strand of hair behind her ear and looked thoughtful. "Listen, I was wondering about something, but feel free to say no if it's a terrible idea and you'd rather just be by yourself."

Seeing her awkwardness at whatever it was she was about to say, Adam gave her an encouraging smile. "I'm intrigued."

"I was thinking about what you said the other day, about dreading the day your wedding was supposed to happen and how you were planning on just working at the shop and then hiding away in your flat until it was over, and..." She shuffled her feet and glanced at the floor before looking back up at him. "Well, I wondered if instead of doing that, you'd like to do something else instead?"

Adam hadn't expected this. "What did you have in mind?"

"I thought you might like to get out of Hollyford for a while. We could catch the train to Stratford-upon-Avon, do the touristy Shakespeare thing, and maybe have a pub lunch somewhere. I've never been to Stratford-upon-Avon, and I thought it might be fun."

The invitation caught him by surprise. For weeks, he'd anticipated the day of his cancelled wedding on December twenty-first, which was a Friday. He'd planned to work in his shop, keep his head down, then go home and vegetate in front of the television with many beers until midnight struck and he could finally move on and leave it all behind him.

Spending the day, or at least part of it, doing something other than wallowing in self-pity and humiliation struck him as attractive.

"I like the sound of that," Adam said. "But I'll have to see if I can get my mother to cover a few hours in the gift shop first."

"Of course. I'm off work that day anyway, but I know it's not so easy for you to just abandon your business."

"Let me talk to my mother and I'll give you a ring and let you know."

"No problem."

Millie's cheeks flushed and that awkward expression he'd come to know crossed her face again. He hoped she didn't think he was trying to fob her off, because he wasn't.

"Thanks for thinking of me," he said. "That's really kind. And I think you're right—getting out and about for a bit is a great idea."

She smiled shyly. "Well, let me know if you can make it."

"Will do." He scrubbed a hand through his sticky hair. "I better get cleaned up before this icing sets any harder."

With a laugh, Millie waved him off and returned to help Mrs Wishmore at their gingerbread icing table. Adam headed for the exit. His stint of volunteering with the Christmas Village event might have ended before it had barely begun, leaving him covered in sticky icing goo, but it hadn't been a complete waste of time.

Far from it.

As he hurried towards his flat, where he planned to

shower and wash the icing sugar out of his hair before returning to the gift shop for the last few hours before closing, he pushed his hands into his coat pockets. His fingers brushed against the angel bauble still tucked inside and he realised he'd once more forgotten to return the item to Doris Wishmore.

Adam made a mental note not to forget the next time he saw Doris. The older lady must surely miss the little trinket she said she liked having with her during the festive season.

He scooped the little bauble into the palm of his hand as he walked, liking its comforting weight against his skin and the soft texture of the pearly surface. He'd almost be sorry to return the bauble to its rightful owner, he thought with a laugh and picked up his pace.

CHAPTER ELEVEN

The day after the gingerbread icing event in the village hall, Millie sat on a bench in Hollyford market square, cradling a hot chocolate in one hand and her phone in the other. She'd just finished a shift at the care home and wanted to enjoy the last of the daylight before the wintry sun disappeared and darkness fell. With midwinter approaching fast, the days were getting shorter and shorter, and when she finished her day shift at three o'clock, the light was already fading fast from the sky.

Sitting outside in the brisk wintry air would, she hoped, spur her into taking the action she'd decided to take after her conversation with Mrs Wishmore yesterday in the village hall. Last evening, she'd thought long and hard again about whether to contact her father and ask if he'd like to meet up over coffee. Despite having already made the decision, she hadn't yet got in touch.

Every time she'd grabbed her phone, nerves got the better of her. What if her father didn't want to meet up? What if he didn't want to get to know her better? Millie wasn't sure how she'd feel about that sort of rejection. After all, he'd had her whole life to get to know her and had chosen not to.

But maybe Derek Hill had no idea that she wanted them to be in touch more. How could he know unless she told him? Perhaps he only kept his distance because she kept hers.

Millie sat on the market square bench, staring at her phone. There was only one way to find out if there was the possibility of a relationship with her father, and that was to ask him.

She reminded herself of the nerves she'd felt yesterday afternoon when she'd plucked up the courage to ask Adam if he'd like to spend time together on the day that would have been his wedding day. She'd felt her usual awkward self as she'd made the suggestion, fearing tripping over her words or making a botch of what should have been a simple invitation to a friend. But she'd pushed on and made the offer, despite her clumsy awkwardness, because she hated the idea of Adam dreading the impending day of his cancelled wedding and ploughing through it alone. He'd already told her how hard he found it, spending time with friends and family because he hated seeing their sympathetic looks and knowing they felt sorry for him.

Maybe time away from Hollyford would help him get through the wretched cancelled wedding day and put it behind him? As they'd become friends of sorts, she thought she ought to help him through what she was sure would be a difficult few hours.

She was pleased Adam had said he liked the idea of an afternoon in Stratford-upon-Avon, although he still hadn't been in touch to say if he could get cover in the gift shop. Hopefully his mother could lend a hand. Millie was already excited about the prospect of visiting the lovely town in the company of her new friend. She'd always wanted to go there and wander along the banks of the River Avon and through the old cobbled streets while admiring the beautiful Tudor buildings and…

Millie sighed, knowing she was allowing her mind to wander so she didn't have to think instead about the actual reason why she'd plonked herself down on this bench in the first place.

Taking a sip of hot chocolate, she peered at her phone. Was she contacting her father or not?

Millie tapped at the screen and found the last text message she'd received from Derek. It had been a couple of months since their last strained exchanges of *How are you? I'm fine, how are you?* After staring at the messages for a long moment, she took a deep breath and started typing.

Hi, Dad. How's things? Hope you're well. Wondered if you'd be interested in grabbing a coffee sometime before Christmas? Might be nice to catch up. Let me know if you're free.

Her heart pounding with every word she typed, Millie added her name and an 'xx' to the end of the message and then sent it before she could change her mind. Draining her hot chocolate, she couldn't help staring at the phone screen for any sign of a reply, even although she knew it was unlikely that Derek would respond straight away.

Still, that bubble of hope bounced around inside her heart just the same and she couldn't help imagining the two of them meeting up in the not too distant future, huddling together in a café as snow fell outside and they nursed coffees and began the task of getting to know one another as father and daughter…

"Stop it," Millie muttered to herself. No good could come from fantasising about a relationship that didn't even exist yet, a relationship that might never exist. Derek Hill was a stranger, even if he was her father. She knew next to nothing about the man. Just because she hoped that might change didn't mean it would.

Her phone pinged with a message, startling her with its chirpy tone. Grabbing it up from her lap, she almost knocked it to the frosty ground in her haste to read the message that had arrived.

When she realised it wasn't a message from her father, she felt a pang of disappointment—but only for a second, because the message was from Adam, and her heart did a little flip of happiness when she read the text he'd sent.

If the offer still stands, I'm up for that trip to Stratford-upon-Avon on Friday. Mum can cover the gift shop from eleven o'clock. Does that sound okay? Cheers, Adam.

It sounded more than okay. It sounded brilliant. Typing a quick response, she told him so. When her phone pinged again a few moments later, it was with another message from Adam.

I'll drive us up there. It's a bus and train journey otherwise and it takes forever. Cheers, Adam.

After a few more messages back and forth, they settled their arrangements. Smiling, Millie tucked her phone away. Things were looking up.

She'd contacted her father and asked if he'd like to meet for coffee, and it had taken courage to do that after so many years of distance between them. She'd invited her new friend for a day out, and that hadn't been easy, either, considering how bad she was at social stuff, but Adam had agreed and the trip was all set.

Millie felt more than a little proud of herself. For someone who was painfully shy in social situations, she'd pushed herself out of her comfort zone and taken risks. She'd joined in with the Christmas Village activities, made new friends with Doris Wishmore and Adam Carter, and reached out to her father.

Perhaps this move to Hollyford was finally helping her find the new life she longed for. Glancing across the market square to the Christmas tree with its bright twinkle lights and silver star on top, she thought of her mother and the promises she'd made before she died.

Life without her mother wasn't easy and losing her still hurt her heart. But maybe this Christmas would be like the one Caroline had hoped Mille would have, one filled with hope and happiness.

Just a few months ago, Millie hadn't thought such a thing possible. Now, she knew differently.

With one last glance at the gorgeous Hollyford Christmas tree, Millie turned for home before the afternoon grew any chillier.

CHAPTER TWELVE

When Adam opened his eyes on the morning of Friday the twenty-first of December, a few blissful seconds passed during which his brain was still waking up and he hadn't yet remembered the significance of the day. Sketchy fragments of the dreams he'd had during the night floated through his mind as he savoured the comforting warmth beneath the duvet, and heard a car drive by outside his bedroom window, and thought about what the day ahead might have in store…

And then it hit him. If things had turned out differently, this would've been his wedding day.

He let the thought sink in. He thought of the suit he would've worn, the white rose buttonhole his mother would have fussed with on his jacket, the rings he would have asked his best man about to make sure they were safe.

He thought about the sweet Cotswold church where he would've waited for Heidi to walk down the aisle towards him. He imagined the dress she would've worn, a dress he'd never seen and never would see, and how it would've felt to slip that wedding ring onto her finger and promise to be hers forever.

He imagined their first kiss as a married couple. Their car journey to the reception. Their first dance as husband and wife.

Each image played out inside his head like a video reel of sparkling moments from what would have been the happiest day of his life. For weeks, Adam had dreaded this day, and had dreaded these exact thoughts spinning through his head in some terrible loop of regret.

Which was why it came as a surprise to realise that he could see those images unfolding in his mind, and imagine the wedding day he'd never have, and yet not feel the grinding humiliation and dread that he'd expected to feel.

Searching his heart, he wondered what he *did* feel.

Sad. He felt sad that things had ended the way they had with Heidi, sad that she'd betrayed him with someone else. He felt sad that the wedding day they'd planned together had been abandoned. He felt sad that all his hopes and dreams for the future he'd imagined with his fiancé had been torpedoed, casting him adrift.

He felt anger, too, and wondered for the millionth time how he could have missed Heidi pulling away from him, and how he could have missed the fact that she'd been seeing someone else and betraying everything they'd supposedly meant to each other. Realising he'd been so blind and oblivious made the anger fizz inside him.

He reminded himself that he'd been angry about all this for weeks and all it had done was leave him spent and exhausted. And the person he wanted to be angry at—Heidi—wasn't even around, so what was the point?

Well, that wasn't quite true, because there was someone else he couldn't help feel anger towards—his sister, Angela. How could she have known about Heidi's betrayal and not told him about it? Why had she kept things to herself? Why on earth hadn't she told him the moment she'd found out that Heidi was cheating?

If you'd given her a chance to explain properly, maybe you'd already have the answers to those questions.

Adam knew that little voice of reason inside his head made a lot of sense, but he couldn't listen to it right now. This wasn't the day for thinking about his sister and what she had or hadn't done once she discovered the truth of what Heidi was up to behind his back. Today was about grinding through the hours until the day of his cancelled wedding was over and he could finally square his shoulders again and think about moving on with his life.

As he threw back the covers and got out of bed, he remembered he'd agreed to go with Millie to Stratford-upon-Avon today. The prospect of the day trip cheered him up. Getting out of Hollyford, getting away from his gift shop, getting space from his gloomy thoughts was just what he needed, and he was glad Millie had suggested the idea.

She was becoming a good friend. After weeks spent hiding from everyone in his life, a new person arriving in his world felt like an unexpected gift, and one he needed more than he'd realised.

A thought flashed in his head, of the way Millie's hand had touched his face when he'd found himself covered in icing during the gingerbread decorating event at the village hall, and of how her skin had seared his as she'd helped wipe the sticky mess away. His stomach somersaulted at the memory.

Easy, he told himself. Millie was a friend, and he badly needed a friend right now. He wasn't about to risk that budding friendship by imagining feelings that simply weren't there.

He was a jilted fiancé whose emotions were shattered and

untrustworthy, and Millie was a friend who was generously helping him through a tough day and helping take his mind off his doomed Christmas wedding. His moods were confused enough without conjuring non-existent attraction into the mix between them both.

If he'd felt something when Millie's hand brushed against his face that day, then it was nothing more than a sign of how badly he needed to connect with other people again after so long spent avoiding everyone. He reminded himself that even his father's fierce bear-hug the other night when he'd gone to his parents' house for dinner had prompted an odd bubble of emotion to well up inside him at the display of affection and the empathy underpinning it.

He was an emotional disaster zone, clearly. That's what Heidi had turned him into. Well, after today, perhaps he could finally push his ex-fiancé out of his head and get on with living his life again, free from embarrassment and free from the fear that anytime someone reached out and touched him or hugged him, he'd dissolve into a pool of stupid helpless tears.

Adam showered and dressed, then bolted breakfast before heading over to the gift shop to open up. He'd only be there for a few hours of work this morning and then his mother would arrive to hold the fort with his assistant, Lorraine, so he could escape from Hollyford for the day.

He could hardly wait. The sooner he saw the back of this horrible day and closed the door on it forever, the better.

THE MORNING SPED by at the gift shop.

After greeting him when he arrived to unlock the doors, Lesley kissed his cheek and forced him to accept a hug, told him to stay strong, and then surprised him by not mentioning anything further about the non-wedding day for the rest of the morning. It helped that the shop was busy with a flurry of Christmas shoppers, meaning there was little time to chat, anyway. Adam had feared Lesley would want to dwell on the significance of the day and commiserate with him, but that wasn't to be.

Instead, she got stuck into serving customers and restocking the shelves and dealing with an order that had arrived at the shop late the night before from a local organic soap artisan. As Lesley sniffed the beautifully wrapped bars of soaps while running a constant commentary about their wonderful scents and clever aroma combinations, Adam was surprised to discover it was already eleven o'clock and time for him to leave. Glad of the backlog of paperwork he'd been able to deal with while his mother and Lorraine worked at the front of the shop and served the customers, Adam grabbed his jacket.

"I'm so pleased you're getting out and about again," Lesley told him as he headed for the door. "It'll do you the world of good to have a change of scenery, especially today."

"I'm looking forward to it," Adam replied.

"That Millie is a lovely young woman, and it's so thoughtful of her to invite you out for the day. You be sure to tell her I said so."

"Will do. I'll be back in time for closing up. Any problems in the meantime, just ring my phone."

"Yes, boss."

Lesley gave a mock salute as Adam opened the shop door, but before he could step outside, his mother gently grabbed his arm.

"Your father and I are here if you need us, Adam. Don't forget that."

"Thanks, Mum."

Adam patted his mother's hand and left the shop. He

knew his parents were there for him, and he also knew how lucky he was to be able to say that and to be able to count on it. As he walked to his car, his thoughts turned to Millie and what she'd told him about losing her mother and starting again in life without any family to support her or cheer her on.

How had she done it? And with the anniversary of her mother's death undoubtedly at the front of her mind this season, how had she found space in her heart to take pity on a sad case like himself and help take his mind off things today?

Adam was glad to know her.

When he steered his car around the market square, Millie was waiting for him as arranged. She hopped into the passenger seat with a smile.

"Hey, how are you holding up?" she asked.

"I'm okay. Looking forward to getting past today and putting it behind me."

"In that case, are you ready for a pleasantly distracting day trip?"

"Absolutely."

"I brought sweets for the journey." Pulling two bags of sweets from her coat pocket, she waved them in the air. "Shall we start with toffees or rhubarb and custard?"

"Has to be rhubarb and custard."

"Right answer. We'll keep the toffees for the drive home."

She opened the bag of sweets and held it out so Adam could help himself to one of the pink and yellow treats. It had been ages since he'd eaten a boiled sweet and the sugary confection exploded on his tongue like a firework.

"Good sustenance choice," Adam said around the mouthful of sweet as he pulled away from the kerb. "Okay, next stop Stratford-upon-Avon."

"I can't wait," Millie grinned. "This will be fun! I went

online and checked out what's happening and what we could get up to. There's a Victorian Christmas market running today, and special outdoor performances of scenes from Shakespeare, and live music, and a hog roast, and..."

Her good humour was infectious. Adam laughed as he turned his attention to the road, happy to listen to her chatter about the day that lay ahead.

When they pulled into a car park in Stratford-upon-Avon an hour later, Adam was stunned to discover he hadn't thought about Heidi or his non-wedding day once during the entire journey.

CHAPTER THIRTEEN

Stratford-upon-Avon in winter was even prettier than Millie imagined it would be.

The day was dry and cold, with bright blue skies and a pale lemon sun skipping across the horizon and showing off the town at its best. Ducks quacked and flapped in the river as crowds gathered to watch a Shakespeare sketch being performed on the banks outside the Royal Shakespeare Theatre. Festive lights decorated the cobbled streets and lanes, and the Victorian market was filled with stall holders in fancy dress and selling everything from arts and crafts to Christmas stockings, from luxury cakes to hot drinks, and everything in between. The event dwarfed the Hollyford Christmas Village, but that was only to be expected given the very different sizes of the two towns. They each had their own charm and unique attractions.

After buying hot chocolate to warm them up, Millie and Adam wandered the town, taking in the sights. They pointed out the gorgeous Tudor buildings to one another, enjoyed the street entertainments, savoured the smells from the food stalls, and admired the wares for sale from the traders. When

Adam took particular interest in one stallholder who was selling hand painted teacups and mugs and other tableware, he spent a few minutes chatting with the woman about stocking her products in his gift shop, and seemed pleased when they agreed to meet in the new year to take things further.

"You never switch off," Millie teased him as they resumed their walk along the high street.

"Occupational hazard. Those teacups were too nice to ignore, and they'd be a great fit for my shop. But I promise I won't chat up anymore traders while we're here. I'm officially off the clock now."

"Chat up as many traders as you like. There's no big agenda for the day. I'm just happy to finally visit Stratford and have a nice wander around."

"It sounds like you've wanted to come here for a while?"

Millie gave a soft shrug. "Not long before my mum fell ill, we talked about visiting Stratford for a couple of days. We'd been clearing out some boxes from the back of a cupboard, and my mum found a stack of her old schoolbooks she'd forgotten she still had. She had a flick through them, and told me about how much she'd loved studying English at school, and how much she'd loved reading Shakespeare. Her favourite was *Macbeth,* and even years later she could still remember many of the lines she'd learned in school."

"That's impressive."

"She had a great memory, and she always loved reading and could remember whole passages from some of her favourite books. Anyway, as we chatted about how much she'd once loved reading Shakespeare, she said she'd never seen a live performance of any of the plays and how much she would've loved to. By the time we'd cleared out that cupboard and sorted through those old boxes, we'd decided we'd save up and book an overnight stay in Stratford and see a Shakespeare play together."

When she glanced Adam's way, she knew he understood how the story ended.

"But you never made the trip," he said.

"Mum started feeling unwell a few months later. She thought she was just a bit run down from working at two cleaning jobs and always being run ragged. By the time she went to the doctor and got the diagnosis from the consultant, we'd forgotten all about the little overnight stay to Stratford we'd talked about."

"I'm sorry you never made the trip together," Adam said, and Millie was touched by the tender tone in his voice.

"Me too. I think she would've liked it here."

As they meandered the streets, Millie glanced at the Victorian-style stalls and the beautiful old buildings and cobbled lanes, knowing her mother would have loved seeing all this.

"There were lots of things my mother never got to do because time ran out," Millie said. "I feel bad about that and wish things were different. Even before she became ill, we didn't have money for day trips or holidays. Don't get me wrong, we were happy with our lot in life because we had each other. But I sometimes wonder if she wanted more out of life than what she got."

Millie hadn't meant to tilt the conversation in such a melancholy direction, especially considering the whole point of this trip was to take Adam's mind off things.

"Sorry, I'm supposed to be helping you get through this rubbish non-wedding day, and instead I'm yapping on about my own sad stuff."

"You're not yapping on at all. You're talking about things that matter to you."

She smiled, grateful for his words.

"If I'd known any of this before we agreed to come here today," Adam continued, "we could've looked into getting a couple of tickets to see a Shakespeare play. Do you want to walk over to the theatre and see if there's any going spare?"

"You're sweet to suggest that. But I'm enjoying just wandering around and getting a feel for the place."

"Fair enough. Maybe next time?"

"Yeah, next time."

She liked the idea that there would be a next time, that there might be more day trips with Adam and that this wasn't just a one-time thing. The more she got to know him, the more she liked his company and appreciated this new friendship they were forging.

"So, if you're willing to see a play, does that mean you're a fan of Shakespeare?" she asked.

His lips quirked. "Actually, no. I'm a bit of a philistine when it comes to that sort of stuff. When we did our Shakespeare in school, I hadn't the foggiest idea what any of it was about. The words might as well have been written backwards in our textbooks for all I understood."

Millie burst out laughing. "Then why did you suggest grabbing late tickets for a theatre performance?"

He gave an easy shrug. "It sounded like something you might like to do in memory of your mum."

His answer left her a little stunned. "That's incredibly sweet, Adam."

A blush coloured his cheeks. Millie couldn't help wondering what on earth was wrong with this ex-fiancé of his, this Heidi person, to have made her walk away from a man as kind and thoughtful as Adam Carter. The woman had to be off her head.

"Anyway," Adam said after clearing his throat. "We'll come back some other time and go to the theatre, and you can watch people prancing around on stage in tights while uttering completely incomprehensible lines of dialogue."

"It's a date." The words were out before Millie realised it. Now it was her turn to blush. "Not a date, I don't mean an actual date, I mean we'd go as friends, that's all, and..."

Adam's chuckling halted her embarrassed attempts to backtrack. "Relax, Millie, I knew what you meant."

"Good. All right then." Her stomach rumbled just then, loud enough to be heard even above the crowds wandering the streets around them and causing Adam to lift an eyebrow in amusement.

"I think it's past your lunch time," he said.

"I think you might be right. What time is it?"

A surprised expression crossed his face when he looked at his watch. "Almost one-thirty."

Millie saw his surprise turn to something more thoughtful and sombre. "Are you okay, Adam?"

For a moment, he said nothing, a faraway look in his eye. "I just realised I would've been married already by now, if things had turned out differently."

It was impossible not to see the mixture of sadness and pain in his expression. But Millie saw, too, that he was trying to shake those feelings away.

"I'm sorry," she said. "But I happen to think you had a lucky escape, Adam. She obviously wasn't right for you. But you already know that."

He nodded, still looking thoughtful. "I know that now. I didn't know it a few months ago."

The sadness on his face cracked her heart in two. She didn't want him to disappear into those feelings, not when he'd been having such a lovely time so far.

"Here's something else you didn't know a few months ago," Millie said. "There's a hog roast stall across the street that claims to be the best in the entire county, and that's where we're buying lunch today."

Adam looked puzzled for a minute before laughing. "You're right. I didn't know that a few months ago."

"Well, now you do know it, what are we waiting for?"

"All right, let's see about this hog roast. Lunch is my treat, by the way."

"Nope, this is on me."

"Listen, I was supposed to be buying roast turkey dinners for a hundred wedding guests today. Since I'm not doing that anymore, I think I can spring for a couple of hog rolls."

"Fair enough," she laughed, pleased to see his expression lifting. "In that case, I'll buy dessert. Those mince pies on that cake stall over there look too good to resist."

"It's a deal."

Sharing a smile, they turned towards the hog roast stall. As they joined the queue, Adam thrust his hands into his pockets and nudged Millie with his elbow.

"Thanks for this," he said. "I didn't realise I needed to get away from Hollyford and do something fun like this today until you suggested it."

"I'm glad our little day trip is helping you through a tough time."

"It's not just the day trip. It's you, too. You're being a good friend and I need that right now. Thank you."

His words once more did something funny to her heart, folding it over inside her chest. But before she could think about it, a man working behind the hog roast counter waved them forward and asked what they wanted to order.

Millie turned her attention to the hog roast and the vast choice of chutneys and sauces on offer, pleased for the distraction from her confused and fluttering heart.

THEY ATE lunch on a bench overlooking the banks of the River Avon in pretty gardens that ran alongside moored canal boats. The hog roast rolls and hot tea warmed them up as the afternoon chill descended.

"Good lunch choice," Adam said as they ate. "These rolls are pretty spectacular."

"I thought we'd end up with a cosy pub lunch, but I think this is nicer. Freezing cold, but still, it's nice."

"How's your winter spiced chutney?"

"So good I might have to go back to the hog roast stall and buy a jar. What about your apple sauce?"

"It's fantastic. If you're going back to buy something, then I'll get some of this for my dad. He'd love a jar of this apple sauce as a Christmas stocking filler."

Millie finished her roll and wiped her hands with a napkin. "It sounds like you're close to your family and see a lot of them."

"Not as much as I used to. I've had trouble looking my parents in the eye ever since the wedding was called off. It might sound stupid, but I'm too embarrassed, you know? I keep thinking about all the village gossip they must have been subjected to these past couple of months. I feel bad about that."

"I'm sure they'd hate knowing you feel that way."

"Believe me, I know this is all in my own head. I'm working on it and trying to be less of an idiot."

Millie let out a soft laugh.

"They're good people, my parents. It was bad enough the wedding being cancelled without them having to put up with me behaving like a twat for all this time."

"They know you're doing your best, I'm sure of it."

Adam looked uncomfortable, a frown creasing his forehead as he shifted on the bench. "I wish that was true, but it isn't. I don't think I have been trying my best."

Millie wagged a finger. "You're not allowed to give yourself a hard time, Adam, not today."

"There are things I maybe deserve a hard time over." He sighed and scrunched up the paper wrapper from his lunch roll. "There's something I didn't mention when we had coffee last week and I told you about Heidi leaving me and the wedding being called off."

Millie waited for him to say more. His expression made it clear that, whatever he was about to tell her, he wasn't finding it easy.

"Okay, I'll give you the short version," Adam said. "My sister, Angela, found out that Heidi was cheating on me a week before I did. She knew Heidi planned to leave me and cancel our wedding. But she didn't breathe a word of it to me."

Millie stared for a moment, processing what Adam had said. "Wow, Adam, that's... that's pretty harsh."

A memory flickered from the first time she'd met Adam at his gift shop, right after she'd been hoodwinked into decorating the place by Evelyn Fox. Once Adam had calmed down after seeing what had happened to his shop while he'd been gone, his mother, Lesley, had tried to mend fences by inviting him over to dinner. Adam had accepted the invite, only to backtrack when he realised someone called Angela would be there. The awkwardness and frustration between mother and son had been too obvious to miss. At the time, Millie hadn't known who this Angela person was when her name had come up. Now, that strained moment made much more sense.

Millie watched Adam's face as he continued his story.

"When I first realised Angela had known what Heidi was up to behind my back and hadn't told me, I thought it was more than harsh," he said. "I thought it was unforgiveable."

She couldn't miss his use of the past tense. "But now you see things differently?"

"I don't know." He let out a long sigh and looked across the river where the low winter sun was casting amber sparkles in the dark water. "Angela only found out about what Heidi was up to because she happened to see her in a bar with the guy she was having the affair with. She confronted Heidi the next day about what she'd seen, and the whole sorry story came out. Angela said Heidi begged her not to tell me. Heidi had said she knew her relationship with me was over, and that she had to tell me herself. Angela agreed to keep quiet about what she'd seen so long as Heidi told me straight away."

Adam shook his head, the memories obviously painful to recount. "But it was another week before Heidi broke the news and left me. All these wretched timelines came out in the wash when Angela admitted she'd found out about the whole mess before I did, but hadn't said a word about it because she'd promised *Heidi* she wouldn't."

He almost spat out the name of his ex-fiancé, before holding up his hands in an apology. "I'm getting worked up about it and I don't mean to."

"It sounds like your sister found herself in a horrible situation when she discovered what Heidi was up to."

"I keep reminding myself of that. But she knew for an entire week before I did. I actually saw Angela at my parents' house during that week, when I was there discussing some ceremony arrangements with my mother. I was *talking about the wedding plans* and Angela didn't say a word about what she knew!" He shook his head and gave a sad laugh. "I can't tell you how much of an idiot that made me feel, and how much of an idiot it still makes me feel. It eats away at me, the fact that my own sister knew my fiancé was a cheat and that our wedding was about to be cancelled, and yet she sat there in my parents' kitchen listening to me wittering on to my mother about the ceremony arrangements and which hymns Heidi had chosen for the church."

On another long and frustrated sigh, Adam leaned back on the bench and looked out at the river view once more. Sensing he needed a moment to settle down, Millie waited before she said anything.

"Has your sister tried to explain why she didn't tell you what she'd found out once it was obvious that Heidi hadn't told you right away like she promised?"

Shrugging and shaking his head at the same time, Adam waved his hand at nothing in particular. "After Heidi finally told me she was leaving, I went to my parents' house the next day to break the news. Angela was there, and I could tell from her expression that there was something she wasn't telling me. When she finally told me she'd already known, I thought my head would explode. I was already reeling from Heidi's bombshell, and then it turned out that my own sister knew all this already? I blew up at Angela and started shouting about how she should have told me the same night she found out Heidi was cheating. Angela is my family and I should have been able to count on her to look out for me. I'm usually pretty even-tempered, but not that night. I got really angry and…" He gulped and closed his eyes as he finished the sentence. "I got so angry that I told Angela she'd made me look even more of a fool than Heidi had, and that I could never forgive her for it."

He looked away, but Millie saw the shame on his face.

"You were upset," she said quietly. "You were upset and caught by surprise. Your fiancé left you and then you found out that your sister had known it was coming and hadn't told you. Anyone would get angry and shout about something like that."

"But I said something even worse. I told her… I told her I never wanted to see her again."

His head dropped and he blew out a breath. Sharing this last terrible part of the story about his doomed wedding seemed to drain all the energy from him.

"You blew up and said something in the heat of the moment," Millie said. "We've all done that at some point. You made a mistake, and it sounds like your sister made a mistake, too. But that doesn't mean you and Angela can't make things right again between the two of you."

"That's what my mother keeps telling me. But the honest truth is that I just can't bear the idea of even looking at Angela right now. All I can think about is how she *knew* Heidi was cheating and planning to ditch our wedding, and yet she didn't tell me. I can't get past that. I don't want there to be bad blood in my family. But I can't get past what Angela did. It doesn't matter why she didn't tell me. There's no excuse. And maybe there's no going back because of it."

Unable to look at the pain etched on Adam's face, Millie reached out and laid her hand on his. "This is eating you up inside and that isn't healthy."

"I know."

She squeezed his hand, and he squeezed hers in return before giving a rueful smile. After a moment, he pulled his hand away and raked it through his hair, his jagged movements jagged and edgy.

"For weeks, I've dreaded today because I was supposed to be walking down the aisle to marry the woman I loved. Now that day is here, I know things will be better once I'm on the other side of it and I can put it behind me. All the love I felt for Heidi disappeared the moment she told me she was leaving me for someone else, and, in some horribly grim way, the fact I don't love her anymore has helped me get to this point. I'm humiliated and hurt, yes, but at least I'm not still in love with someone who doesn't love me."

Frowning, he drew in a deep breath before continuing. "But it's not that simple where Angela is concerned. Heidi might be gone from my life for good, but Angela is my sister and that isn't a relationship you can just walk away from."

"So, don't walk away from it."

"You make it sound so easy."

"I might not be easy. But it doesn't have to be so hard, either."

Pausing, she wondered if she ought to say anymore. Considering what Adam had just told her, he might not welcome any thoughts or advice she might have to offer. He'd just described an upsetting and traumatising rift inside his family, and the last thing she wanted was to say something that would come across as naïve or sentimental.

But Adam had started talking about this for a reason. There'd been no need to bring it up, but he had. Maybe he wanted—or needed—a push in the direction he knew he had to go in, but wasn't sure where to start.

"Do you want to know what I think?" Millie ventured.

He looked at her and nodded. "Yeah."

"Okay. It's been weeks since you lost your temper at your sister, and maybe enough time has passed to start talking again. You've calmed down and got over the shock of Heidi leaving. Once today is over, the wedding date will be in the rear-view mirror, and you already said that will be a big help in moving on. With that big step out of the way, maybe it will be time to take the next one, and mend fences with your sister?"

"I don't know."

"The fact that you're even talking about any of this makes me think you *do* know, Adam. You don't want there to be bad blood. I'm guessing this falling out has been tough for your parents?"

He looked pained at her words. "That's an understatement."

"You're the only one with the power to change things. You're the only one who can choose to talk to Angela again and get past this."

After staring across the river for a moment, thinking about what she'd said, Adam nodded. "I know you're right."

Millie's heart ached for the pain this man had endured. An unfaithful fiancé and a cancelled Christmas wedding were bad enough, but adding a terrible family fight into the mix was even worse. Adam needed his family at his side right now, but instead they were all at loggerheads.

"You've talked about the humiliation and embarrassment you feel about what Heidi did, and I understand how the part your sister played in all this only made things worse. But maybe you have to grit your teeth and find a way forward before it's too late. I mean, how would you feel if you actually never saw your sister again?"

Adam blinked and his colour paled. When he spoke, his voice was tiny. "I'd be devastated."

"In that case, you already know what you have to do."

He nodded, but then waved his arms again, as if trying to illustrate his dilemma because she'd failed to understand it. "I don't want to shut Angela out of my life. But I also can't get past what she did and the embarrassment it caused me. I can't square the circle."

Millie saw Adam's torment and wondered if there might be another way to help him with this terrible problem. "Were you close to your sister before all this happened?"

His expression softened at her question. "Yeah, we were close. Angela's only a year younger than me, so when we were kids, we played together and hung around together.

Things were different when we hit our teenage years and wanted to spend more time with friends, but once we grew up, we became good friends ourselves. We'd catch up over pizza at the weekend, grab coffee together if we had a spare evening during the week. We always knew what was going on in one another's lives. When I was made redundant from my job at the department store and decided to open my gift shop, Angela was the one cheering me on the loudest."

He let out a slow, sad sigh. "Maybe that's what makes this even harder. I needed my sister through this whole sorry mess more than I needed anyone, and yet she was the one person I couldn't stand to be in the same room as."

The look of loss on Adam's face said it all. Millie stayed quiet, understanding that he needed a moment to think about what he'd just said. Out on the river, a group of ducks flapped their wings and quacked at one another. Christmas music drifted from the streets and lanes behind them. The wintry air was scented with crisp frost and hot chestnuts and mulled wine.

After a few moments had passed, Millie gave Adam a thoughtful look and shared something she hadn't intended sharing with him.

"I don't have siblings, so I have no idea what you've gone through with all of this," she began. "But I do know something about how hard it can be to take the first step in a relationship. In my case, the situation is different, obviously, but not so different that it might not help, if you'd like to hear about it."

Adam's expression turned curious. "Okay."

"I've already told you about how my mother and I were always on our own, just the two of us, but I didn't tell you anything about my father. He separated from my mother when I was a baby, and moved away. There was only occasional contact between him and my mother while I was growing up. He'd send presents sometimes for birthdays or Christmas, but mostly he was a stranger to me. I didn't think much about him, to be honest. At least, I didn't until after my mother died."

Adam watched her, his expression curious. Perhaps he was wondering how any of this fit in with his terrible story of family discord.

"Last weekend, after a lot of soul searching, I contacted my father and asked if he'd like to meet for coffee sometime before Christmas. I was more than a little terrified of taking that step, because I couldn't help thinking about how bad I'd feel if he said he didn't want to get together, or, worse, if he just didn't respond at all. Part of me wants to reach out to the only blood relative I know I have left and see if there might be the chance of a connection there. But another part of me is hurt that my father never wanted to be in my life in the first place. I struggled with those warring thoughts and how to resolve them."

"And then you took the big step and contacted him."

"I did, but it wasn't easy. I chatted with Doris Wishmore about it for a bit before I made up my mind, and chatting helping organise my thoughts. Maybe chatting with me will help organise your thoughts, too."

A smile crept across Millie's face as she thought about the next part of the story. "But the upshot of all this is that my father got back in touch and we're meeting on Sunday. It's a small step, and I don't know what, if anything, will come of it. But I had to try. I had to set aside the hurt I felt about why he'd never chosen to be involved in my life. I had to reach out. I had to find out if there might be the chance of a relationship between us, even after all these years of not knowing one another."

Adam looked away again, his gaze distant. "You took a risk."

"I took a risk."

"You think I should take a risk, too."

Millie shook her head. "I'll tell you what Doris Wishmore told me when I asked her if I should contact my father. She said it wouldn't be right for her to tell me what to do, one way or the other, and it wouldn't be right for me to tell you what to do, either. But I started talking to Doris about all of this because I think I knew, deep down inside, that I'd already decided to reach out to my father. I just needed to say it out loud to someone who'd listen and be kind while I talked. Doris did that for me. Maybe you started talking about Angela because you also know, deep down inside, that you need to sort things out, and you just needed to say it out loud. What Doris Wishmore did for me, maybe I'm now doing for you."

For a long moment, Adam looked lost in thought. "I don't know what to say to any of that."

Millie smiled. "Then don't say anything." Feeling the chill that was now descending as the light began draining from the afternoon skies, she rubbed her hands together. "Anyway, we ought to get up from this bench before we freeze."

A church bell chimed from across the warren of Stratford streets and lanes, and Adam glanced at his watch in surprise. "I can't believe it's three o'clock already. Do you mind if we start walking back to the car? I don't want to leave any later than three-thirty, to make sure I get back to Hollyford in time to shut up the gift shop for the day."

"Of course. Let's swing by the hog roast stall on the way and buy some of those jars of chutney. You said your dad would like some for Christmas."

Adam nodded, his expression soft. "He'd love it." He shuffled his feet and blew out a breath. "We passed a stall selling scarves on the way over here to eat lunch. One of them caught my eye because it was decorated with a snowman print, and the first thing that popped into my head was, 'Angela would love that scarf and it'd be the perfect Christmas gift for her.'"

Millie couldn't help smiling. "Then let's get it. Your sister has a soft spot for snowmen?"

Adam nodded, and Millie saw his eyes glisten with emotion.

"Snowmen are her big thing at Christmas. She's always buying snowmen decorations, snowmen mugs, snowmen Christmas cards. She can't get enough of them."

"In that case, a snowman scarf sounds like the perfect gift for her, and one she'll love."

When he spoke again, his voice wobbled. "I want to sort out this mess between us, but I don't know if I can."

"Of course you can. She's your sister. That isn't a bond that breaks easily."

He nodded, then let out a gruff laugh. "Today was supposed to be about slogging my way through the wedding day that never was. But now that doesn't seem as important as trying to put things right with Angela. I didn't expect that." Adam's gaze softened as he looked at her. "Thank you, Millie."

"I didn't do anything."

"Yes, you did."

He pulled her into a hug, the sudden embrace taking her by surprise.

But most surprising of all was the way her heart clutched at the feel of his arms around her.

"I couldn't have asked for a better friend today, Millie," he whispered before releasing her.

"All part of the Hollyford Christmas Village service," Millie said with a nervous chuckle, before shaking her head and rolling her eyes. "Sorry, that made no sense at all. I promise I'm not here with you on behalf of the

Christmas Village Committee. That would be creepy and weird."

Adam laughed, but if he sensed her sudden awkwardness and discomfort, he didn't let on. The hug he'd given her had prompted her social ineptitude to put in an unexpected appearance, and Millie was sorry about that because she'd felt relaxed in Adam's company until now.

"If Evelyn Fox is about to pop up out of nowhere and start haranguing me about something Christmassy, better tell me now," Adam said, giving her a wry grin.

"I promise that won't happen. Well, unless Evelyn is actually here and I don't know about it and she sees us and..."

On another soft laugh, Adam patted her arm. "Quit while you're ahead, Millie."

"Good idea." Drawing in a deep breath, Millie focused on transforming back into the sensible person she'd been a moment ago, the person who didn't say stupid things and make a fool of herself. "Shall we buy some chutney and that scarf for your sister, and then head back to the car?"

"Let's do it."

IT WAS dark when they arrived back in Hollyford. As Adam steered the car around the market square, Millie admired the Christmas tree, its lights filling the dark afternoon with cheerful warmth. Stratford at Christmas was wonderful, but Hollyford's Christmas Village had stolen a piece of Millie's heart, and now that the day trip was over she felt an overwhelming sense that she was home.

"You're sure you don't mind if I stop by the gift shop and close up before I run you back to your flat?" Adam asked.

"Of course not."

The traffic on the road back from Stratford had been

horrible, and she knew Adam hadn't wanted to cut things so fine. It was almost five o'clock, and although Adam had called Lesley at the shop to warn her they were stuck in a traffic jam and might be late, Millie understood he didn't want his mother having to lock the shop up in his absence.

"I can walk home anyway," Millie added. "It's only a short stroll away."

"I said I'd drop you off home, and I will." Adam pulled the car to a stop outside his shop. "This will only take ten minutes."

Inside the gift shop, Lesley was serving a customer at the counter. As she bagged the purchases, she smiled as Adam and Millie came in. After thanking the customer and wishing her a merry Christmas, Lesley turned her attention to the two of them.

"How was your day? Did you enjoy Stratford?"

"It was terrific, thanks," Adam said. "Did everything go okay here while I was gone?"

"It went fine. Lots of customers, lots of sales, and Lorraine and I even dealt with a delivery of those handmade chocolates you stock. As soon as we got them out on the shelves, we sold four boxes of the new Christmas flavours you've been carrying."

"Those have been popular this year. I'm glad they're selling well, because they're pretty pricey."

"People will always pay for good quality items." Lesley glanced at the clock on the wall and then pointed to the door. "It's five o'clock, which means we're officially done for the day. Millie, will you be a saint and turn the sign over to 'Closed'?"

Happy to oblige, Millie flipped the sign over.

"Thank you, dear."

"I'll take care of closing up," Adam told his mother. "You've done enough today already."

"Fair enough. I'll get my coat and bag. Your father and I are going round to see the Gibsons tonight to enjoy a festive glass of wine, and I don't want to end up running late."

Lesley turned for the back shop to fetch her coat and jacket, returning a moment later. "That reminds me, Adam. We're having our annual family Christmas get-together on Sunday evening. I haven't mentioned it before now because I know you've been preoccupied with thinking about today and getting through it so you can finally put Heidi and the wedding behind you. However, the day's nearly over and I can see by your face that you've got through it better than you expected to, and that pleases me no end. And so, I'm letting you know our little party is happening on Sunday and that I hope you'll be there."

"Uh, Mum..."

"And before you say you can't make it, I'm telling you that you can," Lesley interrupted, her tone firm. "The shop will be closed for the day by the time all the guests arrive, and everyone will be pleased to see you. All the aunts and uncles will be there and many of the cousins, and some of the great aunts are making the effort to come along, too. Your cousin Ted is even driving great aunt Joy here all the way from Gloucester and then taking her home again afterwards, because she was looking forward to seeing everyone gathered together and insists that at her age she doesn't have much time left, although we all know she's been saying that for years and that she's as strong as a horse. But no matter, she'd love to see you and I told her you'd be there, so you'd better turn up, and that's an end to the matter."

"All right, I'll be there," Adam said, laughing as his mother's harangue finally ceased. "You'll give yourself a funny turn if you keep scolding me like that."

"Pfft." Lesley waved off his comment and turned to Millie.

"Do you have plans for Sunday evening, Millie? If not, I insist you come along to our little get-together."

"Thanks, that's very kind, but it sounds like a family thing, and..."

"And nothing," Lesley interrupted. "You've helped put a smile on my son's face today, and after what happened with that unspeakable ex-fiancé of his, I wasn't sure that was possible. The least I can do is invite you to our house for a glass of fizzy wine and a sausage roll. Come for five-thirty. Adam will give you our address."

It was obvious that Lesley wasn't prepared to take no for an answer, but Millie still felt uncomfortable about accepting the invitation. The party was a family event, and she wasn't family. Knowing what she did about Adam's recent difficulties interacting with family and friends following the cancellation of his wedding, she wasn't sure if he would even turn up at the party, or if he was just telling his mother what she wanted to hear right now in order to have an easy life.

Millie glanced towards Adam, hoping for a cue. Seeing her uncertainty, he gave an encouraging smile.

"If I'm going to this thing, you'd better be there to keep me company," he said.

"All right. In that case, thanks Lesley, for the invitation. I'm looking forward to it."

"Good. Right, I'm off home. See you both later."

Once Lesley had left, Millie turned to Adam. "I'm glad you agreed to go along to your mother's Christmas party. Judging by the look on her face, you made her day."

"I can't hide away forever like some hermit. Turning up to this Christmas thing might be a good way to show my face around family and start getting back to normal. Plus, there'll be lots of people there, and a lot of catching up happening amongst folk who haven't seen each other for a while, which might mean there won't be as much interest in my tale of wedding woe."

"Will Angela be there?"

Adam shoved his hands in his pockets and looked sombre. "I'd imagine so. Maybe that will make it easier to start talking again. I'm not ready for some big sit down heart-to-heart discussion about what happened. My mother's party might help break the ice and start the thaw."

"That's exactly what I was thinking when I asked my father if he'd like to meet for a quick coffee, and… Oh, I just remembered! I'm meeting my dad on Sunday at five. Your mother took me by surprise with her party invitation and I forgot I already had plans."

"Don't worry about it. I'm sure she'll understand."

"Sorry I won't be there."

"It's fine. And these Christmas get-togethers of my mother's usually last until about nine in the evening, so you could always drop by after you've had coffee with your dad. Here, I'll give you my parents' address and then you have it in case you're able to come along for a bit." He scribbled on a piece of notepaper on the shop counter and handed it to her. "Just send me a text if you can drop by."

As Millie tucked the piece of paper into her pocket, her phone rang. When she looked at the screen, she saw the call was from her supervisor at the care home. She answered the phone.

"I'll have to go, I'm afraid," Millie said a few moments later after the call ended. "One of the care assistants has fallen unwell at work and they've had to send her home. They need someone to cover the rest of her shift and they wondered if I could do it. They sound desperate, and as I'm not doing anything else tonight, I said I'd go in and help."

"I'll drive you over there," Adam said.

"No need. They're sending a taxi to pick me up. Like I

said, they're desperate, and it sounds like it's all hands on deck. By the time I get home and grab my uniform, the taxi will be there."

"Let me drive you home, then."

"You've got your shop to close up. Honestly, it'll take me five minutes to get home. I'd better hurry, though, so I'll see you later, okay?"

"Millie, wait!"

Before she could open the shop door, Adam was at her side. "Thanks again for today. It really helped a lot."

"Good. And I had a fun day, too. Thanks for driving us up there."

"My pleasure."

"See you soon?"

"See you soon, yeah."

Millie hurried back to her flat to grab her uniform and prepare for an unexpected few hours of work at the care home. She was glad she had an excuse to leave and turn down Adam's offer to drive her back. Today had been a good day, and they'd had fun together, even although Adam had struggled with the weight of the wedding day that never was. She'd liked knowing she'd maybe helped him with that struggle and helped him through a tough day, and she especially liked the idea that she might have helped him find the clarity he needed when it came to his troubled relationship with his sister.

What she *didn't* like was the way her heart had hammered inside her chest when Adam had pulled her into that hug back in Stratford. They were only supposed to be friends. Friends didn't feel their hearts do somersaults the way hers had when Adam had held her close.

Something had changed today and Millie didn't like it. She found it hard enough making and keeping friends, and developing a crush on Adam was the last thing she wanted. Without doubt, it would be the last thing Adam wanted, too.

She'd just helped the man get through what should have been his wedding day, for God's sakes. Adam didn't have a single emotional marble in his head right now. He was still smarting from his fiancé's betrayal, still embarrassed by the humiliation of his broken engagement and cancelled wedding, still grieving for the married life he thought he'd been about to begin. He could never feel anything for her beyond the friendship they already shared, and she *knew* that.

Her head buzzing with these thoughts, Millie focused instead on picking up her pace so she could get back to her flat, grab her uniform, and be ready for the taxi to pick her up and whisk her off to the care home. A few busy hours of work was just what she needed to keep herself distracted.

CHAPTER FOURTEEN

The last Hollyford Christmas Village event to take place in the village hall was on Sunday afternoon, the day before Christmas Eve, and Millie and Doris Wishmore were there to lend a hand.

Following the debacles caused by the tree bauble decorating and gingerbread men icing events, Millie was relieved to discover that this last event involved nothing more messy than some Christmas colouring-in for the children. While festive music played in the background, children sat hunched around the trestle tables, colouring the specially designed sheets featuring Santa Claus, snowmen, North Pole elves, reindeer, presents, and other Christmassy scenes. With only crayons, pencils and felt-tip pens available for the little artists, there was no danger of any horrible spillages or sticky messes that would need clearing up at the end of the event. Even the festive snack table where parents and children were enjoying drinks, mince pies, cake, and chocolate once their colouring work was finished had remained incident-free.

For that, Millie was very grateful. Much as she'd loved

helping with these events, she didn't want her volunteering time extended on account of an unexpected mass clean-up operation in order to keep Terry the grumpy custodian happy. Today was the day she was meeting her father for coffee and for a chance to rekindle their relationship, and she didn't want to be late.

The Christmas Village colouring-in event was scheduled to end at four-thirty, and Millie glanced at her watch for what felt like the millionth time.

"You seem distracted today, Millie," Mrs Wishmore said as she tidied the pen and pencil pots on the table following the departure of a young family who'd finished their colouring fun. "Is there something on your mind?"

"I'm meeting my dad for coffee after we're finished here," she said. "I'm a little nervous about it."

A look of understanding crossed Doris's face. "Of course, that's today, isn't it? But I'm sure there's no reason for you to be nervous."

"This will be the first time we've got together like this since I was a little girl. I was so excited at the idea of meeting up that I didn't stop to think about what I'd actually say to him once I saw him. Given how useless I am in social situations, I'm nervous and worried that I won't be able to think of anything to say at all."

"That won't happen. When the time comes, you'll both know what to say to one another. And you must stop telling yourself that you're no good in social interactions, Millie. I've thoroughly enjoyed all our little chats since we met and haven't found you in the least bit awkward."

"Thanks, Doris. I appreciate that."

"And even if you do run out of things to talk about with your father, you can always ask about his Christmas Day plans and perhaps share something about your own plans for the big day, too. That seems like easy conversational terrain."

"Hmm, that's a good idea."

Doris tilted her head and narrowed her eyes. "Do you have plans for Christmas Day, Millie?"

"I offered to work at the care home on Christmas Day, so that the staff with children can spend time at home with their families. The care home puts on a big dinner for the residents, along with party games and other fun stuff, and I'm looking forward to being there with everyone."

"That's very generous of you to offer to work on the big day. And I'm sure your father will enjoy hearing about your job at the care home and what it involves. That's another thing you can chat about together."

Millie smiled. "Thanks, Doris. Maybe I should write all this down so I don't get flustered when I see him and forget all these ideas for things to talk about."

But Doris waved this off. "He's your father and you're his daughter. The two of you have agreed to meet and start getting to know one another, which means you're both committed to getting past any initial awkwardness. Once you're both settled with a cup of coffee and the greetings and formalities are out of the way, I'm sure you'll both find your rhythm and will soon get on like a house on fire."

Millie hoped so, but as the time ticked by, her nerves only jangled more and more. It felt like an age passed before Evelyn Fox finally appeared at the front of the village hall to declare the Christmas Village colouring-in event over and thank everyone for coming along. By the time the volunteers had packed up the crayons and pens, tidied away the chairs and tables, and swept the floor, there were only ten minutes to go before Millie met her father.

"I hope this first get-together with your dad goes well," Doris said as they left the village hall together. "I know you're nervous, but I think everything will be fine."

"Thanks, Doris. I hope you're right."

At the edge of the market square, Mrs Wishmore turned to Millie and smiled. "I'll say goodbye here, as I'm heading off to the bus stop. I'll see you tomorrow afternoon for the final Christmas carol sing-along of the season?"

Millie nodded. As she was working on Christmas Day, the care home manager had insisted she take Christmas Eve off instead, which meant she was free to help with the last Christmas Village event of the year—a carol sing-along in the market square—although she already knew there wouldn't be a great deal of work to do for it. The Christmas Village committee had decided against offering hot drinks or snacks for their last event, in order to keep the organisation and work involved to a minimum. There would be a stall selling the Christmas sweetie bags that Millie and Doris had helped put together earlier in the month, and there would be song sheets to hand out to the visitors who'd come to join in with the singing, but there would be no other demands placed on the Christmas Village volunteers. Instead, everyone who'd helped with so many tasks throughout the month would be able to relax and enjoy singing Christmas carols while gathered around the Christmas tree in the company of their family, friends, and neighbours, before heading home to start their own festive celebrations.

It was set to be a lovely way to wrap up this year's Hollyford Christmas Village.

"I can't believe our Christmas Village volunteering is almost over," Millie said. "It feels like December has flown by."

"I've had fun taking part in all the activities. And I've certainly enjoyed getting to know you, Millie."

Doris's kind smile touched Millie's heart. "Same here, Doris."

A thoughtful look crossed Doris's face, and she reached out and patted Millie's arm. "I'm sure things will go just fine when you meet your father. But if you'd like someone to talk to afterwards, you know where to find me."

Millie felt a welcome warmth flow through her as Mrs Wishmore patted her arm. The older lady's bright blue eyes held hers for a long moment, and Millie saw endless kindness there.

"Thank you, Doris."

With another smile and a wave goodbye, Mrs Wishmore turned and walked off across the market square. Millie watched her leave, feeling that strange warmth the older lady had somehow imparted seep through her like a soothing balm that calmed her jitters about meeting her father.

Mrs Wishmore had disappeared from view when Millie frowned at something she'd said.

If you'd like someone to talk to afterwards, you know where to find me.

Millie realised with a start that this wasn't true. Despite knowing Doris for several weeks now, she didn't have the older lady's phone number in order to get in touch. She didn't even know where the woman lived. In fact, she knew nothing much about her at all, except that she didn't live in Hollyford—Doris usually caught the bus out of the village after their volunteering work was over—and that she had an unusual fondness for angel trinkets.

This last thought caused Millie to lift her hand to the little angel brooch pinned to her coat, the one Doris had given her several weeks earlier. She ran her fingers over the smooth enamel of the angel's billowing gown and the curve of her graceful wings.

You know where to find me.

Millie heard these words in her head—heard Doris saying them, loud and clear. She couldn't tell whether she was imagining Doris saying them, or whether…

Or whether they were being spoken from afar by the

mysterious older lady? Was that really what she was wondering? Mrs Wishmore might come across as a bit of a strange bird sometimes, but she wasn't telepathic, for crying out loud.

Millie dropped her hand from the angel brooch and let out a sigh. This coffee meet-up with her father was playing havoc with her ability to think clearly. Checking her watch, she shook off the funny thoughts she'd just had about Doris Wishmore and started walking to the café where she'd agreed to meet her father.

Derek was driving all the way down from Birmingham to see her, and she didn't want to keep him waiting.

THE CAFÉ on the corner just off the high street was busy as Millie sat at a window table, nursing a latte and waiting for her father to arrive.

As she sipped her drink and glanced around, she recognised a few faces from people who'd attended the Christmas colouring-in event at the village hall, now treating their children to hot drinks and cookies to round out their festive fun day. There were lots of shoppers too, comparing things they'd bought at the Hollyford shops during their visit.

She even saw one shopper showing off a piece of framed artwork that Millie recognised as coming from Adam's gift shop, from the collection on display from the artist in Stow-on-the-Wold. It was the same painting Millie had admired the day she'd met Adam for the first time, and he'd shown her the inventory he'd gone there to bring back with him. The new owner of the artwork was clearly thrilled with the painting depicting the bucolic Cotswold scene, and her coffee companion looked downright envious not to have snapped the piece up for herself, which Millie could understand only too well because it was a beautiful painting, and…

Millie sighed, knowing she could only distract herself like this for so much longer before someone took umbrage and told her to stop being nosy and mind her own business and stop gawping at all the other café customers, but she couldn't help it. Glancing at her watch, she saw her father was over half an hour late.

The longer she waited, the more her excitement turned into anxiety.

She checked her phone, hoping he'd sent a message to say he'd been caught in traffic or held up for some other reason. But there were no messages waiting on her phone.

Picking up her mug, she discovered she'd almost finished the extra-large coffee she'd purchased when she arrived. Should she buy another drink or wait for her father to turn up first?

Over at the café counter, the staff began pulling the left-over cakes and treats from the display case and wiping down the shelves. It would be closing time soon, and some of the other customers were already gathering their bags and preparing to leave.

Millie checked the time yet again. Derek was almost forty minutes late now.

This wasn't how she'd thought the afternoon would go. She'd imagined sitting here at the table, peering out of the café window, and seeing her father appear across the street. Maybe he'd be parking his car and he'd glance up and see her, before giving a friendly wave and hurrying into the café where he'd say hello and pull her into a hug and tell her how glad he was that she'd got in touch and asked to see him. They'd be shy at first, making polite conversation, but things would soon thaw and they'd start talking like a real father and daughter would talk, and she'd feel nothing but happiness at the prospect of starting a new relationship with the father she'd never known…

Was that nothing but a stupid and naïve daydream? Was that the reason she was still sitting here alone in this café?

But Derek had agreed to meet her. They'd set the time and the place.

So, where was he?

Her phone pinged and Derek's name flash up on the screen alongside a new message, and Millie felt an awful sinking sensation in the pit of her stomach.

Derek (Dad): Sorry I can't make it for coffee today after all. Maybe some other time instead? Drop me a message in the new year and we'll try again.

Millie stared at the phone, reading the message over and over. The words on the screen blurred into one another as tears pricked at her eyes.

He wasn't coming. After so long spent debating with herself whether she ought to contact her father, and then summoning the courage to invite him to meet for coffee, and then swallowing her nerves and coming here to the café to wait for him to arrive… after all that, he wasn't coming after all.

She'd sat here for all this time, staring out of the window, wondering what might have caused Derek to run late. But he hadn't been running late. He'd never been on his way here in the first place.

As Millie pushed back from the table and turned for the café doors, she wondered if he'd ever intended coming to meet her at all. Had he just accepted her invitation, knowing he'd never turn up? Did he think she didn't care one way or another whether they met for coffee? Derek might not care—clearly, he *didn't* care—but Millie cared. The pain of the rejection was much sharper than she could have imagined.

Stepping out into the chilly night air, she fought the tears that were threatening to fall. She'd been a fool all along, imagining it was possible for them to have a relationship when they were no more than strangers to each other. Biologically, they might be father and daughter, but that counted for nothing without a meaningful relationship to back it up.

What hurt the most, Millie realised as she walked along the street, head down, was the casual tone of Derek's text. *Can't make it after all... maybe some other time?* Had he no conception of what it had cost her to reach out to him? Of course he didn't, because he'd never reached out to her, not once, to try to forge some kind of relationship between them. She didn't matter to him, and she'd always known that, because if she'd mattered, he would have been there in her life all along.

But Derek had barely been a blip on the radar before her mother died, and after Caroline's passing, she'd had nothing but a few brief texts from the man. Not once in the year since her mother died had he asked if she wanted to meet, talk, get to know each other. He'd come to Caroline's funeral, and that was all he'd done—he hadn't hugged Millie, hadn't embraced her, hadn't even asked if she was okay or if she needed anything. He'd sent a couple of text messages later, but so what? A quick, *Hello, how are you?* and the occasional *Hi, hope you're okay?* didn't count for much.

Actually, it didn't count for anything. She'd grabbed onto those brief messages and held them close because she'd wanted them to mean something, wanted them to mean she was connected to someone she could count as family. But the flippant and casual tone of Derek's message just now made it clear that those exchanges had meant nothing at all.

Millie wished she'd never suggested they meet for coffee. It had been a non-starter from the very beginning, and now she felt sad and alone and rejected. She'd been doing fine until she'd got the stupid idea into her head to reconnect with her father, and now she felt awful.

Still walking, her thoughts swirling, she found herself back on the edge of the market square. The Christmas tree was twinkling softly, and it looked so magical and festive, and yet it failed to lift her spirits. The idea of returning to her shared flat held no appeal, either; her flatmate was out for the evening and Millie didn't want to be by herself. She already felt lonely enough after Derek's no-show.

Remembering Mrs Wishmore's kind comments earlier, before they went their separate ways, she wished she had some way to contact her new friend. Doris would have some words of comfort for her, Millie was sure of it, and she cursed herself for not getting the older lady's phone number before now. It was such a stupid oversight.

Standing on the edge of the market square, Millie felt sadness and loneliness pushing down on her like a dead weight. Along with both came a hot spear of loss for her mother.

In that moment, she missed her mother so much. More than ever, she needed her mother's comforting arms around her, needed her unwavering love and support.

Instead, she was alone on the edge of Hollyford market square, wondering what do to next, wondering who to turn to for comfort.

A thought flashed in her head. Tonight was the night of Adam's mother's Christmas party. Millie had turned down the invitation because she was supposed to meet her father for coffee, and had told Adam to explain to Lesley how sorry she was to miss it. Now, she wondered if she could still turn up, after all. Checking her watch, she saw the get-together had probably only just got underway in the last half hour.

The idea of being with Adam this evening was impossible to resist. He was her friend, and she needed a friend right now. More than that, she needed the company of people to drive away these lonely blues. It wasn't easy for her to seek out company and set aside her natural shyness, but that's what her heart told her to do.

Adam's mother, Lesley, had been nothing other than friendly anytime she'd met her, and Millie doubted that she'd mind her turning up at the party after she'd asked Adam to let her know she couldn't make it.

Adam had given her his parents' home address already, when she'd first agreed to go along to the party. Rummaging in her pocket, she found the scribbled note he'd given her and checked the location. The Carters' house was only a ten-minute walk across Hollyford.

Cheered by the idea of popping in to spend time with Adam and his family at their Christmas get-together, Millie started walking again. After stopping at a mini-supermarket on the way to buy a bottle of wine so she didn't turn up empty handed, she picked up her pace.

The evening hadn't gone the way she'd hoped it would. But as Millie had already discovered during those dark days between her mother's cancer diagnosis and death, things often didn't go the way you hoped they would. Life could be that way sometimes. What mattered was that you put on a brave face and kept going.

Her father failing to turn up to meet her for coffee was nothing compared to everything else she'd been through and survived during this past year. Derek had never been in her life, and she couldn't miss something she'd never had. Yes, it hurt that he'd failed to turn up, and yes it hurt that he hadn't even bothered to tell her he wasn't coming until it was so late, and yes it hurt that her attempt to forge a relationship between them both had been met with a shrug of the shoulders on Derek's part when it came to putting in the effort.

But thinking about all of that only made her eyes smart

with tears she refused to shed, and so Millie straightened her shoulders, tucked the bottle of wine she'd bought under her arm, and set off for the Carter family Christmas party.

Her friend Adam would be there, and seeing him would make everything feel much better—she was sure of it.

CHAPTER FIFTEEN

Adam pulled a tray of hot sausage rolls from the oven and transferred them to a plate on the counter. Beyond the kitchen door, his parents' Christmas get-together was in full swing, the house filled with chatter and laughter and festive music. He'd said hello to the aunts and uncles, been hugged to within an inch of his life by some distant relative of his mother's who he'd failed to recognise, and promised to have a drink and a catch-up with a cousin on his father's side before the evening was over.

For the first fifteen minutes of hustle and bustle as guests arrived at the house and shed their coats and said hello and dished out drink requests, it had all gone fine. Adam was happy to run around on behalf of his mother, dealing with the cloakroom and ferrying wine and beer and snacks through from the kitchen and making polite chit-chat with everyone.

And then one of the ancient great aunts had grabbed him to commiserate over his broken engagement and cancelled wedding, and although the old dear meant well as she pontificated about how awful Heidi was to have left him and how he was better off without her and how sure she was that there was someone else out there for him, her words had sent Adam into a cold sweat of embarrassment. The small gathering of relatives who'd congregated around the two of them to nod in agreement with the great aunt before peering expectantly at Adam to see what he'd have to say about the whole thing had left him tongue-tied and blushing furiously.

He'd fled to the kitchen, claiming he needed to rescue his mother's sausage rolls before they burned. For the past ten minutes, he'd been hiding there, pretending to be busy dishing up the food. When his mother appeared and scolded him for not mixing with the guests, he'd promised to get back out there just as soon as the next batch of mini quiches were warmed through, but it remained to be seen whether he'd actually do what he'd said he would.

Adam knew it was stupid to attend a family Christmas party and then hide from everyone in the kitchen. He couldn't expect people to pretend his wedding hadn't been cancelled, and it stood to reason they'd want to say something supportive to him about it. The best course of action was to smile and nod, and maybe make some lame joke about the whole thing before turning the conversation to something else instead.

Yeah, the whole wedding thing. What a fiasco that turned out to be! I had a lucky escape in the end, not quite ready for the old ball and chain just yet! So, what are you up to over the Christmas holidays, Auntie Belinda? Do you have any big plans lined up?

The sooner he started mingling again out there, the more relaxed he'd feel. The more relaxed he felt, the more likely he'd be able to talk to his sister, Angela, when she turned up, and that's all that mattered. That's why he'd come here, after all, to see his sister while surrounded by lots of people, so they could kick off the process of just talking to each other again before jumping into the deeper waters of mending things properly between the two of them.

The door swung open on a loud wave of chatter and laughter from the hallway, and Lesley walked into the kitchen.

"There's someone here to see you," she said. "That young friend of yours, Millie, just arrived." She held up a bottle of wine. "She brought this with her as a gift. Isn't that nice?"

Adam blinked in surprise. He'd thought his mother was about to say that Angela had arrived and he was expected to get out there and talk to her and start behaving like a proper grown-up. Hearing that it was Millie who was here caught him unawares.

"I thought she was seeing her father tonight?" Adam frowned.

Lesley shrugged. "You'd better get out there and say hello to the poor girl before one of the great aunts gets hold of her and starts interrogating her about who she is and how she's related to everyone."

Adam followed his mother out of the kitchen and found Millie in the living room, accepting a glass of orange juice from his father, who'd taken over the barman duties. When she saw him crossing the room towards her, she smiled.

"Hi, Millie," Adam said. "I didn't think you could make it tonight. Weren't you seeing your dad?"

"Ah, there was a change of plan," Millie said.

Adam thought he saw an odd glint in her eye as she spoke, but before he could say anything else, Adam's father thrust a glass of juice into his hand.

"Here you go, son," Roger said. "The key to these shindigs of your mother's is to stay hydrated, or else it's impossible to keep on top of the ten thousand conversations that are happening all at the same time."

"Thanks, Dad."

"Millie was just telling me about the volunteering work she's been doing with the Christmas Village committee," Roger said. "It sounds like a full-time job, if you ask me."

"Not far off it," Millie laughed. "But it's been a lot of fun, too. Have you gone along to any of the events, Mr Carter?"

"I'm sorry to say I haven't."

"Well, there's still time. There's a Christmas carol sing-along in the market square tomorrow evening. Perhaps you and Mrs Carter would enjoy it."

"Perhaps we would." Roger wiggled his eyebrows. "Although don't let Lesley hear you calling her Mrs Carter. She says it reminds her of my mother and makes her feel old."

"Thanks for the tip."

Adam grinned at Millie and his father as the two of them shared a laugh. His dad always knew how to make people feel at ease, and he'd clearly done that already with Millie, even although she'd only arrived a few minutes ago. Remembering all that Millie had told him about her awkwardness when she found herself in unfamiliar social settings, Adam was glad his father had helped her feel welcome.

"Shall we get you some party food?" Adam asked Millie. "If you don't grab a plate soon, the cousins and uncles will polish off the lot and it'll be another ten minutes before the next batch of snacks come out of the oven."

"Thanks, that sounds good."

Adam steered Millie towards the table in the dining room where the food was laid out.

"I'm glad you could make it tonight after all," he said.

"Me too. It looks like a fun party."

Adam gave a wry grin. "Well, so far, the conversation has been mostly about my doomed wedding and great aunt Felicity's bunions, but we'll agree to disagree on our definitions of fun."

Millie laughed softly at that. He was passing her a plate and pointing out the various snacks spread across the dining table when someone tapped him on the shoulder.

"Hi, Adam. Long time, no see."

When he turned, he saw Angela.

After so long spent avoiding his sister, the sight of her right next to him came as a shock. She'd cut her hair short since the last time he saw her, and dyed it a lighter colour, too, making her face look completely different. For a moment, he just stared.

Adam couldn't think of a single thing to say to her. It had been too long and yet not long enough since they'd been together in the same room. She was his sister, but the space between them felt more vast than ever. He wanted to say something, but couldn't get his mouth to work.

"Um, merry Christmas," Angela said, looking at him from beneath hooded eyelids and not quite meeting his gaze. She was struggling with this whole mess just as much as he was.

"Yeah, merry Christmas." Clearing his throat, he turned to Millie, clocking the look she was giving him. She was no doubt wondering how he planned to handle this big step he'd told her only a few days ago he was keen to take. "Millie, this is my sister, Angela. Angela, this is my friend, Millie. She just moved to Hollyford a few months ago."

"Hi, nice to meet you, Millie," Angela said with a warm smile.

"You, too. This is a lovely party your parents have put on."

"Yeah, it's a nice chance for the family to get together." Angela gave Adam a pointed look as she said this. "How have you been, Adam? Have you been doing okay?"

He couldn't help but scowl at her question. The old, familiar anger rose before he could stop it in its tracks. "I've been brilliant, Angela. Just fantastic," he said, sarcasm dripping from every word.

Angela dropped her gaze, and beside him, Millie drew in a sharp breath.

"I thought about you on your, um… well, on the day that would have been the wedding day," Angela said. "I almost phoned to see how you were, but Mum said you went out for the day and that I should just leave it and let you have the time away."

"She was right," Adam said.

He knew he had to do better than this. He *knew* it. But every time he looked at his sister, all he could think about was how she'd known about Heidi's betrayal for all those long days before he had, and how she'd kept it from him. No matter what he did, he couldn't shove those thoughts from his head.

"I'm glad to see you now," Angela said, smiling and obviously keen to persevere despite his bad attitude.

His sister was trying to connect with him, and he was offering surly grunts in response. Millie scowled at him, no doubt appalled by his behaviour. Chastened by her expression, he offered his sister as much of a smile as he could muster, and thought of the snowman scarf he'd bought for Angela during his visit to Stratford upon Avon.

He'd bought that scarf because his sister loved snowmen. How could he be angry at a person who loved snowmen?

"Glad to see you too, Angela," Adam muttered at last.

Angela's eyes lit up at the small morsel he'd offered. As she sipped her drink, a thought seemed to occur to her, and her face grew animated.

"Hey, Adam, do you remember when Mum held this Christmas party for the first time, and we were, what, eleven and twelve? And we hid under the dining table all evening eating those mini chocolate cakes and we both ended up as sick as dogs and—"

"I'm sorry, Angela, I can't do this."

Before he even realised he was doing it, Adam turned and left the room as a terrible mixture of resentment, anger, and humiliation roared inside his head. No matter how hard he tried to hold onto good thoughts about making amends and moving on, no matter how much he clung to those desperate thoughts about the snowman scarf he'd bought and how he'd done it because he wanted his sister back in his life again where she belonged, all the old familiar hurt and embarrassment rose up inside his heart to claim him.

Pushing through the relatives gathered in the hallway, Adam hurried to the kitchen and escaped through the back door. Outside in the cold night air, he closed his eyes and took a deep breath.

A moment later, he heard the back door open again and heard footsteps hit the patio paving. He expected it to be Angela who'd followed him outside, but when he looked around, it was Millie he saw standing there in a pool of light thrown out from the kitchen.

"What was that?" she said, her tone frothing with irritation. "Your sister was trying to talk to you, trying to make an effort, and you just walked out on her."

"I couldn't help it. I had to get out of there."

"What are you talking about? When were in Stratford, you said you wanted to patch things up between the two of you. You said you wanted to start talking to Angela again and move on from all of this."

"I know what I said."

"So, why aren't you in there talking to her and sorting this out?"

"Seeing Angela again after all these weeks of avoiding her was harder than I thought it would be. I tried, but…"

When he tailed off, feeling stupid and foolish, Millie's gaze hardened.

"It didn't look to me like you tried at all, Adam. You barely said a word to her."

"Look, you don't know what it's like to have your own flesh and blood make a fool of you the way Angela made a fool of me."

Millie's hard stare wavered then. She shook her head and gave a sad shrug. "You have no idea what you're talking about, Adam. And you have no idea how lucky you are, either. There's an entire army of family inside that house who are there for you. Your sister wants to make up for her mistake and be part of your life again, but you turned your back on her, and…"

Adam heard Millie's voice catch, saw her gulp and draw in a deep breath.

"She put herself on the line to make things up to you, Adam, and you repaid her by walking away. You should be ashamed of yourself."

A distraught look flashed across her face before she turned and fled back into the house. Adam stood stunned, staring at the open door and feeling the force of her disappointment in him, and anger at him, hit him squarely in the chest.

What had just happened? They might still be getting to know each other, but Adam thought it was out of character for Millie to become so upset about something that wasn't even any of her business, if he was putting it bluntly.

He hadn't handled seeing Angela again the way he would've liked to. But did Millie really have to flip out at him about it?

Puzzled, Adam remembered the coffee she'd arranged with her father tonight, and the way she'd brushed him off when he'd asked about it. A sinking feeling hit him as he wondered if there was more going on with Millie than he'd realised.

Adam hurried back towards the house, wanting to find Millie before she left. But he'd barely made it into the kitchen before Angela appeared and pushed him back outside into the dark garden.

"We need to talk," she said.

"Now isn't a good time, Angela," he said, and made to move around her.

"I don't care if it's a good time or not. This has gone on long enough and we need to sort it out."

"Angela—"

"Adam, I'm sorry. I'm so, so sorry."

Her words stopped him, forced him to look his sister in the eye for the first time since that ill-fated night when he'd told his family that Heidi had been cheating on him and their wedding was cancelled, and Angela had floored him all over again by admitting she already knew the whole awful story.

Now, as he looked into his sister's eyes, he saw deep hurt and raw regret. All the self-righteous anger he'd cloaked himself in just a moment ago dissolved at the sight of Angela's obvious misery.

"I'm so sorry I didn't tell you that Heidi was cheating the moment I found out about it," Angela said, her voice shaking. "I made a terrible mistake and I hurt you, but I didn't mean to."

Tears glistened in her eyes as she looked straight at him. Chatter and laughter floated through the open door from the house, along with the Christmas music Adam's mother was playing on the stereo. Lyrics from *The Christmas Song* lingered in the night air, words that spoke of the hope and joy of the season, and Adam felt a wave of exhaustion wash over him.

He'd held onto his anger for so long and it was time to lay it down to rest. He *wanted* to lay it down to rest.

But one question still burned like an angry fire in his heart.

"Why didn't you tell me, Angela? I don't understand why you left me in the dark. How could you go around for an entire week, knowing what you knew, knowing Heidi was about to leave me for someone else, and yet you didn't say a single word? I'm your *brother*."

Angela sighed and shrugged, as if she scarcely understood it herself. "Heidi said she planned to tell you she'd been seeing someone else, and that she was leaving you for him. She told me she'd tell you right away. When she didn't actually do that, I thought..." Another head shake as she waved a hand in the air. "I thought she'd changed her mind. I thought she'd decided to stay with you and get married, after all."

Adam blinked, trying to process this as a frown burrowed across his forehead. "You would've let me marry someone who you knew had been unfaithful to me? Who you knew had almost left me for someone else?"

"No, of course not!" she cried. "But as the days went past, and Heidi obviously still hadn't said anything, I didn't have the first idea how to tell you what I knew. Should I just blurt it out, tell you I'd seen her in a pub with some bloke and that she'd come clean and told me she was having an affair and planned to call off the wedding, but somehow hadn't quite got around to telling you yet? I knew it would crush you, Adam. I knew how much you loved Heidi and that I'd be crushing you if I told you what I knew. I hated having to be the person who had to bring your whole world crashing down."

She paused for breath, her expression pained. "But I knew that's what I had to do, Adam. I knew I had to tell you. I had no idea what Heidi was up to, or when she was going to tell you the truth, and so I knew I had to do it instead. A couple of days after Heidi told me what she was up to behind your back, I came over to your shop to speak to you before you closed up for the day. I was on the street outside the shop, about to walk inside, when a horrible thought occurred to me."

When Angela stopped talking and closed her eyes, Adam couldn't help wondering what she was about to say and why it was so difficult to get out. "Go on," he said softly.

Angela opened her eyes and sighed. "It had been days since I spoke to Heidi. *Days*. Why hadn't she already told you what was going on? Why hadn't she come clean? I was standing outside your shop with my hand on the door when it suddenly struck me—maybe Heidi *had* already told you everything."

When she didn't say anything further, Adam could only stare in bafflement. "I don't understand."

"I thought maybe Heidi had told you everything, and you'd... decided to forgive her." Angela's voice was a whisper as she said this. "For all I knew, Heidi had come clean. Maybe you'd had a huge argument, but somehow you'd both decided to work things out. She'd decided not to leave, you'd decided to forgive her and go ahead with the wedding."

"Are you serious?" Adam almost exploded. "You thought I'd find out about something like that and just, what? Shrug my shoulders, convince Heidi not to leave me and to go ahead with our wedding, and just carry on regardless?"

"When you put it like that, of course not."

"I'm not a doormat, Angela! You really think I'd have so little self-respect that I'd ignore the fact that my fiancé was cheating on me and marry her anyway, as if nothing had happened?"

"I didn't know what to think!" Angela's loud voice now matched his own. "But who knows what goes on inside a relationship, Adam? Couples have private lives that no one outside their relationship ever knows anything about. All I knew was that Heidi had promised to tell you she was seeing someone else and that she wanted to call off your wedding. Days went by and that obviously didn't happen. So, what had happened? Had she changed her mind? Had she cut her losses with this other bloke and decided to stick with you instead? Because if so, then I had to tell you what I knew. But what if she *had* told you what she knew, and you'd reached some kind of... understanding and forgiveness between the two of you, and you wanted to go on as if it had never happened? Would I be making things worse by admitting I knew what Heidi had done? Would you get angry at me and accuse me of stirring things up?"

"I'd never accuse you of that, Angela."

"But I didn't know for sure either way. And I was terrified of jeopardising our relationship by wading into a situation between you and Heidi that I might not fully understand."

She fell silent, and the tortured expression on her face made Adam ache.

"Look, Adam, I know I got it all wrong. When you came round to mum and dad's that night and told us what had happened and that it was all over between you and Heidi, I knew straight away that I should've told you sooner. That's why I came clean right there and then about seeing Heidi in the pub and confronting her. I'd kept Heidi's secret from you and I shouldn't have, and I wasn't about to make it even worse by pretending I hadn't known about it the entire time. Of course, that *did* only make things worse, because you were already devastated and I only added to all that upset."

Waving a hand at nothing, she shrugged at the situation she'd found herself in, a situation Adam now understood had been far more difficult than he'd realised.

"It felt like one betrayal on top of another," Adam said, his voice now devoid of the anger that had burned just moments ago. "But I held onto the resentment for far too long. I couldn't help being angry at the time. It was a lot to take in, maybe too much. But I was wrong to keep ignoring you and avoiding you. And I was wrong to refuse to listen when you tried to explain all of this."

Angela let out a soft sigh and shook her head. "You had to lick your wounds, I understand that. If the situation had been reversed, I honestly don't know how I would've dealt with it. You're my brother and I'd trust you with my life, and if you kept a secret like this one from me, I'd be gutted. That's what I've kept reminding myself, over and over, these past weeks. You were angry and upset, and you were right to be angry and upset. Anyone would be. But I knew I had to give you time to get over the shock of Heidi leaving, and the upset of having to cancel the wedding. Only then would you be able to start thinking about talking to me again."

They stood for a moment in the darkness of the back garden as everything they'd said sank in.

"I haven't handled any of this very well," Adam said. "I'm sorry for being a twat for all this time."

"I'm sorry for messing up and making a terrible judgement call." She studied him for a long second. "Can we get past this?"

A smile ghosted at Adam's mouth. "We'll have to. We're stuck with each other, aren't we?"

At his joke, Angela let out a long breath and laughed. "I guess we are."

"Come here."

Adam pulled her into a hug. She hugged him back, her embrace fierce, then gave him a playful shove.

"Get off me, you daft lump," she laughed and wiped away a stray tear.

"Can we promise each other something? From now on, we don't keep potentially life-changing secrets from each other."

"Promise. But only if you'll promise me something in return."

"What's that?"

"You'll put your Christmas misery behind you and agree to come to mum and dad's for Christmas Day lunch. After everything that's happened, it'll mean the world to them if you're there."

Adam nodded and smiled. "Of course I'll be there. Unless you're cooking the turkey this year, in which case..."

"Cheeky sod," Angela said, and gave him a playful whack.

"Am I the only one who remembers the Great Turkey Incineration from three years ago?"

"You're never going to let me live that down, are you?"

"Never. I'm your brother. It's my job to annoy you."

"And it's a job at which you excel."

It felt good to be back to the old familiar banter they'd once traded so easily. And it felt, too, like a tremendous weight had lifted off Adam's shoulders. Clearing the air with Angela and talking through what had happened left him feeling better than he had in weeks.

"We ought to get back inside the house before we freeze to death," Adam said.

"Good idea. And you've left that friend of yours, Millie, by herself for long enough. She'll be wondering what happened to you."

"Millie!"

Adam could have kicked himself for neglecting Millie for so long. He'd been so caught up in the much-needed heart-to-heart with Angela that he'd lost track of time. Hurrying inside the house, he scanned the rooms where the family guests were chatting and wandering around, but saw no sign of Millie anywhere.

"Dad!" Adam called to his father when he spied him at the buffet table. "Have you seen Millie?"

"She left, son, about ten minutes ago," Roger said as he piled his plate with cocktail sausages. "Said she had to hurry off for something or other. Seemed strange to me as she'd only just arrived."

Adam yanked his phone from his pocket and dialled Millie's number, but after ringing a few times, the call went to the answer service. After leaving a quick message asking her to phone him back, he hung up, then sent a text message to her saying the same thing. He'd upset her by storming off the way he had earlier, but he wanted to speak to her in person before he started explaining all that had happened with his sister. Millie's reaction had given him the kick up the backside he'd needed to move things in the right direction at last, and he wanted to tell her that, face-to-face.

And he also wanted to know why Millie had become so upset tonight. It couldn't just have been about Adam being a twat to his sister and needing called out on it. Something else was going on with Millie, he was sure of it.

Heading out the front door, Adam peered up and down the street outside his parents' house, just in case there was any sign of Millie around, but the street was quiet. She'd left straight after their argument, by the sounds of it, so it was unlikely she'd still be out here on the street. He wondered if he ought to grab his jacket and head into the village centre in search of her, perhaps see if he might catch up with her on her way home, if that's where she was heading.

Or maybe the coffee meet-up with her father had been delayed, and that's where she was now? When she'd arrived at the house and Adam asked her about it, she'd said there was a change of plan. Was that what she'd meant?

"Adam, what are you doing out here in the freezing cold?"

Turning, he saw his mother on the front door step, peering out at him with a confused look on her face.

"Nothing, I was just coming back into the house."

"Good, because I could use some help serving the cakes and desserts."

"No problem."

As he stepped back inside the house, Lesley tilted her head and smiled. "Angela says you two have talked at last?"

He nodded. "That's right."

"Good. It's about time, too."

"I'm sorry, Mum. I'm sorry for taking this so hard and dealing with it all wrong, and I'm sorry for upsetting you and Dad."

But Lesley shook her head. "You and your sister talking to each other again is the best Christmas present your father and I could have hoped for this year."

Adam threw an arm around his mother's shoulders and brushed a kiss across the top of her head. "Does that mean I should return the luxury food hamper I was planning to give you both on Christmas morning?"

"Absolutely not!"

On a rumble of laughter, Lesley shooed him toward the kitchen to help with the party chores. For the first time in far too long, Adam felt like things were starting to feel right in his life again, and that the dark clouds were at last disappearing and letting the light shine down.

CHAPTER SIXTEEN

Millie sat alone on a bench in the market square, wavering on the verge of tears. Not since her mother's death had things seemed so dark, or the world so hard.

After the disappointment of her father's careless message, cancelling the coffee meet-up Millie had been so excited about, all she'd wanted was to cheer herself up by doing something she knew she needed to do but which she always found challenging—seeking out the company of others. Adam, and the Christmas party his family were hosting, had been her refuge. The friendship they'd forged these past weeks brought her solace and hope.

At least it had until tonight, when she'd watched Adam turn his back on his sister and ignore her pleas for forgiveness.

Millie saw a side to Adam tonight she hadn't imagined possible. After everything he'd gone through with Heidi, and all the hurt his ex-fiancé had caused in his life, how could he treat his own sister so cruelly? He had to know the hurt and damage he would cause by throwing Angela's apologies in her face and walking away. Judging by the look on his sister's face, Angela wanted nothing more than to make amends with her brother. By Adam's own admission, the rift between them had caused much heartache in their family, especially for their parents, which was only one of the reasons why he knew it was time to put things right, to talk openly with his sister about what had happened, and begin moving on.

But when Angela had given him the chance to do just that, he'd blown it.

Adam had no idea how lucky he was to have a family who longed to be in his life, who longed to have a close and loving relationship with him, and who only wanted him to be happy.

"He's an idiot!" Millie muttered to herself as she sat on the bench, her outburst startling a passing dog walker who gave her an uncertain look before hurrying away.

Great, now she was turning into the village nutter, frightening the locals while she grumbled incoherently and sat scowling alone in the dark.

She glanced around the market square, hoping she hadn't alarmed any other innocent passers-by, but there was no one else around. She turned her attention to the beautiful Christmas tree in the middle of the square, hoping it would remind her of the hope and joy of the festive season and cheer her up.

But it didn't. Instead, it just made her think about how she was alone, and how, no matter how much she reached out and tried to connect with people and forge new relationships, she still had no one in her life, no one who cared, no one who wanted her.

She pushed back against the self-pity, knowing it did her no good. Last year, she'd promised her mother she'd be happy this Christmas, and that she wouldn't feel sad because Caroline was gone and no longer around to celebrate the season the way they used to. Realising that her mother's absence wasn't even the reason why she felt so sad only made it worse.

Her plan to throw herself into Christmas, make new friends, reconnect with family, and embrace everything that Christmas stood for had all been for naught. After all she'd done to make this season special, she was still alone.

Millie hung her head, hating this heavy, black sadness that was washing over her, but helpless to stop it. As she gazed at the frosty ground beneath her feet, her eye was drawn to the Christmas tree lights reflecting on the shiny enamel of the angel brooch pinned to her coat. Lifting her hand, she ran her fingers along the smooth edge of the angel's wings and sighed.

I wish I didn't feel so sad, Millie thought. *And I wish I wasn't so alone.*

No sooner had the thought fluttered through her head than a shadow fell across the ground at her feet.

"Hello, Millie. Mind if I join you?"

She looked up to see Mrs Wishmore standing beside the bench, a kind smile on her face, her blue eyes shining. The Christmas tree lights shone behind the older lady, wreathing her in a warm glow.

"Doris, what are you doing here? I thought you caught the bus home ages ago?"

"I planned to," she replied, and gave Millie a mysterious look. "But then I thought better of it."

Mrs Wishmore sat down beside her, and in one fluid move, took Millie's hand into hers. At the older lady's touch, Millie felt a wave of warmth and love flow through her and the comfort of it brought tears to her eyes.

"It's all right, dear," Doris said quietly. "It's all right."

Millie's tears fell then, and the weight of everything that

had happened tonight—her father's no-show, her argument with Adam—came crashing down around her heart.

"Oh, Doris," she whispered, and laid her head on Mrs Wishmore's shoulder. "I wish..." Her voice cracked and she couldn't say any more.

"It's all right, dear," Doris said once more, squeezing her hand. "Just let it all out."

Mrs Wishmore's words brought forth the hitching sob Millie had been fighting against. As the Christmas tree lights twinkled in the dark market square, Millie cried, her head buried against Mrs Wishmore's strong shoulder.

She cried for her mother. She cried for the life she'd lost when Caroline died. She cried for the friends and family she feared she'd never have. She cried for the Christmas hope that had fled from her heart.

Mrs Wishmore held her close through every tear and wracking sob, as the Christmas tree lights twinkled and the stars wheeled across the dark December sky.

At last, Millie sniffed and wiped her eyes. Reaching into her pocket, Mrs Wishmore handed her a crisp, white handkerchief. Unfolding it, Millie wasn't in the least surprised to find an angel design stitched at the corner. With a half-laugh, half-sob, she dried her cheeks and wiped her nose.

"Thank you, Doris."

"My pleasure, dear."

Folding the damp handkerchief, Millie was about to hand it back to Doris when she noticed the streaks of mascara on the fabric and the snotty edge where she'd blown her nose. When she caught Doris's wry grin and arched eyebrow, she couldn't help but laugh.

"You keep that handkerchief," Doris said. "I won't be needing it back."

Tucking the sodden hanky into her pocket, Millie

laughed, but her expression turned serious as she found herself wondering about something.

"It's strange that you found me here, just when I needed a shoulder to cry on," Millie said.

Doris gave her a curious smile. "It's not so strange at all."

The older lady's gaze dropped to the angel brooch pinned to Millie's jacket. Millie remembered how she'd brushed her fingers against the brooch just a few seconds before Doris appeared and remembered how she'd wished that she wasn't so sad and alone.

She'd touched the angel brooch. She'd made a wish. Mrs Wishmore had appeared.

Millie turned to Doris, feeling a swirling mixture of confusion wrapped around a spark of understanding. Touching the brooch once more, a bolt of something pure and wonderful and *good* rushed through her, filling her up from her fingers to her toes.

Her gaze wide, she looked at Mrs Wishmore, really looked at her. Behind her bright blue eyes, Millie saw wisdom that was older than the universe, and love beyond all understanding, and kindness so deep it could fill the oceans a thousand times and more.

"Who are you, Mrs Wishmore?" Millie said, her voice a whisper. "*What* are you?"

Doris laughed softly at the question, but inside Millie's head she heard the older lady's voice strong and clear, even although Mrs Wishmore uttered no words at all.

You already know who I am. In your heart, you've always known.

Millie searched inside herself, wondering if this was true. Did she already know who Mrs Wishmore was, *what* she was?

Yes, she realised—she did.

"Are you… a guardian angel?"

The whispered question sounded ludicrous. Mrs Wishmore only laughed softly again and turned to admire the Christmas tree. The twinkle lights glowed in the darkness, and as they caught Mrs Wishmore's silvery cloud of hair, Millie thought it made her look as if she wore a halo.

"Christmas is a time for hope and joy, for miracles and angels," Mrs Wishmore said. "Perhaps that's all the explanation we need."

Millie smiled. She liked this answer very much. It comforted her more than she could say. Peace descended, stilling her racing thoughts, and it suddenly didn't seem to matter very much whether she knew exactly who Mrs Wishmore was, or what she was, or how any of this strange yet lovely moment could be explained. All that mattered was that Mrs Wishmore was here, and Millie was glad to have her company.

Beside her, Doris patted her arm.

"Things will work out just fine, Millie, you'll see. You put yourself on the line this Christmas, made new friends, reached out to family. The universe rewards those who are scared half to death but take the big leaps anyway, in search of those things their hearts long for."

Millie thought about this for a moment before sighing. "But nothing worked out the way I thought it would. My father didn't show up. Adam turned out to be a jerk."

Doris laughed softly. "Perhaps those two stories aren't yet over."

Millie wasn't sure what the older lady meant. Seeing her confusion, Doris squeezed her hand again.

"You'll see what I mean soon enough," Mrs Wishmore said. "Everything will be fine, just like I said."

Millie hoped so. Turning her gaze to the Christmas tree, she watched the twinkling lights and remembered all the Christmases she'd spent with her mother. She thought about how much she still missed Caroline, how much the loss still hurt.

Beside her, Mrs Wishmore gave her hand one more squeeze. "She watches over you, Millie. Your mother is always by your side, even now. And she loves you so very much."

Emotions surged at Doris's words, and Millie felt her mother's love, felt her presence, felt as if she could reach out and touch her. She closed her eyes, wanting to drink in every drop of the wonderful sensation and hold it close.

Everything will be fine, Millie.

The voice might have been Mrs Wishmore's or it might have been Millie's mother's—right then, she didn't know.

Everything will be fine.

A soft tinkling noise pulled Millie from the dreamy reverie. It sounded like jingle bells, but the soft tinkling turned into harsh ringing as the noise grew louder. Blinking, she looked around, wondering where the sound was coming from. When she realised it was her phone ringing in her pocket, she pulled it out and stared at the name on the screen.

The call was from her father. Her eyes widened in surprise.

"It's my dad," she said, turning to Mrs Wishmore.

But Mrs Wishmore wasn't there.

Millie gaped at the space beside her on the bench. Where had Doris gone? She'd been right beside her, holding her hand, and now she was nowhere to be seen, and…

Her phone was still ringing. Millie looked at the empty space on the bench in total bafflement, then looked at the phone. With a shaking hand, she tapped the screen.

"Hello?" she said.

"Millie, it's me. It's your dad."

The voice on the other end of the line sounded as uncertain as Millie's. Still staring in bewilderment at the space on the bench beside her, Millie cleared her throat.

"Hi," she said, then was once more at a loss for words, still a little startled and confused by the strange dreamy state she'd fallen into for a moment, and the tinkling jingle bell sound that had roused her, and the baffling disappearance of Mrs Wishmore from the bench.

"I'm sorry I didn't turn up for coffee earlier," Derek said. "I was looking forward to it, but the thing is..."

When he trailed off and said nothing further, Millie spoke instead. "Look, it's fine. It was a last minute arrangement and everyone's busy at Christmas. I'm sure you've got loads happening and don't have the time to squeeze in something at short notice."

"No, that's not it at all." There was a long sigh down the line. "I was about to drive down to see you when I wondered if I should be doing it at all."

Millie frowned. "What do you mean?"

A long moment passed before Derek spoke again. "I was a terrible father to you, Millie. I was never there. I never made time for you, never made you a part of my life. After your mother and I separated, I just went off and did my own thing. I was too selfish to think about you or what you might need. The older I got, the more I regretted it, but it seemed too late to change anything."

His words left Millie stunned. She hadn't expected him to say anything like this when she answered the phone. It had never occurred to her that he might feel this way.

Derek sighed, then added, "Here's the hard truth. I've never been any good at relationships and haven't had many in my life that have worked out. I always seem to make mistakes and get things wrong. After a while, it just became easier to be alone and keep myself to myself."

This revelation hit Millie hard. Derek might as well have

been describing her own difficulties when it came to interacting with people. She, too, had so often found it easier just to be by herself rather than forge friendships and relationships that never seemed to get off the ground because of her social awkwardness and tendency to say the wrong thing.

Although she'd never known much about her father, she wondered if they might have more in common than she could have guessed. Millie's mother, Caroline, had always been friendly and out-going with their neighbours and her own work colleagues, at ease in social situations, and it wasn't until this very moment that Millie wondered if her own social awkwardness wasn't just a quirk of her personality but something handed down from her absent father.

Realising Derek might struggle with the same anxieties as she did not only took her by surprise, it filled her with a sudden and deep empathy for the man.

"I'm sorry, Dad," she said. "I had no idea."

"Of course you didn't. I was never a part of your life. How could you know? Sometimes I thought that was for the best, so you didn't have to put up with me, put up with the mistakes I've made. There have been a lot of those."

"I'm sure that's not true," she said, even although she knew from her mother that her father had indeed made a lot of mistakes in his life. He'd walked away from jobs without good reason, lost others because of his all-too-often chaotic lifestyle, and found himself in precarious financial situations far worse than any that Caroline had faced as a single mother working hard to make ends meet.

Down the phone line, Derek let out a sigh. "I haven't had a good life, Millie. I've had tough breaks and made bad calls. But the message you sent asking if we could meet for coffee, well, that brightened up my days more than you could know. I'm not very good with words, Millie. You've probably worked that out by now from the texts I've sent. It's hard for me to say what I feel. And so when it came to this coffee we agreed to have together..."

Millie waited for him to continue. When he didn't, she wondered if he was waiting for her to say something instead. "So, you didn't meet me for coffee because you weren't sure what we could talk about, or...?"

He sighed again before he answered. "I'm embarrassed, Millie. After all these years, you were the one who reached out to me, when it should have been the other way around." He blew out a slow breath down the line. "I think it's too late for me to try to be your father, Millie. I wouldn't know how to do it. I left it too late."

Derek hadn't said anything Millie hadn't thought herself. His absence from her life had hurt once she'd become old enough to think about it. Despite what Caroline had told her about Derek's unsettled life, the fact that he'd disappeared with barely a backward glance for his own flesh and blood had long been a source of pain.

But this Christmas, she'd promised to find the happiness her mother had wanted for her. She'd taken risks and reached out to people in order to find that happiness. Millie had no idea if having Derek in her life would bring her happiness or not—but she knew she had to try.

They both had to try.

"I'm not asking you to *be my father*," Millie said, emphasising the words Derek had used. "Perhaps you're right, and it is too late for that. But I don't think it's too late for us to at least get to know one another. That's all I wanted. That's all I hoped for when I asked if you wanted to grab a coffee sometime."

A moment passed. Millie guessed Derek was thinking about what she'd said.

"I've made a right mess of this whole thing, haven't I?" he finally said.

"Sort of," Millie laughed. "But maybe we can still put things right."

"That's what I want. That's why I phoned."

"Then let's arrange to have that coffee sometime next year, and this time we'll make sure it actually happens."

"Yes, I'd like that." Another sigh. The man seemed to have an endless supply of them. "Why are you giving me another chance, Millie? It's more than I deserve."

She thought about the question. The answer came quickly. "Because it's Christmas."

Derek let out a quiet laugh. "Your mother raised a good kid."

A lump of emotion lodged in Millie's throat. "Merry Christmas, Dad."

"Merry Christmas, Millie."

The call over, Millie leaned back against the bench, a whoosh of air escaping her lungs. After Derek's no-show at the café and now their strained conversation on the phone, she had no idea what the future might hold for them both. But he'd been honest about the mistakes he'd made by failing to be part of her life when she was growing up, and maybe that honesty was the kick start they both needed to find their way to some kind of relationship that would work for them both—whatever that might look like.

The Christmas coffee meet-up with her father hadn't happened like she'd hoped it would, but something else had happened instead, and their brief conversation had erased the upsetting rejection she'd felt earlier. That was a good thing, and Millie would take it.

What had Mrs Wishmore said just a few moments ago? *Everything will be fine.* Perhaps the kindly older lady had been right all along.

Millie turned once more to the empty space beside her on the bench. Where on earth had Doris disappeared to? And how had she got up and walked off without Millie even realising it?

Remembering the strange, dream-like state she'd found herself in when she'd closed her eyes in search of solace and comfort, Millie wondered if it was possible that she'd somehow fallen asleep for a minute or two and not noticed Mrs Wishmore leaving.

But that made no sense. It was freezing cold in the dark market square, not exactly the warm cosy environment needed for a quick nap. And if she had fallen asleep, Mrs Wishmore surely wouldn't have left her here all alone.

It was a mystery. Doris had somehow vanished in the blink of an eye.

Rising from the bench, Millie decided it was a mystery that would have to keep until tomorrow. She was cold and ready for home.

More than that—she was coasting on the lovely warm feeling of having connected at last with her father, of learning something about him that helped her better understand him, and that was a feeling she wanted to cherish and hold close for as long as she could.

CHAPTER SEVENTEEN

Christmas Eve in Hollyford arrived with blue winter skies and a bright yellow sun and an excited rush of activity around the village as everyone hurried to finish their festive preparations in time for the big day.

At Adam's gift shop, a constant stream of shoppers came through the doors from the moment he opened at nine until he closed at two, seeking last minute Christmas gifts for loved ones and treating themselves to festive candles and delicious chocolates and other goodies to add extra sparkle to their celebrations. By the time he threw the lock on the door and closed up, he'd sold out of huge chunks of his seasonal stock and would have very little left over to discount when the shop reopened after Boxing Day.

"Well, this has been such fun!" Lesley said as she tidied the counter. "I'm so glad I got to spend time here this Christmas working in your lovely little shop, Adam. It's been wonderful."

"I couldn't have made it through these last couple of weeks without you, Mum. And I know Lorraine appreciates you stepping in today and working her shift."

His regular shop assistant, Lorraine, had been invited to an impromptu family gathering to celebrate the surprise visit home of a close cousin and his family who had emigrated to Canada. Lorraine would have had to miss out on the reunion if Lesley hadn't covered her Christmas Eve shift.

"I was happy to help. Working here today has made everything feel so Christmassy. I've loved every minute."

Adam smiled at his mother's good cheer. He'd enjoyed today, too. Christmas Eve was supposed to be magical and filled with excitement and expectation, but only a few weeks ago, he wouldn't have thought it possible to enjoy any of those feelings. He'd thought he'd still be mired in gloom, depressed about his cancelled Christmas wedding and counting down the minutes until the season was finally over and done with. But after spending the day of his non-wedding in Stratford with Millie, a cloud had lifted from his life and his heart felt light. Today, as he worked in the gift shop, he'd once more felt that bubbling sense of goodwill and fun that was supposed to be part and parcel of any happy Christmas.

"Don't let me forget to grab a bottle of fizzy wine at the corner shop before we head over to Angela's for our late lunch," Lesley said.

"I need to pick up a few things at the shop anyway, so we'll go there together."

After the family party finished at his parents' house last night, Angela had invited Adam and their parents to her flat for a late Christmas Eve lunch before they all headed over to the market square for the Christmas carol sing-along. Attending the carol singing was his father's idea. After hearing Millie talking about the event when she'd stopped by their party, Roger had insisted they all go along as a family to support the efforts of the Christmas Village committee.

"I know I've said it a thousand times already, but I'm so

glad you and Angela are on talking terms again," Lesley said as she pulled on her coat and picked up her bag. "This is going to be a very happy Christmas because of it, I'm sure."

"Don't speak too soon. If Angela's cooking lunch today, we might all be spending Christmas in the hospital with food poisoning."

With a laugh, Lesley swatted at him. "I suppose that means you'll take on turkey duties tomorrow for Christmas lunch?"

"If it keeps us out of intensive care, no problem."

That earned him another playful swat. Content that the shop was squared away, the ceiling lights off, and the till now silent after a busy Christmas shopping season, Adam stepped outside with his mother and locked the doors, glancing at the window of the gift shop as he turned the key. The pretty lights strung up by the Christmas Village committee when he hadn't been looking were still twinkling in order to bring festive cheer to the high street as Christmas Eve grew dark and to welcome Christmas Day when it arrived.

Adam breathed a sigh of relief. He'd made it to Christmas without losing his mind.

A frown creased his brow. He might not have lost his mind, but he feared he might have lost Millie.

During the few short weeks he'd known her, he'd come to appreciate and treasure her friendship. But after their cross words last night at his parents' party, when Millie had called him out about the situation with Angela, she hadn't returned his text messages or answered his calls.

With the gift shop closed for the day and his work now done, there was nothing stopping him from going in search of her and apologising face to face for how he'd behaved. It seemed like he'd made a habit of doing that—behaving stupidly around her and then having to say sorry. She was a good friend to put up with his rubbish.

In Stratford, there'd been a long, delicious moment when he'd thought they might even become more than friends. As they'd sat on the bench eating lunch and looking out at the water, he'd felt the fizzle and snap of something sparking between them. Just like he'd thought it was impossible to enjoy Christmas after the disaster of Heidi and their cancelled wedding, he'd thought it would be months, maybe years, before he got over the break-up enough to even think about feeling attracted again to another woman.

Yet, something about Millie made his entire world light up. He hadn't expected that, and he didn't want to lose her on account of a stupid argument that had been his fault, anyway.

Worse, he'd felt sure Millie was upset about something more last night than just his bull-headedness towards his sister, but hadn't got the chance to ask her. He wanted to be as good a friend to Millie as she'd been to him, and he felt bad for not pulling his weight. Perhaps nothing would ever come of that fizzle and snap he'd felt in Stratford, but he owed Millie the same support and comfort and friendship she'd given him these last few weeks.

"Adam, stop staring at the shop window, for goodness' sake. We need to get a move on."

Blinking, Adam realised he'd been lingering at the shop door with the keys in his hands, lost in a day dream. Lesley was staring at him quizzically.

A thought occurred to Adam, one he wanted to act on before it was too late.

"Uh, listen," he said to Lesley. "You go on and buy your bottle of fizzy wine and I'll catch up with you over at Angela's. There's something I left behind in the shop and I want to fetch it."

"All right, I'll see you there."

Once his mother had set off up the street, Adam unlocked the gift shop again and stepped inside, throwing the bolt across the door just in case any passing shoppers thought he was still open, and came inside. Walking to the area near the back that he liked to think of as his gift shop 'art gallery', he looked up at the framed paintings by the artist who lived in Stow-on-the-Wold.

The watercolours had proved popular with his customers. Over the course of the last few weeks, he'd sold over three-quarters of the stock he'd brought back with him when he'd visited the artist in her quaint painting shed at the bottom of her garden. But there was one small watercolour that remained for sale, and which had leapt into his head just a moment ago as he'd stood outside his shop, thinking of Millie.

It was the watercolour that depicted a Christmassy scene featuring a snow-frosted woodland landscape at night, the bright December moon shining down on the magnificent fir tree in the centre of the painting. The boughs of the snowy fir sparkled beneath the moonlight as a young woman stood to the side, gazing up in obvious wonder. Amongst the trees in the background there was a bushy-tailed fox, and a bright-eyed rabbit, and a little red-breasted robin hopping around in the snow.

When Adam had chosen the watercolour for his stock, the artist had laughed at first, telling him she doubted he would find a buyer for it. She explained how she'd painted the original with a mind to use it for a line of Christmas cards she'd hoped to produce but hadn't got around to. No one would want such a whimsical and much-too-cute painting such as this one hanging on their wall at home, the artist assured him. If he displayed it as stock, it would only waste space.

Adam hadn't agreed, insisting that someone would fall in love with the little painting and buy it as a Christmas gift. He hadn't expected that someone to be him. Now, he was glad no one had bought the watercolour, because he knew exactly who would make the perfect owner for it.

The young woman staring in wonder at the snow-dusted fir tree in the woodland painting made him think of Millie, he now realised. The warm and open expression on her face, the hope she saw in the world when she looked around her, the bright joy in her eyes… that's how he saw Millie, and he wanted her to have this whimsical painting. With its sweet and innocent view of the world, it could only belong to her.

Removing the framed painting from the art gallery wall, Adam gift wrapped it at the counter. That job done, he pulled out his phone and rang Millie's number, hoping she'd answer his call at last so he could ask her to meet him somewhere and give her this present and say sorry for last night and tell her he hoped she'd have a great Christmas and…

"Hello there, Adam."

The unexpected voice behind him in the shop almost had him dropping his phone to the floor in fright. Fumbling to keep the mobile in his hand, he turned in surprise.

Doris Wishmore stood there, smiling at him.

"Uh, Doris, how did you get in here?"

She gave him a surprised look and pointed behind her. "I walked in through the door, of course. How else would I get inside?"

Adam frowned and peered at the gift shop door. "But I locked the door."

"You must be mistaken." Mrs Wishmore turned and walked to the door, pulled it open, and gave him a shrug. "See?"

Adam shook his head. He'd only just walked back inside the shop less than two minutes ago and he remembered throwing the bolt at the top and bottom just in case any shoppers wandered inside when he was already closed. The door had been locked. There was no doubt about it.

And yet there was Mrs Wishmore, standing inside the shop. Before he could get to the bottom of the mystery, the older lady picked up a box of hand-decorated chocolates and carried them to the counter.

"I'd like to buy these, thank you so much, Adam," she said, pulling a purse from the big blue handbag she carried around with her before removing a twenty pound note and sliding it across the counter. "I forgot to pick up a present for an old friend of mine I'm planning to visit tonight and I think these chocolates will be just perfect for her."

Adam glanced at the till, which was turned off. "Give me a second while I grab the coin float from the safe so I can give you some change."

But Mrs Wishmore held up a hand. "I wouldn't dream of inconveniencing you when it seems like you're ready to leave for the day. Just pop my change into your charity tin."

"That's very generous, thank you."

Mrs Wishmore placed the boxed chocolates into her blue handbag and then nodded at the wrapped artwork Adam had set on the counter. "It looks like you're taking care of some last minute Christmas shopping, too." A smile creased the edges of her mouth. "I'm going to hazard a guess and say that you're planning to give that to Millie. Am I right?"

Adam's eyes widened in surprise. "Good guess. How'd you know?"

"Just a lucky hunch. So, when are you two exchanging gifts?"

"Just as soon as I can get her to answer my calls." Adam punched Millie's number again on his phone, but it went straight to the answer machine. "I think she's ignoring me."

"Why would she do that?"

"She called me out on something last night and I didn't respond too well to what she had to say. I owe her an apology."

"Ah, I see. Well, for what it's worth, I'm sure she isn't ignoring you. She's not petty that way. But I do happen to know there was an unfortunate misunderstanding with her father last night and it knocked her off her axis, so to speak."

Adam frowned. "Is she okay?"

"She's fine. Millie is a fighter and doesn't stay down for long."

"I know she was meeting her father coffee, and I wondered if it maybe hadn't gone the way she hoped it would. What happened?"

Mrs Wishmore waved a hand as if to dismiss his question. "I'm sure Millie will fill you in the next time you see her. I believe it's all sorted between them now anyway."

"Okay, well, that's good to hear." He glanced at Doris, thinking about what she'd just told him. "It sounds like you were there to chat to her about whatever happened. I'm glad."

"I was only with her for a quick moment." Doris gave him a thoughtful look. "Millie was upset last night at your parents' party, when you had cross words with your sister, Angela."

"She told you about that?"

"Not in so many words. But not much gets past me." Doris gave a warm chuckle before saying, "She sees you surrounded by a loving family and can't understand why you'd push them all away. Family is precious."

Adam nodded. He now understood that only too well.

"And friends are precious too," Doris added. "I think the friendship you and Millie have found is too lovely to let it wither."

"I couldn't agree more." He nodded at the wrapped artwork on the counter. "Which is why I want to make amends."

"Good," Doris said with a nod. "I think Millie has generously agreed to cover another unexpected staff absence at the care home today. That may explain why she hasn't answered her phone."

Adam let out a breath he hadn't realised he'd been holding. "You don't think she's ignoring me?"

"Not for a minute." Doris laughed, then gestured in the general direction of the market square beyond the shop. "I know she's excited about the final Christmas carol singalong of the season and won't want to miss it for the world. I'm sure you'll catch her there in a few hours, if you can wait that long."

"Thanks for the tip."

"Perhaps the extra time will give you a chance to think about what you want to say to her?" Doris said.

"I've got my apology all lined up," Adam laughed.

"And perhaps something else, too?"

Doris's mysterious grin and knowing blue eyes brought a sudden rush of heat to Adam's cheeks. He found himself thinking about what he wanted to say to Millie—that he was sorry, again, for being an idiot, that he valued their friendship and didn't want to lose it, and that he wanted…

What did he want? The answer blew through his heart in an instant.

One day, he wanted more than just friendship, if that's what she wanted too.

As this terrifying and exciting idea raced around his head, Adam's blush turned thermonuclear.

Mrs Wishmore laughed as she studied his expression. "I think my work here is done."

He wondered what she meant, but the older lady was already turning for the door. She was about to step outside when Adam remembered the little angel bauble he'd found in the market square.

"Doris, wait. I think this belongs to you."

Digging into his coat pocket, he pulled out the pearly bauble and held out his hand. Knowing her quirky fondness for angels, he thought the older lady would be glad to have the trinket returned. So when Mrs Wishmore only glanced at the bauble and shook her head, he couldn't hide his surprise.

"You keep it, Adam," she said. "I think you might still need it to bring you some festive good luck and Christmas courage."

Doris reached out and closed his fingers around the little angel bauble, and he found himself relieved that she wanted him to keep it. With a smile, he slipped the bauble back into his pocket, wondering at the luck and courage it might yet bring.

"I hope you enjoy tonight's carol singing," Doris said as she stepped out into the street. "The weatherman said there might be snow later. Wouldn't that be the perfect way for everyone to welcome Christmas as they gather and sing around the tree?"

Adam smiled at the picture the older lady had painted. "Yes, I think it would."

Mrs Wishmore smiled and hitched her big blue bag up on her shoulder. "Well, I really must skedaddle. Take care, Adam, and merry Christmas."

"Merry Christmas, Doris."

He watched Mrs Wishmore shuffle off along the street. There was something about the older lady, something mysterious he couldn't quite put his finger on. With her warm smile and cheerful demeanour, she almost seemed like some sort of wise old Christmas elf.

CHAPTER EIGHTEEN

Millie made it to the market square just in time for the final Christmas Village event of the season. The afternoon was already growing dark as the setting sun disappeared behind a bank of heavy grey clouds blowing in from the north-east. She'd heard on the weather forecast that there might be snow on the way and was keeping her fingers crossed they might be lucky enough to enjoy a light dusting of snowflakes before the Christmas carol sing-along was over. Snow on Christmas Eve, while everyone was gathered around the Christmas tree in the market square and singing their favourite carols, sounded too perfectly festive to miss.

Millie checked in with Evelyn Fox when she arrived in the square and was handed a stack of printed Christmas carol lyrics to distribute amongst the people gathered and waiting for things to start. As she passed around the song sheets, the church choir turned up and began lining themselves up in front of the Christmas tree in preparation.

While everyone jostled and shifted around, stamping their feet on the ground to ward off the wintry chill and adjusting scarves and hats to stay warm, Millie looked around at the lovely village scene. The magical Christmas tree with its white lights glowing in the dark afternoon. The hustle and bustle of the villagers chatting to each other about their plans for Christmas Day. Children running around the cheerful plastic Santa Claus and his sleigh and reindeer, shrieking with excitement fuelled by the prospect of Father Christmas's visit later that night. The scent of the cold air and the promise of snow. The feeling that there was festive magic all around.

Less than a month ago, Millie had no idea how she'd create a happy Christmas for herself, the way she'd promised her mother last year she would. She'd felt too alone in the world and too anxious about reaching out and making the connections she so desperately wanted to make. But in just a few weeks, she'd turned a corner.

She didn't have the vast social circles some people seemed to gather around themselves so naturally, and Millie knew she never would have that—it wasn't her style, it wasn't who she was, and it wasn't how she approached the world.

But she'd made some friends, good friends, friends she'd come to cherish, such as Doris Wishmore, not to mention many other people she'd met while helping on the Christmas Village committee. Evelyn Fox had emailed all the committee volunteers just this morning, inviting everyone to her house the day after Boxing Day for refreshments in order to say thanks for all the hard work people had put in. Millie was already looking forward to the event and the opportunity to chat with folk and make more connections in the village.

There was another friend she'd made these last few weeks who she thought of now with a mix of sadness and irritation —Adam Carter.

Although it seemed like they'd forged the beginnings of an unexpected friendship between them, Millie wondered if that friendship might now have gone as far as it could. Every time she thought of the way Adam had turned his back on his sister, Angela, at his parents' party last night, her blood ran cold. Just when she thought she knew who Adam Carter was and what sort of man he was—warm, funny, kind—she found herself surprised by his darker side.

She understood the hurt and humiliation he'd experienced since his fiancé left him and his Christmas wedding was cancelled. It stood to reason that something like that would leave the man reeling, and that it would take time to recover and find his feet once more. She saw for herself the progress he'd made in getting over what had happened, and during the time they'd spent together in Stratford-upon-Avon, she'd been so happy to see the obvious transformation in him as he'd talked not just about moving on from Heidi but about putting things right with his sister and with his family.

He said that was what he wanted—to move on and put things right. So why hadn't he done it when his sister had come to him, almost pleading for his forgiveness?

Adam's heart must be far harder than she'd realised, and his empathy for others was far less than she'd realised, for him to behave the way he had. Although she and Adam had shared many fun moments together during the last few weeks, she wasn't sure she wanted to get much closer to a man who let resentment eat him up and who held onto grudges at the expense of those closest to him.

Millie's thoughts were interrupted by Evelyn Fox clapping her hands and drawing everyone's attention. After welcoming the gathered crowds to the last Hollyford Christmas Village event of the year and thanking all the volunteers for their hard work during the last few weeks, Evelyn introduced the church choir one last time and invited them to kick off the Christmas carol sing-along with a much-loved favourite, *Once In Royal David's City.*

As the choir rang out the first line of the carol and the assembled villagers and visitors joined in, Millie smiled at the festive scene around her and was determined to stop thinking about Adam Carter for the rest of the day. She wanted to enjoy this last carol sing-along of the season, and wondering about Adam wouldn't help her do that.

Millie joined in with the singing while keeping an eye out for any late arrivals who might need a song sheet. They were onto the second verse of the carol when she felt a tap at her elbow.

"Hello, Millie."

When she turned, Millie saw Mrs Wishmore at her side. Tonight, the older lady's usual red coat was accessorised with a bright red woollen hat along with a soft ivory scarf decorated with little silvery angels, making her look especially festive.

"Doris, I was hoping you'd be here," Millie said in a quiet voice so as not to interrupt the nearby carol singers.

"I wouldn't miss it for the world." Doris smiled and looked around the market square. "What a wonderful turnout, especially considering how cold it is. I hear that snow is coming."

"Everyone's wrapped up, so if it does snow, we'll all be ready for it."

Millie didn't want to dwell on the weather. There was something else on her mind she wanted to ask Doris about.

"Doris, thanks for being there for me last night when I was a little upset about things."

"Oh, think nothing of it. I was happy to help. Are you feeling better today?"

Millie nodded. "My father called, and we chatted about things. He explained why he hadn't turned up for coffee and… well, it helped to talk and understand him better. We've agreed to meet in the new year and hopefully we'll manage to do it this time."

Doris smiled. "That's wonderful news, dear."

"I wanted to ask you about something, though." Millie paused, knowing her question would sound crazy. "Last night when we were sitting together on the bench, it seemed like you just… disappeared all of a sudden."

Mrs Wishmore looked astonished. "Disappeared? What do you mean?"

"One minute you were comforting me because I was upset, and the next minute I looked up and you were gone. It was as if you'd vanished into thin air."

For a long moment, Doris only stared. At last, she let out a startled laugh, her blue eyes twinkling. "My goodness, I can assure you I didn't vanish into thin air. How on earth would I do that?"

"Well, I don't know, but it seemed to me like, um, that's what happened."

Millie cringed as she said this. It sounded ludicrous, and she knew it. But she also knew that's exactly what had happened.

At least, she *thought* she knew. Looking now at Mrs Wishmore's astonished expression, she wasn't so sure anymore.

"Perhaps you became a little muddled on account of being so upset about things and forgot exactly what happened," Doris said, her tone kind. "We were talking together, you and I, and then your phone rang. You were surprised to see the call was from your father. As your father was part of the reason you were so upset in the first place, and it was obvious the two of you needed to talk, I said I'd leave you alone so you could answer the call and chat in private. I took my leave, you answered the phone, and that's how we came to part ways last night." Doris tilted her head as she studied Millie's face. "Do you remember now?"

There was no denying the plausibility of the account Doris had just provided. There was also no denying that it sounded far more convincing than Millie's take on last night's events.

She'd thought Mrs Wishmore had just… disappeared into the night? That she'd been sitting beside her on the bench one minute and had vanished the next? Obviously, that wasn't what happened. People didn't just vanish into thin air, not even at Christmas time, when there was a sweet sprinkling of magic in the air and all kinds of wonders were possible…

Millie gazed at Mrs Wishmore as the Christmas carollers sang around her. The older lady's bright blue eyes twinkled and her kind smile warmed her and in a flash Millie remembered the question she'd asked Doris last night.

Are you a guardian angel?

Mrs Wishmore had only laughed softly at the question. But in her heart, Millie knew the answer now just as she'd known it last night.

"Christmas is such a magical time, don't you think?" Doris asked as she gestured to the Christmas carollers and the twinkling Christmas tree across the market square. "Sometimes instead of trying to explain the magic, I think it's best to just let it be."

Mrs Wishmore brushed her hand against Millie's arm. Instantly, she knew the older lady was right. Why try to explain the magic of Christmas when you could just enjoy it in all its mysterious loveliness?

Millie glanced at Doris and realised she'd completely forgotten what they'd been talking about just now. Was it something about last night or… no, it had entirely slipped from her mind. Her unexpected shift at the care home today combined with the excitement surrounding the Christmas Eve carol sing-along had left her thoughts a little scrambled.

The carollers reached the end of *Once In Royal David's City* and moved on to *Ding Dong! Merrily On High*. The upbeat tempo of the carol brought fresh energy to the gathering.

"Oh, look over there," Doris said to Millie and pointed across the market square. "Isn't that Adam and his family?"

Millie looked up from her song sheet to where Mrs Wishmore was pointing and saw Adam slipping into a free space near the Christmas tree, with his parents and his sister, Angela, beside him. Evelyn Fox passed song sheets to them and the Carter family found their place in the music and joined in with the singing.

Millie's eyes widened at the sight of Adam in his sister's company. When he slipped his arm around Angela's shoulders and gave her a playful hug as they sang the carol together, Millie couldn't help a huge smile spreading across her face.

Somehow, Adam and his sister had made peace and resolved their differences. It was the only explanation. After the terrible scene she'd witnessed last night at Adam's parents' house, she'd thought that was impossible, and had thought Adam was foolishly determined to make himself and his family miserable by refusing to talk to his sister and sort things out.

Now, they were gathered together, singing Christmas carols together, and happy to be with one another as a family once more.

"They worked things out!" Millie said in a whisper. "Adam and his sister must have worked things out between them. I'm so happy for them."

"Me, too." Doris slanted her gaze towards Millie. "How lovely to know that we've had at least two happy Christmas stories in just the last few hours. First, you had a heart-to-heart conversation with your father and began the process of getting to know the man, just like you hoped you would. And second, Adam has had a heart-to-heart with his sister, cleared the air, and finally allowed his family back into his life where they belong."

Mrs Wishmore's lips quirked in a smile. "So many lovely Christmas miracles."

Millie nodded at Doris's sweet way of describing what had happened, her gaze still focused across the market square on Adam in the company of his parents and sister.

"Perhaps there will be a third little Christmas miracle before the evening is over," Doris added.

When Millie turned, wondering what the older lady could mean, she saw a strangely knowing grin on Doris's face.

"Like what?" Millie asked.

Doris only shrugged. "Last night you were very upset with Adam, and with good reason. Maybe you two will also clear the air, in keeping with the spirit of Christmas."

"There's nothing to clear. We're just casual acquaintances, after all."

"If that was true, you wouldn't have become so angry at Adam last night when he walked away from his sister."

"Well, I…" Millie frowned. "How do you know that's what he did? I didn't say anything about the specifics when we spoke last night."

Millie remembered describing Adam as a jerk when she'd talked last night to Mrs Wishmore, but hadn't said anything about the unhappy scene at the Carters' Christmas party—of that, she was sure.

But Doris waved this off. "This Christmas has been a trying time for you, and for young Adam over there. You've helped each other through these past weeks more than either of you realise. I only hope that when you speak to him later, which I'm sure you will, you'll listen to what's inside your heart."

Millie had no response to this. Listen to what was inside her heart—what did that mean? Adam was a casual acquaintance, barely a friend. Okay, that wasn't true, he was definitely a friend, and she'd hoped he'd become a good friend in time, had even wondered if maybe…

Heat warmed her cheeks at the thought forming inside her head.

She'd wondered if, one day, Adam might become more than just a friend.

Millie glanced at Mrs Wishmore. The sparkle in the older lady's bright blue eyes made her wonder if Doris had somehow read her thoughts. That idea only made her blush all the harder.

"Well," Doris said, "I think it's time for me to go."

"Go?" Millie said, blinking at the surprising turn in their conversation. "Aren't you staying for the rest of the carol sing-along?"

"I'm afraid not, dear. I promised an old friend I'd drop by to see her this evening and if I don't hurry, I'll miss the last bus out of Hollyford."

"I'm sorry you're leaving so soon." She was sad Doris wouldn't be around to enjoy the carol singing, especially as it was the last event the Christmas Village was holding. But she knew Christmas was a busy time for everyone, and that people had plans and festive celebrations to begin. "But I hope you have a lovely Christmas, Doris. Will I see you at Evelyn's Christmas Village volunteer thank-you get-together in a couple of days?"

"Unfortunately, I won't be able to come along. I'm spending the holidays back home, and home is rather a long way away from here."

"Oh." Millie let this sink in. "I thought you lived in one of the nearby villages?"

Mrs Wishmore shook her head. The tender expression on her face made Millie ask another question.

"Will I see you again, Doris?"

With a kind smile, Mrs Wishmore laid a hand on Millie's arm. "I don't think so."

A bolt of sadness rushed through her. She hadn't expected to be saying goodbye to Mrs Wishmore. She'd thought she'd made a new friend in the mysterious but kindly older lady.

"We'll always be friends, Millie," Doris said, as if she'd once more read her thoughts. "And whenever you need me, you know how to find me."

Mrs Wishmore's gaze dropped to the little angel brooch pinned to Millie's coat. Lifting her fingers to touch the soft gold rim along the angel's wings, Millie felt a warming surge of comfort roll through her.

With a smile, she looked back at Doris. "Yes, I know how to find you."

Mrs Wishmore pulled her into an embrace. Millie wrapped her arms around Doris, sensing that this would be the last time she'd see this strange and lovely woman who she'd been so fortunate to meet and so lucky to call her friend.

"I wish you a very happy Christmas, Millie."

"You too, Doris."

The Christmas carollers switched to a new song as Mrs Wishmore stepped back and peered over Millie's shoulder. "I think someone is coming over to see you."

When she turned, Millie saw Adam stepping away from his sister and parents before making his way through the busy crowd of carol singers. His gaze was fixed on Millie as he walked.

"Farewell, Millie," Mrs Wishmore said.

Looking once more at Doris, Millie smiled. "Goodbye, Mrs Wishmore."

With a tinkling laugh, the older lady turned and shuffled off across the market square. When she reached the far edge, she turned and waved.

Millie waved back, already missing Doris Wishmore's cheery presence and kind-hearted wisdom.

"Hi, Millie."

Adam stood beside her when she turned, a shy smile on his face. Before greeting him in return, Millie looked one last time in the direction Mrs Wishmore had departed.

When she saw no sign of the older lady anywhere, she wasn't much surprised. Mrs Wishmore was a mystery, Millie knew that now, just as she knew that her sudden appearance in her life had been more than just a happy Christmas coincidence.

Something wonderful had happened this Christmas, just as Millie had hoped it would, and there was now peace in her heart for the first time in much too long.

Feeling that peace inside herself, and treasuring it, Millie looked one last time at the spot where Mrs Wishmore had disappeared before turning to Adam with a smile.

"Hi, Adam. Are you enjoying the carol sing-along?"

He nodded, then gestured behind him towards where his parents and sister stood across the market square. "My family are enjoying it, too."

Millie's smile softened. "Does that mean you and your sister are on talking terms again?"

"That's right, and it's all thanks to you." Adam glanced around at the nearby carol singers before taking Millie's arm and gently pulling her to a quiet spot at the edge of the crowds. "What you said last night was painful to hear, and it hit home hard, but I needed that, more than you know."

Although she'd meant what she'd said, Adam's words still

made her drop her gaze and blush. She'd never spoken to someone before the way she'd spoken to Adam last night. It wasn't in her nature to be confrontational. "If I was a little harsh..."

"You weren't," Adam interrupted. "And nothing you said was news to me. My mother's been saying the same thing for weeks, but I wasn't listening. Hearing you say it is what drove it home. I was being stupid, punishing Angela for something that was never her fault. I was hurt and angry, but I was also wrong. After you left the party, Angela forced me to listen to what she had to say. If you hadn't just given me that wake up call, I might have pushed her away again. Instead, we talked and sorted things out at last. The truth is, there wasn't much to sort out once I started acting like a proper grown-up."

Millie offered a bright smile. "I'm glad things are on the mend, Adam."

"I'm sorry I ruined the party last night for you, Millie. I'm sorry I caused you to leave. I feel terrible and I apologise."

"It all worked out in the end and that's all that matters." Millie pointed to the carol singers and waved her stack of song sheets in the air. "I'd better take a walk around the crowd and make sure everyone has a song sheet or Evelyn Fox will be after me. See you later, Adam."

She stepped back towards the carol singers, but Adam caught her arm before she could leave. "Millie, wait. Look, I want you to know I really am sorry about last night."

"It's fine. I'm just glad you've sorted things out with Angela."

"Now I need to sort things out with you, too. I *want* to sort things out with you, Millie." He blew out a breath and frowned. "I was so busy thinking about myself I didn't stop to think about what was going on with you. Did something happen last night when you went to meet your father? If it did, I'm sorry I wasn't there to be a friend, the way you've been a friend to me these last weeks."

Millie saw the remorse in his eyes. Despite wondering if a friendship with Adam was worth the trouble after seeing how he'd behaved last night, she couldn't walk away from him.

Something in her heart wouldn't let her.

"My dad didn't turn up for coffee last night like we'd planned," Millie said, wanting to explain, needing to explain. "He left me sitting in the café by myself for ages before he sent a message to say he wasn't coming. I was upset about it, which was why I blew up at you at the party. I was feeling sorry for myself."

He shook his head at her description. "Your dad didn't turn up like you hoped he would, and then you had to listen to me whining about Angela. No wonder you yelled at me. I deserved it." Adam frowned and let out a slow sigh. "I wish I'd known. I'm sorry I was no use to you when you could've used a friend. But I bumped into Doris Wishmore earlier and she said you and your father had sorted things out?"

"We ended up speaking on the phone last night. It was the first time we've spoken so honestly to each other. He shared things with me that helped me understand. We're meeting early next month with a clean slate."

Adam smiled. "That's fantastic."

"It's a start. I doubt we'll ever have a real father-daughter relationship. I think we both know it's too late for that. But we might have some kind of relationship and I want to see what might be possible."

For a long moment, Adam didn't speak, his gaze roaming her face. "You have a big heart, Millie. You blow me away."

Millie's cheeks flooded with heat and she couldn't help dropping her gaze, the expression in Adam's eyes too much for her. Just a few minutes ago, she'd resigned herself to letting Adam slip out of her life, not so desperate for a friend that she'd put up with someone who couldn't let go of resentment against those who loved him in order to move on with his life.

But seeing Adam with his family, their ease with one another obvious, made her see he could move on, after all. He *had* moved on. He'd let go of the hurt and anger, made amends with his sister, and he looked lighter for it, as if the tension had lifted from his shoulders and erased the pain from his frown.

"Are we still friends, Millie?" Adam asked.

His eyes told her he didn't know the answer to that question and that he wasn't sure whether he'd like her answer.

"We didn't get off to the best start since we met," he continued, intent on pleading his case. "I've spent most of the last few weeks behaving like a twat."

The matter-of-fact way he said this caused Millie to laugh. Encouraged, Adam's expression lifted.

"We're still friends," Millie said.

Adam blew out a long breath of relief. "I'm glad."

"Me, too."

Digging his hands into his coat pocket, Adam smiled as a thoughtful look crossed his face. Removing his hand from his pocket, he opened his palm to show her what he held there.

"I tried to return this little angel bauble charm to Mrs Wishmore, but she said I'd need it and she was right. Before I came over here and talk to you, I slipped my hand in my pocket and held onto this little trinket of Doris's, and it gave me the courage I needed to say sorry and to say…"

His gaze roamed her face before he looked down at the angel bauble and laughed. "Anyway, Mrs Wishmore was right. This is now officially my good luck charm."

Millie tapped a finger against the angel brooch on her jacket. "I know just what you mean."

They smiled at each other and shuffled their feet. Millie was glad they'd cleared the air and were once more back on familiar territory. But it still felt like there was something still unfinished between them.

The carollers began singing *Silent Night,* the sweet notes swirling in the cold December air. Millie wanted to return to the crowd, but it was hard to step away from Adam when he was looking at her that way, his dark gaze mesmerising and rooting her to the spot.

"I almost forgot to give you this." Adam reached into an inside pocket in his coat and pulled out a slim wrapped gift. "Happy Christmas, Millie."

"You got me a Christmas present?" she said in surprise.

"It's a Christmas present and an apology present, to make up for last night. And it's a thank you present, too."

"Thank you? For what?"

His gaze held hers for a long beat before he answered. "These last few months, I've been the worst possible version of myself. You helped me find my way back to the man I used to be."

Adam's words left her speechless. He held out the Christmas gift. When she unwrapped it and saw what was inside, she stared in surprise as her heart filled.

"This is the pretty Christmas watercolour I saw in your shop that day we met." Running her fingers across the frame, she admired the twilight woodland scene with its snow-covered fir trees and the lone young woman gazing up in wonder. "I love this." she said, the words catching on account of the gesture.

"I knew you would," Adam said.

His voice was filled with intent as their gazes met. As the notes of *Silent Night* rang out around the market square and the Christmas tree lights twinkled and glowed, snow began falling. For a long moment, Millie stood unmoving, her eyes on Adam.

Unspoken words passed between them as snowflakes swirled.

Adam stepped closer, searching her gaze as he took her hand in his. The touch of his skin was electric. As Millie slipped her fingers into his and looked deeper into his eyes, she glimpsed what their friendship was already turning into.

When Adam brushed his lips against hers, Millie was lost.

The Christmas carols filled the market square with joy as the snowflakes floated around them and the air sparkled with the magic of the season. As Adam's arms wrapped around her and their kiss deepened, Millie realised she'd found everything she'd hoped for this Christmas, after all.

Everything and more.

EPILOGUE

Mrs Wishmore walked along the high street, the Christmas songs of the carollers becoming quieter as she left the market square behind. Festive lights shone in the closed shop windows and twinkled where they garlanded between the lampposts, illuminating the soft snowflakes that were falling and heralding the last few hours of Christmas Eve.

She was sorry to leave Hollyford behind. The little town had lived up to its Christmas Village name and Mrs Wishmore had loved every moment spent here these past weeks.

She'd especially loved making friends with Millie and Adam, and helping them find their way to each other. When she'd met them, she'd known only that friendship was what they both needed as they navigated challenging times in their lives and reached for the happiness they wanted so desperately but doubted they could find.

By leaning on one another, they'd found their way to Christmas, albeit with a few ups and downs. Mrs Wishmore was delighted that the friendship that had kindled between Millie and Adam was already sparking into romance. She hadn't seen that coming, and neither of her young friends had been looking for it. But as Doris had long ago learned, the ways of the heart were often mysterious—and thank goodness for it, too.

As she walked, Mrs Wishmore thought about all that lay ahead for Millie and Adam once they surfaced from that beautiful Christmas kiss they were sharing right at that very moment back on the market square. Catching glimpses of the future was one of the great perks of Mrs Wishmore's job and one she always looked forward to when her work was done.

Mrs Wishmore smiled as the images flickered through her mind.

She saw Millie and Adam blushing as they shared another kiss before stepping back from each other, wondering what had come over them but liking whatever it was very much. The excitement in their eyes warmed Mrs Wishmore's heart even more than the wonderful singing of the Hollyford Christmas carollers.

What would happen next? Mrs Wishmore saw it all unfold. Adam's family walked over as the carol sing-along finished, and soon Lesley and Roger were inviting Millie to join them for Christmas Day dinner when her shift was over at the care home, both of them refusing to take no for an answer. Doris saw the festive day they'd all share, content in good company and enjoying good food. Millie would think of her mother often throughout the day, and think of how Caroline would have loved the Carters' company, but she wouldn't be sad. Instead, her heart would fill with joy at the Christmas happiness she'd found and the new relationships she'd begun.

Adam, already fascinated by Millie and by the promise of what they might have found together, wouldn't think of Heidi or his heartbreak at all, although he wouldn't realise this until late on Christmas night, when he'd kiss Millie goodbye after dropping her at home, and he'd think to himself, *This really is a wonderful Christmas.*

Mrs Wishmore looked a little deeper into the future, hoping to see what the rest of their lives would look like.

She saw the many moments Millie would spend with her father in the years to come. Their bond would grow, and although they'd never have the father-daughter relationship that others might enjoy, what they did have would be enough for them and they'd be glad to have that much when for so long they'd had nothing.

Mrs Wishmore thought once more of Adam and Millie, glimpsing scenes of their unexpected romance as it bloomed deep and true. She saw two friends falling in love. She saw happy time shared and wonderful memories made. She saw many Christmases ahead that they would celebrate together… and with the family they'd create.

In one last glimpse, Mrs Wishmore saw the baby daughter Millie and Adam would welcome one snowy Christmas Eve a few years from now, a child who would fill their hearts to overflowing and fill their lives with joy beyond measure.

Pausing on the street, Mrs Wishmore smiled as her glimpse of the future disappeared into the snow falling all around. What a wonderful life Millie and Adam had ahead of them, she thought to herself.

And what a wonderful thing it was to take sorrow and loss, betrayal and heartache, and turn it all into a beautiful life of hope and love. If that wasn't a Christmas miracle, then Mrs Wishmore didn't know what was.

Laughing softly, she continued walking along the high street. Doris would treasure her memories of the young friends she'd made here this Christmas, even although she knew that Millie and Adam would soon forget all about her.

Whenever the young couple thought back to the Christmas when they first met, neither would remember the old lady who'd briefly come into their lives and become their friend for a few lovely weeks. Mrs Wishmore's face would disappear from their memories, every trace of her erased.

That was just how it was.

But Mrs Wishmore wouldn't forget. As she continued on her journey, she would take her memories of Millie and Adam with her and treasure them always.

Mrs Wishmore reached the bus stop and had only a few moments to wait before the last bus of the day arrived and stopped to let her on. Taking a seat by the window, she gazed one last time upon the sweet Hollyford Christmas Village she was now leaving behind.

The snowfall grew heavier as the bus pulled away. Above the twinkling festive lights wrapped around the town, stars shone bright and brilliant between the gaps in the clouds. Mrs Wishmore smiled as Hollyford disappeared into the distance. A new adventure waited at the other end of her journey, just as it always did.

For now, though, she was content to sit back and let the peace of the season flow through her. It was Christmas Eve, the most magical night of the year, and Mrs Wishmore smiled at the wonders and miracles still waiting to unfold as people everywhere opened their hearts to hope and love.

A MESSAGE FROM ALIX

Dear Reader

Christmas is such a wonderful and magical time, filled with so much joy and hope. I love everything about the season, from the fairy lights and festive food (especially the festive food!), to the carol singing and gift-giving. But it can also be a hard time too, especially if we are grieving for loved ones we've lost or are struggling with difficult challenges in our lives. Sometimes Christmas can be just a little too merry and bright, and Christmas miracles impossible to find. Thinking about the tough Christmas that both Millie and Adam were going through was how I started writing this book, and although there were many ups and downs along the way, I was so happy when they at last found their way to the happy Christmas they longed for.

I've always loved Christmas stories featuring helpful angels or other guiding spirits. From the ghosts who show Ebenezer Scrooge the error of his ways in *A Christmas Carol*, to the angel Clarence helping George Bailey understand the true value of his existence in *It's A Wonderful Life,* to the angel Dudley appearing out of nowhere to help Henry remember his true priorities in *The Bishop's Wife,* I can't get enough of stories where mysterious visitors turn up and guide people towards a happy Christmas and a richer life. I like to think that stories such as these remind us to bring love and joy to those around us, because those are the two greatest gifts we can ever hope to give.

Thank you for joining me in Hollyford and taking part in the Christmas Village festivities, alongside Mrs Wishmore. I wish you a very happy Christmas filled with all the comfort and peace of the season. Until next time…

Alix Kelso
October 2022

What to read next

Join Mrs Wishmore for more Christmas adventures in my festive short story collections:

A Dream Of Christmas And Other Stories

and

The Magic Of Christmas And Other Stories.

Each collection contains a Mrs Wishmore tale along with many more stories filled with Christmassy warmth and fun.

Stay in touch

If you'd like to hear about new book news, then join my Reader's Club and I'll also send you an exclusive and heartwarming story to enjoy. Pop over to my website at www.alixkelso.com to sign up.

Please consider leaving a review

If you enjoyed this book, I'd be so grateful if you'd leave a review at the store where you bought it. Reviews are very helpful for readers searching for new books and for authors hoping for new readers. Thank you!

ABOUT THE AUTHOR

Alix Kelso writes warm-hearted stories about romance, friendship and family. She's happiest with her nose in a book and loves being whisked off to imaginary story worlds. Alix lives in Glasgow with her husband, where she enjoys pottering in the kitchen, exploring the great outdoors, and buying far too many Christmas decorations.

Alix loves to hear from her readers, and you can find her online on Facebook, Instagram and Twitter at @AlixKelsoAuthor

Visit her website at www.alixkelso.com

ALSO BY ALIX KELSO

The Fairhill Series

The Perfect Moment (Book 1)

The Next Forever (Book 2)

The Magic Hour (Book 3)

A Little Romance (Novella)

The Story Collections

A Dog's Heart and Other Stories

The Food Of Love and Other Stories

A Dream Of Christmas and Other Stories

The Magic of Christmas and Other Stories

Home Sweet Home and Other Stories

Mrs Wishmore Series

A Wish At The Daffodil Cafe

A Wish On Star Castle Lane

A Wish At The Christmas Village

Printed in Great Britain
by Amazon

23746886R00182